THE BROKEN

Written by Rachel Marshall

"In Him we have redemption through His blood, the forgiveness of our trespasses, according to the riches of His grace which He lavished upon us, in all wisdom and insight making known to us the mystery of His will, according to His purpose, which He set forth in Christ as a plan for the fullness of time, to unite all things in Him, things in heaven and things on earth." Ephesians 1: 7-10 ESV

CHAPTER 1

SADIE

She flipped her ponytailed brown hair over her shoulder and took a deep breath. The night was surprisingly cold for early May, and the air burned her nose and throat. Sadie Thompson stared at her bat without actually seeing it, letting the mantra calm her mind. *Stay focused, have confidence.* The nervousness in her chest that generally accompanied stressful situations, like public speaking or any unwanted attention, was noticeably absent. This is what she lived for. This is when she was at her best. Down one run, runners on second and third, two outs, bottom of the seventh inning. A base hit scores one, but most likely two, as the fastest girl on the team stood at the ready on second base. A win would send the team to the state championships. Only a junior, Sadie had already established herself as the unspoken leader of the team and was rewarded for her overall efforts by being named 'captain' by her teammates. She would never acknowledge it, but she probably deserved the title. She worked her butt off for this sport. Because she loved it. Loved the competition, loved the hard work, loved the mental side, loved winning. And every fiber in Sadie's entire being desperately wanted to win a state championship. And so did everyone else. Last season ended in this very game, against this very team, with a walk off homerun after a ten inning pitchers' duel. Heart wrenching was probably an understatement. This season had been a revenge tour of sorts, hammering out win after win to get back to this very spot, only this time with their school getting the opportunity to host and therefore get the last at bat. Now here they were, here she was, with the opportunity of a lifetime, in a situation she had practiced so many times in her back yard or at the rec field with friends. She took one more deep breath, hearing none of the screaming crowd behind her, and stepped into the batter's box.

She was six years old the first time she stepped onto a softball field. The memories are only there in photos but according to her parents, it was love at first step. She played numerous other sports as a child; still played volleyball and soccer for her high school, but softball was her first love. Something about the clay, the smell of freshly cut grass, the difficulty in hitting a ball moving at ridiculous speeds from forty-three feet away; it gave Sadie a sense of excitement and purpose that she probably would never be able to explain. The softball field was one of only two places in which Sadie felt insulated from the outside world. No matter what was going on at home or in school or in her very limited social life, when she stepped onto the field, all of that disappeared. On the field, and in the waters of the river that bifurcated her town, is where she found solace. Sadie couldn't imagine a life without either.

Your zone, crush it. First pitch coming in low and outside, close but not her pitch. Ball one. Sadie stepped one foot out of the batter's box and looked down the third base line at her coach. His mouth was moving but she had no clue what he was saying. Partly because the crowd was so loud, but mostly because she was locked in. No signs, so swing away. Which, with the current situation, was a given. Deep breath, bat stare, mantra, back in the box. Her mind was so clear that not even her anxious subconscious could dirty it up. There was only extraordinary focus on that yellow ball and its raised red seams. Next pitch, low and outside. *Crap,* she thought. *They're not going to give me anything to hit. I want to hit.* She thought about moving closer to the plate to make the outside pitch hittable but nixed the idea. *Focus on your pitch only. Do not overthink this.* The next pitch was also a bit outside, but it was higher in the strike zone, a drop ball

2

that didn't drop, and Sadie took a hack. The ball clanged against the backstop with such force that the crowd congregating behind the plate flinched and let out an array of "whoa, she's on that," or "dang, she just missed that one."

"C'mon Sadie, you got this. Here we go, Sev," her best friend Kat O'Malley hollered from the third base bag, referencing Sadie's jersey number.

"Your pitch, kid, your pitch." Her coach was clapping his hands and nodding his head at her as she stepped back out of the box.

Sadie heard none of it. She took a deep breath and looked at her bat. *Just freaking missed.* She looked out at the pitcher and glared, the intensity in her eyes saying all that needed to be said. *I got you. I'm all over it.* Without even thinking, Sadie knew that the pitcher was going to try to jam her up and on the inside part of the plate. To change her eye level, to move her off the plate; whatever the reason, it didn't matter. Sadie was ready for it. And the slightly elevated inside pitch was her jam. She dug her back foot in just a little bit more, getting her back leg ready to turn and explode on the next pitch. One more deep breath. And then the pitcher did exactly what Sadie expected her to do; throw the ball in and just a little up. Sadie let out all her breath as the bat struck the ball: a blistering line drive to the left center field gap. Sadie took off from the batter's box, internally yelling at her teammate on second to haul butt home. Off the bat, everyone knew Sadie had just won the game. Her coach was windmilling the runner around third. His shoulder was going to be sore tomorrow. Teammates were jumping up and down both in and outside of the dugout, screaming at the runners to score. Sadie was watching the ball sail toward the gap as she ran to first. *States, here we come.* Just as she was about to hit first base, something flashed across her field of vision. Not something, someone. The left fielder. It was as if a portal opened and spit her out, full Superman dive in effect, in the exact same spot as the ball. As she landed, so did the ball, into her glove. Game over. Just like that, a state championship was gone. Sadie stopped just beyond the first base bag and crumpled to her knees as the other team ran ecstatically by on their way to leftfield. She looked out toward the ruckus, too stunned to even process what just happened. She felt the hand of her first base coach on the top of her helmet. She was saying something. But Sadie's mind was just blank. Shock turned into sad realization as Sadie's head slowly tipped forward until the bill of her helmet was touching the clay. Heartbreak yet again.

CHAPTER 2

Sadie could be classified as a typical Type A first child: hardworking, competitive, and opposed to both losing and failing; in sports as well as in her schoolwork. It propelled her to superb grades and all-county athletic awards despite an extracurricular calendar that could only be described as insane. She somehow managed to keep up with all the chaos without concern. But in the week following the regional final loss, Sadie found herself forgetting about tests and finishing her homework in the period before it was due. To be fair, a small amount of procrastination was to be expected; she qualified as a procrastinating perfectionist, but this was a different type of postponement. The 'perfectionist' part of the prior self-assessed moniker tended to take a strong hold on Sadie's brain when she was faced with failure. And not playing for a state championship was potentially the biggest failure of her young life. She found herself constantly analyzing every play of the game, from the first pitch to that last, devasting out. Her last out. And therein lay the bigger issue. It was not just a loss; it was a personal failure. Never mind that she couldn't have put a better swing on the ball if she had one hundred chances, or that the left fielder made a ridiculous "SportsCenter Top 10" play, she made the last out and her team was now sitting at home. Sadie's torment was evident all over her features. A strange mix of sadness, anger and hopelessness seemed etched into her face like the sculptures on Mt. Rushmore. Her body slumped as if her best dog had just died. Even finding out that she had the highest cumulative grade point average of anyone in her class could not quell the disheartened spirit within her. Between her teammates and members of the community at large, she'd probably heard a thousand times how great of a season it was and that they'd be playing this weekend if it weren't for that "amazing catch." Basically, telling Sadie that she wasn't to blame without speaking those actual words.

But the only opinion that mattered to Sadie Thompson was that of Sadie Thompson, and the lack of a state championship ring on her finger rang louder in her brain than any outside platitude. Even if they were true.

With her travel softball season not starting until the end of May, Sadie had some both necessary and undesired down time. Her body had taken a beating over the past nine months as volleyball season ran into soccer season which ran into softball season. The physical rest was a good thing. The mental "rest," however, was an absolute disaster. Sadie had spent far too much time replaying that last game, wondering what she could have done differently to facilitate a better outcome. Not that it mattered. There are no do-overs. But that didn't stop her brain from agonizing over every play.

On Saturday, well over a week since the loss, Sadie had had enough. She didn't think her heart could handle losing that game in her head for the thousandth time, so she decided to do the thing that always helped her clear her mind: go fishing. Between the tranquility of the water, the unobtrusiveness of nature and mindlessness of casting and reeling, Sadie figured she could find at least a modicum of peace for her overworked brain. She walked the eight blocks to her grandfather's dock where he kept an old twelve-foot Jon boat with a ten-horsepower motor tied up opposite his brand new twenty-four-foot Carolina Skiff. Her grandfather, one of the most respected physicians in the area, lived in an old, turn-of-the-century house separated from the Broken River by a small road that was only traversed by homeowners. The house, along with the surrounding land, was family property, passed down by multiple generations. Her family had been in Edgewater since the late 1700s. To most, her family history was stuff of legend; Sadie merely wondered why no one left. She asked her grandfather once. He only pointed to the river and said nothing. He could be a bit peculiar at times.

To make things more accessible for his grandchildren, and frankly, easier for him, he had put up a shed on the strip of land opposite his house and adjacent to the dock to serve as a storage facility for all his marine equipment. He owned all the land next to river, as well as the land by his house, for nearly a ½ mile so if he could do pretty much whatever he wanted with the property. But he was also a simple man who had very little use for "things." The exception was the boat. The acreage remained earthen soil.

Sadie lifted the rock by the side of the door and snagged the spare key that was stuck to the bottom of it. After grabbing a fishing pole, tackle box and an extra two-gallon gas can, Sadie tacked a note to the door letting her grandfather know it was she who had taken out the *Johnny Pesky*. Named for his favorite childhood baseball player, the boat was about as old as the real Johnny Pesky probably was. Rusted, dented and plastered with remnants of fish guts and hole plugs, it was a wonder that the boat was still buoyant. Because of the relative grossness, and the fact that it was a *Jon* boat, most of her cousins and friends simply referred to it as "The Toilet." She couldn't deny that the name fit.

At this point, the note was merely a matter of politeness, as she was usually the only one of her fellow grandchildren who took out the boat. Her aunt and uncle owned a big Yellow Fin that they kept at the marina, along with a couple of jet skis that her cousins much preferred over the tiny old hunk of metal. Occasionally, her brother would ask to take the boat out, but he and his buddies spent most of their time either fishing near the marina or engaging in massive backyard football games. Sadie pushed off the dock and used the oar to paddle out a bit before cranking up the pull cord motor. She looked downstream toward the marina and beyond that, to the mouth of the river.

Nearly a mile wide at its outflow, the Broken River had one of the largest mouths in the state. It had not always been that way, however. When the first European settlers landed in the area, the river had two narrow entry points: the water bifurcated by a wedged shaped barrier island, the crust of the pie facing the ocean. It funneled into what looked like a lagoon. Both points of access were too shallow for large boats to enter so many of the people sailed further north, finding the aptly named Broad River more suitable for their liking. A few boarded smaller vessels and navigated the narrow passageway. That was their first mistake. The area that they found just beyond their "lagoon" was a broken mess of tributaries and streams permeating the riverbanks for miles. The swampy land was nearly uninhabitable by anything other than waterfowl, alligators and snakes. For reasons lost to history, the people stayed and started a settlement about a half a mile from the barrier island, at another fork in the river. It's where the marina is currently located. As with every settlement, disease took a fair share of lives, but here, so did wildlife. And then came the storm. A massive hurricane blew through the region and completely decimated the area. Gone was most of the settlement, along with most of the people, and the entirety of the barrier island. What were once two small punctures on an otherwise unbroken coastline was now a gaping hole of deep water, allowing a new assembly of settlers to access the area unimpeded. But legend has it that the original settlers, or perhaps the natives before them, put a curse on the river. Because that was apparently the only explanation for what has happened since. Over the last two hundred years, the river overflowed its banks at least ten times, each time taking several lives with it. It also had a history of causing people to outright vanish, venturing out into the seemingly placid waters only to never be seen again. One such victim was Sadie's own grandmother, ten years ago. She was a former competitive swimmer and had gone out, as she had nearly every day for forty years, for her morning swim. Only this time she didn't return. Her body was never found. Sadie wasn't sure if the river was named for its physical appearance or for the mental anguish it doled out. It didn't really matter; the name fit either way.

Sadie often wondered why her grandfather still enjoyed the river so much. He would always quote something from *Moby Dick* and then follow it up with a smile and say that the river is where he could hear her voice. She didn't know about all of that - she was not a fan of Melville - but her grandfather was a cerebral man, and the smartest person she'd ever met, so she took him at his word. Sadie would admit, however, that there was something about the river that spoke to her and pulled her towards it despite its sordid history. Maybe it was her grandmother, or the long-standing family obsession with the water. Maybe it was the sense of peace that the river seemed to endow on her. Or maybe peace was her own white whale, and this is where the hunt always took her.

Boats and jet skis were out in droves, enjoying the beautiful late spring weather. The chill from the previous week had vanished and the sun was showing off in both beauty and warmth. No cloud dared impede the brilliant blue sky. The Banks, upstream and off to the left by the old bridge, looked quiet, but after sunset it would be ripe with her high school classmates living what they assumed was their best lives. Lots of beer, bonfires, hook ups; it was like a 90s teen movie, sans the beach and the insanely rich teenagers. Sadie herself had never been to the Banks at night for one of the parties. Her parents forbade her and, to be honest, she had no interest in all that craziness. For her, it was school and sports. And church on Sundays. Sports, ugh, not right now. Sadie tried to clear her mind and let it drift with the current. She turned the boat upstream and to the right, toward one of the quieter tributaries that broke from the main branch, navigating both the water and the labyrinth that was her mind.

CHAPTER 3

*T*here was a figure sitting on the edge of her grandfather's dock. Sadie could make out the silhouette as she rounded a bend and headed back home. At first, she thought it was her mother or her grandfather out to reprimand her for being out so long but the messy bun on top of the silhouette's head gave her cause for relief. Sadie wasn't sure how she managed to do it, but Kat was able to wrap her long, sandy blonde hair up into the messiest bun and still make it look cute and stylish. Popular, beautiful, athletic and extremely extroverted, Kat O'Malley was the envy of nearly every girl and the desire of nearly every boy, yet somehow completely untouchable. And she was "best friends" with the quiet, cerebral, introverted Sadie. To most people, they were quite the juxtaposition, but they understood each other on a level that few others did. Kat was the only person to whom Sadie felt comfortable allowing glimpses inside her complicated mind. And while Kat may be open and gregarious, it was Sadie who made her feel known. And loved.

Kat's family dynamic was always in flux. She and her mom had a small house on the east side of town, in an area where there were more cars on blocks than on tires. It was far away from the splendor of the river, both in distance and appearance. But neither Kat nor her mom seemed to spend much time there. Kat's mom was a serial dater, seeing a guy for a few months, but then quickly moving on to someone with more money or more status. Or both. During the periods in between men, she'd be home. But then, with the speed of a hummingbird's wings, she'd be gone, presumably living with whomever she was dating. And then the cycle would repeat. And repeat. Kat also had two older half-brothers who would randomly reenter the picture and then leave just as quickly. Sadie had never met Kat's dad, and neither had Kat. As a result, Kat spent most of her time with Sadie and her family. She was far more a part of their family than her own, finding not only food and shelter but also support, stability and love. It had been that way for years. Sadie and Kat may not have shared any DNA, but they were sisters, nonetheless.

Kat was gently kicking her feet back and forth, toes lightly grazing the water with each swing of the leg. The little splashes she created looked to Sadie like golden flecked minnows jumping from the top of the water. As she neared the dock, Sadie had to shield her eyes from the setting sun.

"Catch anything?" Kat hollered out, not taking her eyes off the sunset.

"What if it wasn't me pulling up to the dock?" Sadie asked in reply.

Kat turned to face her, slightly rolling her eyes in the process. "I can hear that rust bucket from a mile away."

"Whatever. It's not that loud." Sadie cut the motor and the whine that accompanied it disappeared.

"Whatever you say."

With the sun in her eyes, Sadie misjudged the distance from the dock and had to use the oar for an assist. She hooked the cleat on the dock with the knob of the oar, and pulled the boat in. The knob then stuck in the cleat, and Sadie found herself having to dodge the blade that was taking aim at her stomach, all while trying to grab the dock and prevent the boat from slamming into the side. She succeeded but looked ridiculous in the process.

"That was graceful. I thought you've done this before." Kat teased from her spot at the end of the dock.

"Thanks for the help," Sadie replied sarcastically.

"Hey, you like to do things on your own, my friend," Kat retorted, throwing her hands up in mock surrender. "I'm merely complying with your unspoken request."

"Ugh," Sadie growled as she tied up to the dock. She put the now empty gas can and the tackle box up on the dock. Grabbing the fishing pole, she climbed out of the boat.

"You didn't answer my question," Kat said, still refusing to move.

"Couple of cats, an undersized red, and one small jack. Tossed 'em back."

"How 'bout your sanity?"

"What's that supposed to mean?" Sadie said, nearly stumbling over the gas can. "And how'd you know I was here?"

"'Cause I'm an all-knowing genius," Kat said with more than a hint of sarcasm. She turned to face her friend and saw Sadie roll her eyes and shake her head. "Sade, really? You've been stone faced and silent for over a week. Which may not be all that abnormal for you but this time, it's abnormal. There are only two places you go when your brain takes over your body." Kat looked back out over the water. "And the field was empty. So, number two." She patted the dock next to her. "Sit."

"I went out to clear my head and to try not to think. I certainly don't want to talk."

Kat once again patted the dock next to her, saying nothing and keeping her eyes out over the river. Sadie shot a menacing look towards Kat's back.

"Don't look at me like that," Kat said.

Sadie clenched her jaw a few times and then let out a long sigh, slightly annoyed that Kat knew her well enough to recognize her irritation without even looking. She also realized that this was a battle she wasn't going to win. "Let me put this stuff in the shed," she relented.

After she locked the door and stuck the key to the bottom of the rock, Sadie meandered back across the dock and sat down next to her best friend. They both sat in the stillness of the evening; Kat watching the sun disappear below the horizon and Sadie staring at the darkening water below her feet. This was Kat's modus operandi: sit in silence until Sadie decided it was time to tell her what was going on in her self-proclaimed 'messed up brain'. Sometimes they sat for minutes, other times it took much, much longer. Sadie was just about to break the silence with a nonsense statement when Kat turned to her and spoke.

"Remember the first time we met?" Kat asked.

"How could I forget? First day of first grade and I'm confined to a picnic table during recess because I had broken my arm jumping out of a tree. This tall, skinny kid with ocean blue eyes and her blonde hair in braids, whom I had never seen before by the way, walks up and says, 'My name is Katherine Anne O'Malley, but you can call me Kat."

"The start of a beautiful friendship."

"Had I known this was how it was going to go, I'd have walked away from you instead of letting you sit down," Sadie joked, knowing full well that she never would have done such a thing. Sadie couldn't have prevented Kat from joining her at the picnic table even if she wanted to. Even at so young an age, Kat did whatever she felt like doing.

"Yeah, uh huh," Kat said sarcastically.

"I also think you said something like, 'we're best friends now, just accept it'."

Well, I do speak the truth, so," Kat shrugged her shoulders in a manner that indicated that Sadie should already know this. "Now, what were you getting ready to say? And don't say 'nothing' or give me some lame excuse about having to get home. Your mom already knows we're here."

Sadie rolled her eyes and huffed a little laugh. Kat's eyes glinted with humor as she flashed a look that could only be read as 'don't even try to lie to me.'

"You know me way too well," Sadie said, shaking her head and looking out over the river toward the setting sun. "Why'd you ask about the day we met?"

"Remember what I did every day for the next four weeks?" Kat asked.

"Sat down at my picnic table with a deck of cards and taught me to play Texas Hold 'Em," Sadie said.

Kat laughed and said, "I think it was rummy, but ok." Her voice then became serious. "I sat with you then; I'm going to sit with you now. For however long it takes. But sooner would be better." Kat nudged Sadie with her pointy elbow.

It was true. Kat did sit with Sadie then. She sat with Sadie a few months later when her grandmother disappeared. And again, at the funeral. Kat had been with Sadie for every significant event in her life, and all the insignificant ones as well. And vice versa. They had just started second grade the first time that Kat's mom left. No one came to pick Kat up from school that day and the school couldn't reach her mom, so they called Sadie's mom. When they took Kat home, Kat's eleven-year-old brother was there alone. He said that he had no idea where their mom was. Sadie's mom took Kat and her brother to Sadie's house. They stayed a full week, after which her brother left the state to go live with his father, who was not Kat's father. And that was the first of many sleepovers at Sadie's house, of both the planned and unplanned variety. Theirs was a bond unlike most, and consequently, they knew each other better than they knew themselves.

When Sadie remained silent, Kat took it upon herself to direct the conversation. "Look, I know how much that loss hurt you. And not just because you hate losing. You made it your goal to win states this year and now you feel like you failed and let everyone down. Listen to me when I tell you that you have failed absolutely no one. Life doesn't always work out the way that you want it to. And just because you do everything 'perfect'," she said, complete with finger quotes, "that doesn't guarantee you'll win."

"I didn't do everything 'perfect.' There's so much I could have done better."

"Stop. Softball isn't an individual sport. Not everything depends on you, whether you do everything great or not. It's a team sport and even undefeated teams don't do everything perfectly. And sometimes teams with mediocre records win championships. That's sports. Shoot, that's life. Sometimes you win, sometimes you lose, and sometimes it rains, right? You can only control what you can control, and you just have to figure out how to deal with the stuff you can't. And stop trying to be perfect. Because that's not real. Excellence, not perfection."

"I wasn't excellent either," Sadie mumbled, which elicited a series of groans and eye rolls from her friend. Realizing that Kat was probably right, and being eager to move on from this conversation, Sadie asked, "Okay, anything else, o wise one?"

"Yeah, there is. This 'I expect way too much out of myself because I think I'm better than everyone else' crap is super annoying."

Sadie whipped her head in Kat's direction, mouth agape at the words she just heard spilling from her best friend's mouth. "I do NOT think I'm better than anyone else."

"I know," Kat replied. "You think you're way worse than everyone else because you're not living up to your standards of perfection. And I know how much that torments you. But you don't hold anyone else to those same standards, which could be interpreted as you thinking that you're better than everyone else. And I know THAT makes you feel even worse."

Sadie thought for a second and then dropped her face into her hands. "I came out here to feel better," she mumbled into her hands. "And you knew that," she snapped at Kat as she lifted her head. "Yet here you are making me feel like the worst person in the entire world. Some friend you are."

Kat just looked at Sadie. "You done?" she asked.

Sadie stared back at her and scoffed.

"Sadie, you are one of the best softball players I know. You are also one of the best people that I've ever met. You are extremely talented, you're basically a genius, you genuinely care about other people, you're loyal to a fault and you are exceptionally kind-hearted. Except when you lose. Kindness goes flying out the window when you lose." Kat smirked and then continued. "Yet, you keep all of that hidden behind a hard exterior and lots of sarcasm. Because you think you're not deserving of good things because you're not perfect. Newsflash my friend, no one is. And logically, you know all this already." Kat took a deep breath and Sadie hoped that she was finished with her diatribe. She was not.

"You realize what you mean to this team, right? And not just in your talent. You're a leader, even though you say very little. You work harder than anyone else in every single thing that you do and everyone around you is better for it. You do things the right way and even though that may prevent you from participating in the 'popular' things surrounding high school, people notice, and it makes a difference. So, stop trying to be perfect and just keep being the you that God made you. Because that you is pretty awesome."

Sadie sat there in stunned silence. Even though Kat was pretty much dead on with everything she said in her compliment sandwich, it was still difficult for Sadie to hear. Even the compliments.

"Just accept it. I speak truth and there's nothing you can do about it." Kat teased with a smile on her face. "Accept it like I'm about to accept a Mama Tess dinner tonight." She reached her hand into the river and flung a handful of water into Sadie's face. And then she started howling in laughter.

As stunned and angry as Sadie felt a split second before, by both the words and the water, it was as if the water had a mind wipe effect and made her forget all those emotions. "You're about to accept a bath in the river," she hollered as she formed both hands into a big scoop, shoved them wrist deep into the river and tossed a heap of water all over Kat. The ensuing water fight left them both drenched and exhausted from laughing. When they had calmed down, Sadie punched Kat in the arm with a bit of force behind it.

"I can't believe you said all that stuff to me."

"Me neither." Kat replied, rubbing her arm where Sadie hit her.

Sadie gave Kat a confused look.

"I just got tired of waiting for you to say something. So, I opened my mouth and all that came out," Kat confessed. "Plus, I've been devoid of people all day, so I've had way too much time to think and not nearly enough time to exercise my jaw. I don't know how you do it. My brain hurts from just a couple of hours of thinking. If my brain didn't shut off, I'd collapse from exhaustion."

"That's how I feel about talking. And being around people. How are we friends again?" Sadie asked jokingly. After a pause, she asked, "Where's your mom today?"

"No clue," Kat replied. "Hence the reason I'm staying with you tonight."

Sadie finally put two and two together. "And the reason my mom knows where I'm at."

"I stopped by after I checked the field. Wanted to make sure it was ok. And let her know that I knew where you were and that you wouldn't be back for a while."

"I'm sure my grandfather called her too. The note I left wasn't on the shed door anymore."

"Stopped to say hi to him too."

"I thought you said you didn't talk at all today," Sadie exclaimed.

"I said I didn't spend enough time exercising my jaw, not that I haven't talked. Can you imagine me not talking? Ever?"

"I cannot." Sadie chuckled at the thought and looked toward the horizon where the last vestiges of sunlight were losing their battle with darkness.

"We better get going. Eight blocks isn't that far but you know how slow I walk. We don't want to make Tess mad. And Kat," she paused, giving herself a moment of seriousness, "thank you."

Kat put her arm around Sadie's shoulder and pulled her a little closer. "Now was that so hard say?" she joked. "But seriously, I will always be around to drop truth bombs. And," she said as she dangled keys in the hand she had around Sadie's shoulder, "you know I refuse to get on Mama T's bad side. Wherever my mom happens to be, she didn't take her car. We'll be home in no time." Kat flashed her biggest smile as she hopped up from the dock.

"Sweet," Sadie said as she followed Kat off the dock. "And can we not make a habit out of truth bombs, please? That kind of sucked."

"Then just do what I tell you to do. And don't take so long to start talking." Kat hip checked Sadie as she stepped off the dock and nearly sent her crashing into the shed. "Also, don't say 'sucked.' Your mom will get mad."

Sadie rolled her eyes. "Just drive."

She climbed into the passenger seat of Kat's mom's beat up Geo Storm, a little two door coupe with the rear seat so tight to the front that a back seat rider would be far more comfortable sitting lengthwise across the fabric. Luckily, she didn't have to ride back there. She wasn't overly tall, but her five foot seven frame didn't fit well. Watching Kat fold her extra three inches into the back seat, which she had done only once and probably never would again, was like a comedy show. As Kat put the car in drive and headed for Sadie's house, Sadie found herself full of gratitude for that nutty first grader who chose to sit and play cards with her instead of run around the playground.

CHAPTER 4

*S*ummer passed like an unremembered dream. Aside from getting a few offers to play softball in college, which should have been the pinnacle of a lifetime of work, Sadie's summer had been a completely uneventful blur of work, softball and fishing. Kat had disappeared for nearly the entire three months and when she would pop back into town, it was only for a day at a time. Kat's mom was currently not involved in a relationship and was therefore attempting to be the doting, attentive mother that she had never previously been. Which meant multiple vacations, college visits, and various other things that could be defined as 'quality mother-daughter time.' Kat confessed to Sadie that she was a bit concerned about where the money to pay for college was going to come from, but she also knew better than to try to ask her mother. Sadie sometimes caught herself wondering how Kat's mom was paying for anything now, let alone college in the future. It was a ridiculous thing for her to be concerned with, probably spurred from the irritation of her best friend being missing in action for an entire summer. Kat was a tremendous athlete in her own right, especially in basketball, but she didn't play on any travel teams so Sadie didn't know how she would be recruited. Her grades could probably qualify her for some academic scholarships but, according to the internet, college was still absurdly expensive. Maybe the reason for all this melancholy on Sadie's part was the subconscious realization that there was a very big chance that this was the last year that she and Kat would be together.

On the Saturday before her senior year was scheduled to start, Sadie was up in her room half preparing for school, half getting ready to take out the *Johnny Pesky*. She heard the front door shut followed by a very loud bounding up the stairs. Thinking it was her annoying younger brother, she shut her bedroom door in hopes that he wouldn't bother her. The voice that she heard in response was clearly not her brother.

"That's how you're going to greet me after I've been gone all summer."

Sadie's heart leapt with joy at the sound of her best friend's voice, but she decided to play along. "You were the one who bailed on me. I'm still a little bitter," she said through the closed door, although the excitement in her voice defied her words.

Kat opened the door and wrapped Sadie in a big bear hug that lifted her off her feet. "Geez, it's good to see you too, Kat," Sadie laughed. "How was, wait, where were you these last two weeks? I don't think you ever said."

Kat plopped down on Sadie's bed, effectively messing up the half-folded clothes that Sadie had been in the process of putting away. "Apparently my mom was going to take me to some theme park, but we never made it. She met a guy and left me to my own devices in the hotel. You know that I can't sit still for longer than ten minutes, so I went on a little adventure and ended up at a college party. And guess who was there?"

"College kids?" Sadie replied. "You know I hate guessing games."

"JJ," Kat said smiling.

"JJ? As in the just graduated, super-rich, super popular, football star, JJ? The same JJ who you've been not so secretly flirting with for the past two years?"

"One in the same. He plays football there. And he looks even better after a summer of lifting weights. So, I spent the better part of two weeks hanging out with him. And yes, a bunch of college kids too."

"Kat," Sadie said somewhat disapprovingly. "Seriously? JJ? You know his reputation."

"Yes, I know. Nothing happened. It was all innocent. But he did invite me back there this coming weekend for his first football game. Maybe we're starting something."

"And maybe I'll win the lottery."

"Wow, Sade, jealous much?"

"Of you and JJ? Absolutely not. But do you think his country club, yacht club, uppity parents are going to approve of his dating you?"

"Tell me how you really feel," Kat retorted, more than a little hurt.

"That's not a reflection on you," Sadie said as she walked to her bed to sit down next to Kat. "That's one hundred percent a reflection on them and their super exclusive ways. They look down their noses at everyone. They would go apoplectic if their 'pride and joy' of a son was dating someone outside of their status circle. That would be the one thing that he actually could do wrong. Kat, I know you've had a thing for JJ for a while. You're not exactly great at hiding it. At least not from me. It's why you haven't dated any of the hundreds of guys who have asked you out over the past few years. I honestly thought with him leaving for college, maybe you'd forget about him. Kinda hoped for it because I don't want you to get hurt. By him or his snobbish parents."

"Maybe you're right," Kat confessed. "But, maybe you're wrong. I guess we'll just have to find out." Kat jumped up off the bed. Her boundless energy was a wonder to Sadie.

"You're going back there this weekend, aren't you?" Sadie sighed.

"Yep. Now let's take the boat out."

"I'm not going to be doing much fishing, am I?"

"You keep asking me questions that you already know the answer to. Just get ready. We have a whole summer to catch up on. Plus, I got these." Kat tossed a set of keys toward Sadie, which she snagged out of the air. The keychain was a custom-made quarter note, red and blue in color, with the note looking like a baseball.

"You got my grandfather to let you take out the *Sweet Carolina*?" Given her grandfather's affinity for the Boston Red Sox as well as for Carolina Skiffs, it seemed a most appropriate name for his boat, of which he was extraordinarily protective.

"What can I say, people like me. A lot. But I convinced him to let you take out *Sweet Carolina*. He may like me, but it's you he trusts. Besides, we can't roll up to the Banks in the toilet boat."

Sadie huffed and rolled her eyes. There were always so many people at the Banks. Technically, it was the sandbar opposite the actual Banks, but everyone just lumped them together when referencing them. She tried to avoid both like the plague.

"I know you hate it, but you have to hang out with people from time to time," Kat said.

"I do. I just spent all summer with my travel ball teammates."

"Playing softball. You just spent all summer with your travel ball teammates, playing softball. Not hanging out. C'mon. It's just some of the girls from school. And maybe some of the boys, maybe one named Tyler. Or maybe even Ethan." Kat admitted guiltily, a devilish grin spreading over her face.

"Kat, you didn't." Sadie could feel her cheeks redden with embarrassment. Tyler Richards had had an unrequited crush on Sadie since their sophomore year. But Sadie had one on the very attractive Ethan Sanders. She was fairly certain it, too, was unrequited because she felt as though Ethan was out of her league. Sadie would also probably never know because she would never admit to having feelings for him. But of course, Kat knew. Which probably meant that Ethan knew too.

"I did," Kat admitted proudly. "But I promise that if it gets crazy, we'll leave. Promise."

"My definition of crazy, or yours? Because those are two wildly different things."

"Split the difference. Now let's go. I'll get a cooler from your garage and meet you in the kitchen." Kat paused, looked at Sadie with a grimace and said, "But you may want to change first." She then bounced out the door and down the stairs.

"What's wrong with my fishing shirt?" Sadie hollered after Kat, not expecting a response. When Kat hollered back, "Everything," Sadie grunted and fell back onto her bed. As annoying as Kat could sometimes be, especially with her extrovertedness, if that was even a word, Sadie could not help but marvel at the person that was Kat O'Malley. Not only had Kat subverted Sadie's plans for fishing and convinced her to go to the Banks, of all places, she'd also managed to talk Sadie's own grandfather into letting her take out his most prized possession. Kat would never divulge her methods and that was probably for the best. Not that she was doing or saying anything that was illegal, immoral or unethical. Kat just had a way of framing things that made everything sound better than it was. Or at least better than Sadie saw it. But hey, Sadie got to share the benefits of her friend's overly enthusiastic approach to life. Which, given Kat's background, was a wonder all in itself. Sadie tossed the keys up into the air and caught them, trying to motivate herself to stop thinking and start doing. She took Kat's advice and changed into a swimsuit, her Roxy boardshorts with matching tank and a cute Billabong hat and headed down the stairs after her. Sadie hoped Kat would limit the potentially embarrassing moments with Ethan, but she wasn't going to hold her breath. She'd probably die if she did.

CHAPTER 5

BECCA

"It's a brand-new day. It's a brand-new year. And it's going to be a great one." Becca Scott high-fived her mirrored reflection as she turned to leave the bathroom. Her honey-colored brown hair bounced off the back of her shoulders as she hopped down the stairs two at a time. The butterflies residing in Becca's stomach decided this was as good a time as any for a gymnastics meet and, as she reached the last step, she thought she might be sick. First day jitters. Today was the last first day of middle school and although she had been at the same school with the same kids since kindergarten, eighth grade was the year to undo the horrors of seventh grade and try to have a clean slate for high school. Realistically, her social status was probably fine. But at thirteen, no one looks at life realistically. Becca certainly didn't and, in her mind, she had a lot of work to do. With every inch she grew last year, and there were four of them, the boys seemed to shrink at least two. She was already a better athlete than most of the boys and now she was taller than nearly all of them. Tall, smart, athletic girls were not high on the middle school popularity food chain. Not much she could do about that other than pray the boys finally hit their growth spurt. Then there were the hormones and everything that came with that. Ugh. What a miserable time. And it happened every month? God couldn't have figured out a better way for a girl to enter womanhood? Seriously. All that grossness wasn't going to stop any time soon, but maybe she could manage it all better. Her mom was very doubtful as to Becca's ability to do such a thing. But Becca was determined to prove her mom wrong. Altogether, seventh grade was an awful and uncomfortable year, and she was eager to move on.

"Becca, lunch," her mother called out as Becca grabbed her bookbag from the entryway hook.

"Mom, can't I just buy lunch?" she moaned.

"You know the rules, Bec," her dad gently reminded her from the doorway. "Grab it and let's go. Your brothers are already in the truck." Buying lunch was a 'special privilege' according to her parents, and she was allowed two lunch purchases a month. Same for her younger brothers. Primarily because their school didn't have a cafeteria, so lunches were brought in from local restaurants. And were 'too expensive,' according to her father. It was a dumb rule. Maybe not for her brothers who still ate lunch in their classrooms, but she was in middle school and that meant lunch with all of 7th and 8th grade. *No one brings lunches anymore. I'm so getting made fun of.*

Becca rolled her eyes and let out a purposefully loud and obnoxious sigh that sounded more like a growl than she had intended it to. Her mom, having a somewhat unique ability to say things with her face without her mouth uttering any words, stared at her with a look that screamed "was that really necessary?" She grabbed her lunch box somewhat angrily from the counter and sulked out of the door.

"Love you Bec. Have a great first day," her mom called out, using actual words this time. She shut the door behind her without acknowledging her mother and climbed into the front seat of her dad's truck. It was amazing how quickly her parents could change her mood. Still fuming as she adjusted her backpack in the space underneath her legs, she heard her name being called from the backseat. She tried to ignore it.

"Hey Becca, want to see my drawing of Spiderman?" her eight-year-old brother Brendan asked from the backseat, flipping through his artwork to find the page. Brendan was the youngest of her two brothers and was quite talented with the pencil. And with the piano. Which was a source of both pride and irritation for Becca, probably in equal amounts. Becca possessed a negative level of artistic skill and, where

Brendan could play nearly anything by just throwing the sheet music in front of him, Becca struggled playing with both hands simultaneously. It was quite obvious that his fine motor skills were on a level far superior to most, including hers.

"Not really," she stated bluntly.

"Becca? Please Becca, it's my best one yet," he pleaded. She didn't answer.

"Becca?" he pleaded once more, this time with a hint of sadness in his voice.

"No," she replied with more than a hint of annoyance.

"Becca," her dad admonished with a look that, even hidden behind sunglasses, meant she better oblige.

"Fine. Let me see it." She reached her hand to the back seat without taking her eyes off the road ahead. She glanced down half-heartedly at the drawing and had to do a double take. The detail of the drawing was not comic book level by any means, but it looked more like something she'd find in the hallways of her middle school instead of in the sketchbook of a child. *Dang, that's pretty incredible*.

"Wow, Bren, that's pretty good," she encouraged, turning toward him to give back the sketchbook. His face beamed with delight at her compliment.

"Drawing's for nerds," Bryson remarked from the seat behind their dad. "And you're the biggest nerd around."

"You're one to talk," Becca retorted as Brendan screamed at Bryson to shut up.

"We can't even make the five-minute drive to school without you three fighting. Seriously Bry, can you try being kind to your brother?" Becca's dad asked.

"Why? He's a nerd and an embarrassment to me and my friends!"

Becca watched through the rearview mirror of the truck as Brendan shrunk in his seat, curling as close to the window as possible. Bryson, on the other hand, was sitting tall, staring out the window as their dad scolded them for their behavior. Two years older than his brother, Bryson was starting to separate himself and define his independence. He was starting fifth grade, which to him was an incredibly big deal, and he was ready to leave Brendan behind. Aside from sharing DNA and a nice sized bedroom, he had nothing in common with his artsy brother. Bryson raced dirt bikes and played every sport imaginable; Brendan preferred music, movies and drawing. The two brothers fought constantly, although usually in the privacy of their own home. Lately, however, Bryson had started to publicly tease and then shun Brendan. Outwardly, Brendan took it in stride, but Becca knew that it was taking its toll on him. On the occasions when she decided to intervene, it was always on Brendan's behalf, although she found that her 'good deeds' would not go unpunished. She was the oldest and 'supposed to set a good example'. She'd argue her case, that she was standing up to the bully and looking out for the less fortunate, only to get told that her methods needed improving. Becca disagreed, but since her methods of standing up for the little guy included punching, shoving and locking Bry out of the house for hours, her parents may have had a point. Whatever, he deserved it. Becca would try cheering Brendan up when they got out of the truck at school. She really did love her brothers, especially Brendan. It was just easier to ignore them. She had her own life to live.

Her dad brought the truck around the car rider circle at school and eased to a stop in front of the overhang on the side of the main building. Becca spotted her best friend EJ waiting for her in front of the double doors to the middle school.

"Bye Dad," Becca hollered behind her as she jumped out the truck, already forgetting about her brother and his hurt feelings.

"Bye Becca, have a great. . .day" he finished as the passenger door slammed shut. "Well then, you boys have a great first day" he said looking into the backseat, only to find that Bryson had jettisoned as well. Brendan was taking his time fitting his sketch book into his backpack.

"Wow, ok. Guess I know where I rank in the lives of those two. At least I still have you. And don't listen to anything Bryson says. You are exceptionally talented and a genuinely great kid. Have a great day buddy. Love you."

"Thanks Dad. Love you too."

CHAPTER 6

"**B**ecca!!" EJ squealed as she saw Becca racing toward her.

Becca and EJ, formally named Evelyn Jane Jones, had been inseparable since they were old enough to walk. According to their parents, since neither of them could remember being that young, EJ's mom brought her to the church nursery, and she promptly walked to the table where Becca was playing and stole her doll. Becca angrily took it back and just when the teacher thought she'd have to separate the two, they started playing together with said doll. Every Sunday, the two would gravitate together and refuse to play with anyone else. Not much had changed, although they weren't quite as exclusive as they were back then. The girls still did nearly everything; school, church, sports, and last year even vacationed together when Becca's parents allowed her to go on a ski trip with EJ's family. Whatever envy or ridiculous fighting that generally affected all middle school friendships had yet to change theirs at all. Becca hoped it never would.

The two best friends hugged and squealed as though they hadn't seen each other in years when in fact they had spent the previous week together at volleyball camp.

"Ok, I know we don't have homeroom together but what's the rest of your schedule? I have Mr. Drews first period history and then French. Oh, and I have Mrs. Anson for English. A plus here I come!" EJ said while pulling out her phone so that they could compare schedules.

"I have science first period then math. And honors English with Mrs. Bellemare." Becca retorted with an emoji type frown covering her face.

"Mrs. Nightmare? Harsh. Why do you have to be so darn smart?" EJ asked. "Can't you just pretend not to know everything so we can be in class together? And so I don't feel dumb."

"Whatever EJ, you're not dumb. You just choose not to do the work for some weird reason. By the way," Becca said, changing the subject effortlessly, as teenagers often do, "your makeup is fire today. You look like Zendaya."

"Oh, stop it," EJ said as she flipped her long chocolate brown hair over her shoulder. The pure white color of her school issued polo made her caramel skin look even darker. With EJ's dark brown eyes, she truly did resemble the aforementioned actress/singer. EJ's mom, Elisabeth, was a Swedish born former model who now worked in fashion and interior design. Ms. Elisabeth was by far the most stunning woman Becca had ever seen, and EJ inherited not only her mother's looks but also her fashion sense, which sadly was stifled by their current dress code. EJ's caramel skin came from her dad's side of the family. Mr. Jones himself did not share the skin tone; it came from EJ's grandmother, who was from a wealthy Bermudian family with ties to an English shipping empire. EJ's grandfather met and married her while stationed there during his short stint in the Navy. Upon the very early death of his father, EJ's great-grandfather, they returned to Edgewater to run the family real estate business. EJ's grandfather had passed away when she was very young, but her grandmother had lived until this past year, when, upon her death, she left a substantial portion of the family fortune to EJ's dad. Not that they needed any help in the financial department. Becca remembered EJ being momentarily sad, but her grandmother was kind of cold and mean, so she wasn't heartbroken.

Around Edgewater, the Jones family had been synonymous with wealth for many generations, and the pattern continued with EJ's father, even without the inheritance. They lived in the biggest house in town, were members of the most exclusive clubs, drove the most expensive cars, and took the most lavish vacations. Becca sometimes fought twinges of jealousy over EJ's perfect life. She was beautiful, rich, had the most amazing wardrobe and could do just about anything she wanted without significant parental oversight. Luckily, being EJ's best friend for most of her life gave Becca near family status. She got to enjoy the house, the jet skis and the fancy brunches at the country club. As well as the ski trip to Jackson Hole last winter.

"We do have lunch together. And third period debate," Becca noted looking at EJ's schedule. "But why did you choose French instead of Spanish? We've been taking Spanish since Kindergarten so it would have been an easy 'A'."

"Because French is the language of love," EJ replied, drawing out the 'o' in love to make it sound like a swoon. Becca watched EJ's eyes track toward the doors, following a tall, broad shouldered boy with golden hair as he entered the building. "And because I heard Will Stevens was taking French."

Becca smiled and nudged her best friend with her hip. "Someone's crushing on the new kid!" Will's family moved to the area about a month ago. Becca had seen him once at church but didn't know much about him. Apparently, EJ was already getting the inside scoop on all things Will.

"Wanna talk about crushing? Here comes Golden Boy right now." EJ had turned back toward the front car rider lane and spotted a group of boys walking toward them. One stood out above the rest, and not just because he was about six inches taller than everyone else: Weston Gold, a freshman and the source of Becca's secret affection for the past year. EJ had used Weston's last name to come up with their pseudonym for him so no one would know who they were talking about. Becca was unsure about how well that plan was working.

"Shut up EJ," Becca whisper yelled, once again nudging her toward the building doors while stealing another glance at the tall, very cute boy with floppy brown hair. He just happened to be flipping his hair from his face with a quick toss of his head. Becca couldn't help but smile as she felt the resident butterflies flitter in her stomach. *He is so cute!*

"Becca! EJ! Hey, wait up!" Cooper Cunningham's friendly voice brought Becca out of her daydream. "Excuse me. Sorry. Coming in hot." Cooper deftly navigated his wheelchair through the growing mob making their way toward the doorway. Diagnosed with osteosarcoma in his left leg when he was 10, surgery had taken a chunk of Cooper's femur and quadriceps muscle. A metal rod had been inserted to stabilize his upper leg, but the muscle strengthening had been slow, primarily because of nearly two years of chemotherapy. He moved around fairly well, albeit with a limp, but the stairs at school still gave him some issues. Hence the wheelchair. But Cooper was a resilient and determined kid with a goal of ditching the wheelchair by the end of the month. Becca knew he'd achieve it; she'd watched firsthand as he'd conquered every goal so far.

The Cunningham family had moved onto the same street as Becca's family about the time that Becca and Cooper started kindergarten. Cooper had some older siblings that had aged out of the 'playing' stage, but his younger brother and sister were almost the same age as Bryson and Brendan, so the kids often found themselves roaming from house to house. Both families intermingled comfortably and did quite a few things together. And even though Cooper and Becca were of opposite sex, they had always gotten along exceptionally well. Partly because Cooper was the most sincere, kind-hearted person Becca had ever met. He was also hysterically funny and had no shortage of friends. Cooper bounced from friend group to friend group like a politician working a room. When he was first diagnosed with cancer, Becca's family spent even more time with him and his family. Her mom was a rehab specialist who did a lot of work in oncology early in her career and helped his family navigate the medical terminology, gave advice to help in decision making and created strengthening programs to help him after surgery. Occasionally, his younger siblings would stay with Becca's family during long hospital stays or when things got a little rough for Cooper at home. 'Anything to take a load off or give the kids a sense of normalcy,' she'd once heard her mom tell her dad. They'd been through a lot together in their relatively short lives. But Cooper was currently cancer-free, a cause for immense celebration. There was a huge block party this summer when he got his all clear.

"What's the daily goss?" Cooper asked excitedly, always eager to be in the know about everything.

"Bec was fantasizing about becoming Gold."

"Hey!" Becca retorted, feeling the heat rising into her face, knowing that her cheeks must be cherry red. To deflect, she said "I wasn't the only one fantasizing. Evelyn Jane's crushing on the new boy."

"Becca!" EJ yelled.

They were conveniently interrupted by the ringing of the school bell.

"Ooh, saved by the bell," Cooper said, eyes cutting to EJ with an 'I need details' look before continuing, "Did you know that used to be a TV show? Apparently, my mom watched it."

"Old shows are so cheesy," EJ quipped.

"So are you," Cooper teased back.

And with that, they joined the masses heading through the doors of Edgewater Christian School, ready to conquer day one.

CHAPTER 7

After what seemed to be days instead of hours, the clock finally struck three. Becca grabbed her nearly full backpack from the floor next to her locker and headed out to round up her brothers. As she turned the corner of the middle school building, she nearly collided with another body heading quickly in the other direction.

"Easy!" she yelled.

"Oh, hey, sorry. I'm really sorry. Are you ok?" It was Will Stevens, the new boy that EJ had her eyes on. And it was easy to see why. He was taller than most eighth-grade boys, had a beautiful head of golden hair and bright blue eyes that seemed to captivate Becca. Suddenly, the butterflies were back.

"It's Becca, right?" he asked, and then smiled sheepishly as Becca nodded the affirmative but also gave him a strange look. "Volleyball – my sister Lindy. She was at volleyball camp with you last week and happened to mention you a few times."

Oh yeah, his sister. Twin sister to be exact. Lindy Stevens was tall, taller than her brother who was already looking down a bit at Becca. She guessed Lindy was probably close to six feet tall, as she pretty much towered over Becca's five-foot six frame. From what Becca saw at camp, Lindy had pretty good command over her long arms and legs, and she was probably the best volleyball player there. Which made Becca secretly loathe her. She'd always been the best athlete on whatever team she played for so having that status suddenly challenged triggered a whole world of negative emotions that Becca was not used to. To make things worse, Lindy was really nice and seemed to get along with everyone. It was so much easier to dislike mean people.

"I'm trying to find the boys locker room. Football practice starts at 3:15 and I have no idea where I'm going or to how to get the equipment."

"It's on the far side of the high school," she replied, pointing in the direction that Will had just come from. "Through the double doors and I think it's on the right."

"Awesome. Thanks Becca. See you around." With a parting smile that made her heart tingle and the butterflies jump, Will Stevens jogged away, leaving Becca feeling a little stupefied at the entire encounter. "What just happened?" she said aloud to no one at all. At least she thought there was no one there, until the spinning wheels of Cooper's wheelchair announced his arrival.

"What *did* just happen?" he asked. "You're looking a little flushed. Don't let EJ see you like that." He gave her a wink to let her know he was joking with her, but her defenses still went up.

"Flushed? Seriously?" Becca tried to regain her composure. "C'mon Coop, no one says flushed unless they're referring to the toilet. And nothing happened. Will was just looking for the locker room and was going the wrong way."

"If you say so. I was just echoing your words. And your face is a little red so. . ." Cooper gave a little shrug of consent.

Becca rolled her eyes as Cooper flashed a devilish smile and chuckled.

"You're so annoying," she said. As they made their way to pick up their respective siblings, Becca could not help but think about Will. There was something about him, something mesmerizing yet oddly comforting, that she couldn't quite put her finger on. It made her want to get to know him more, but that was something she wasn't sure that she should do, given her best friend's current obsession. She shook her head to clear her mind as EJ raced up with Becca's brothers, EJ's brother Xan, who was the same age as Bryson, and Cooper's siblings.

"Kiddie pickup is complete. Congregating at Becca's house?" EJ asked.

"Ice cream time!" shouted the younger kids. Mrs. Scott had a long-standing tradition of taking Becca and her brothers out for ice cream after their first day of school. Over the past couple of years, it had evolved into an ice cream party for the entire group.

"So today was the best day ever!" EJ said as they all made their way to the car rider circle. "Not only do I have French with Will Stevens, he's also in my history class and I sit, like, right behind him! Well, off to the side one row, but that's even better because I can see his face and he has no idea I'm staring at him. Which I did A LOT today. OMG, he is gorg!"

Cooper glanced back at Becca with a knowing look that, unfortunately for Becca, did not escape EJ's eyes.

"What am I missing?" she asked, alternating her glance between Becca and Cooper. "Seriously guys, what is going on? You better tell me. No secrets, remember."

"It's absolutely nothing. Will asked me where the boys' locker room was, and I told him. And Cooper somehow thinks I'm 'into him'," Becca replied, complete with finger quotes.

"Wait, you talked to Will? Will Stevens? The very Will that I was just talking about. When? Where? Why wasn't I invited?" EJ gave Becca a withering stare while her hand landed on her hip, striking a most defiant pose.

"It just happened," Becca explained almost apologetically. "I was walking out of the middle school building, and he ran into me. He asked, I answered and that was the end of it. Seriously." Becca then turned to Cooper and gave him her own withering glance, to which he cringed and kept on moving.

"I cannot believe you talked to Will Stevens before I did. So unfair," EJ huffed.

"You had TWO opportunities, in TWO different classes. And he talked to me first!" Becca retorted, slightly exasperated and ready to end the current conversation. "Can we just get in the car and go? And since when have you had an issue talking to anyone? You're the queen of flirt."

EJ's mouth dropped in mock horror at Becca's comment but they all knew that it was true. Becca breathed a silent sigh of relief and climbed into the waiting SUV, vaguely aware that her mother was talking. Her mind was a million miles away and the only thing she could hear was her own swirling thoughts. Apparently, Weston Gold wasn't the only boy who awakened the butterflies. And that made her very nervous.

CHAPTER 8

SADIE

"**I**'m holding off on college for a semester or two. I'm going to go down near JJ and find a job and see what happens."

Kat had first announced her intentions to Sadie shortly before graduation. They had been sitting in Sadie's car after graduation practice, chatting about the coming summer and the life events to follow. Sadie had told her that she thought it was the most ridiculous idea she had ever heard. Kat had shrugged her shoulders and moved on to something else. Sadie had hoped that she'd either forget about it or, at the very least, change her mind. Yet, here they were, sitting on her grandfather's dock, Sadie getting ready to leave the following morning for college and Kat once again saying that she was going to bypass college for a boy. The disappointment was clearly written all over Sadie's face, to which Kat replied,

"You're leaving tomorrow to fulfill your dream. What am I supposed to do, stay here with all the other college rejects?"

"That's the thing, Kat. You're not a college reject. You got offers to play basketball at three different schools and decided not to take any of them. I know, I know, small private schools, you couldn't afford the rest of the tuition, blah, blah. But you could have gotten into my school with just your grades if you had only applied. And you know my parents would have helped pay for an apartment for us to share so that would have been taken care of. Instead, you are choosing to follow a guy who you're not even really dating."

"We're kind of dating. And once I'm there, it will be better."

"It's been almost a year of you going to visit him. Has he ever talked about dating you exclusively? Or introduced you to his family? No. And the only way I've ever heard him refer to you is 'Hey this is Kat, the girl from back home.' That doesn't inspire a whole lot of confidence in him being committed to you."

"Maybe you're right. But maybe you're wrong."

"This again? C'mon, Kat. You're better than that. You're better than him and you deserve better than him. Just because he has everything in life that you don't have but probably want, doesn't mean it's good or right. Or that he's good or right for you. He's still a playboy who takes zero responsibility for his actions. That, in and of itself, is bad enough. But he's also a rich, whiny jerk too."

"You've never liked him, Sade. I still remember when you told him not to choke on his silver spoon," Kat said, chuckling.

"Well, yeah, he was, as always, being a jerk. And if I remember correctly, he was being a jerk to you."

"He was just flirting with me. You take things way too seriously."

"And sometimes you don't take them seriously enough," Sadie countered, frustration and anger apparent in her voice.

"Sade, I know you're upset that I'm not going to school with you. College will naturally push you out of your comfort zone, so you won't need me to do that for you. But you'll be ok. I'll visit any time that I can, and you can call me whenever you want. But I know you'll be fine."

Sadie paused to think about the obvious truth in Kat's words. Was her anger about the JJ situation stemming from her being scared about a future without her best friend? She shook her head when she realized what Kat was trying to do.

"Nice try, Kat, but this conversation is not about me. Yes, you know I'm a little scared. I'm working through that. But I'm more concerned about you. I'm worried about you."

"I'm not my mom, Sadie. I promise if I get there and what I think is real isn't, I will come home. I won't keep chasing. I won't keep searching for the next best thing."

"I know you're not your mom. That's not what concerns me. My concern is that you think he is your best thing and that, even on the rarest of chances he may actually feel something real for you, you will never be his best thing. His circles are at the top of the food chain. Ours don't even intersect."

"Your mom ran in those circles, and she married for love and not for money."

"Don't I know that," Sadie said exasperatingly, pointing at the dirty little Jon boat tied up next to them and then to her grandfather's much nicer water craft. "But my mom and JJ are two very different people. And his money trumps my grandparents' money by a lot."

"Truth bomb?" Kat asked.

Sadie suddenly felt a wave of nervousness wash over her. "For you or for me?" she questioned.

"I'm proud of the way you handled the end of our softball season this year."

"I know that's a lie," Sadie responded. She had handled the regional loss far better than the previous year but that didn't mean she had handled it well. There was a lot of silence and a few concealed tears, privy only to Kat. But it only took two or three days to move on instead of over a week. "Try again."

Kat was silent for so long that Sadie had to nudge her to make sure she hadn't fallen asleep. As she did so, she noticed a small tear sliding down the side of Kat's face. Reaching over, Sadie draped her arm around Kat's shoulders. They sat like that for some time, both feeling the range of emotions that come with saying goodbye to the person that knows you better than you know yourself. Kat was the first to break the silence.

"You and your family have been my family for as long as I can remember. I am who I am because you have been here for me. With me. And it does scare me a bit to leave the safety net that is your family. Because that means it really is just me from now on. But I really want things to work out with JJ."

"I know you do. But you know I'll be here. Always. Forever. Whether this thing with JJ works out or not. And you're not alone, even if you feel like it."

"And neither are you. Even though you're not going to know what to do with yourself without my constant optimism and overly outgoing personality that you love so much," Kat teased, lightening the moment, if only for a second before she continued. "For real, Sade, you have to remember that it's ok to put yourself out there, to open up. That life is way too short to keep trying to be perfect in every single thing you do. We are not best friends because you are perfect. Because you most certainly are not," she prodded lovingly. "We are best friends because you're not perfect. Because you've let me inside those ridiculously high walls you've put up so I can see your imperfections. And I love the imperfect person that you are. Just like you love the imperfect person that I am. We are the most perfect, imperfect, not real but should be real sisters around."

"You know that makes no sense whatsoever," Sadie replied through tears of her own.

"I think it makes perfect sense," Kat said with a heavy emphasis on the word 'perfect.'

"Ugh." Sadie rolled her eyes and gave Kat a little shove. "How do we always start a conversation talking about you and then end up on my issues?"

"Because you have a lot of issues," Kat said bluntly but her face betrayed her seriousness. She burst into one of her silly bouts of laughter.

"I'm not going to miss these dock talks," Sadie said, shaking her head at Kat.

"I'm going to miss you too," Kat said as she leaned her head against Sadie's.

Sadie took a deep breath and let it out slowly, allowing her head to rest against Kat's.

"Are you driving up with us tomorrow?" Sadie asked.

"Nope. I would absolutely bawl my eyes out. So instead, I will be packing up my stuff and driving off in the other direction. But not before getting one more home cooked dinner from Mama T, keeping you up until all hours of the night giggling like 13-year-olds and filling my belly with a hearty breakfast of pancakes, eggs and bacon."

"I would expect nothing less," Sadie chuckled. "Hey Kat," Sadie paused, struggling to find the right words. "Thank you for being you. For telling me the hard stuff. And for really knowing me and still wanting to be my friend."

"Love you too, Sadie."

Sadie took another deep breath as the two friends slowly stood and walked from the dock towards Sadie's waiting car. Sadie wanted to linger here a little bit longer, both on the dock and in the moment, but her brother had his first varsity football game tonight so her mom wouldn't be holding dinner for anyone, even on Sadie's last night at home. She glanced up at Kat, who was always two steps ahead of her. It never ceased to amaze Sadie at how well Kat knew her. She was excited about the prospect of playing softball in college, something she had dreamed about nearly every day for the last twelve years, but that excitement was currently subdued by the knowledge that she'd be separated from the one person who kept her from allowing her mind to screw everything up. The next four years were going to be hard. How hard, she couldn't even begin to imagine.

CHAPTER 9

BECCA

*F*ridays were for The Grove, a one-hundred-yard stretch of undeveloped riverside land that separated EJ's sprawling waterfront estate from the county park and boat ramp. The land was owned by EJ's family and Becca assumed that the reason that it was still a bunch of massive mangroves, overgrown foliage and a broken seawall was because Mr. Jones wanted plenty of space between his house and the rest of the world. Occasionally, some wayward teenagers would sneak over from the Banks, the infamous party spot on the opposite side of the river, to engage in whatever behavior teenagers involved themselves in, but for the most part, the only people invading the waterfront habitat were Becca and her friends.

On a typical Friday, Becca would come home from volleyball, complete any homework that she had, (a mandate from her parents for all three kids), grab her bike and pedal the mile to EJ's house. Cooper was always waiting for her, usually biding his time shooting hoops in her driveway. Today was no different. Becca could hear the basketball bounce off the pavement as she opened the garage door. He nodded his head in acknowledgement of her presence, tossed one more shot through the hoop and then rolled the basketball into the grass where it found temporary residence next to his bike. It made Becca's heart happy to see Cooper returning to the Cooper of old. He couldn't yet play a game, but standing and shooting didn't give his legs any problems. And lately, he'd been able to endure the mile long trek to EJ's without much of an issue, only stopping once last time, and that was to readjust his foot on the pedal. He'd be out of the wheelchair for good real soon.

The afternoon air was sticky, the humidity not caring at all that it was September and fall was starting soon. Becca's face was wet from sweat and she could hear Cooper breathing heavily behind her. She hoped the shade from the mangroves would keep the Grove from being miserably hot, or that an evening sea breeze would kick up. Anything to cool them down a bit. As they pedaled through the gate to the Jones estate and up the driveway, a black Jeep came hurtling from the opposite direction, away from the house. Becca and Cooper had to swerve hard into the grass to avoid being run over. The driver, either not looking or not caring, was EJ's older brother Gavin. He was a senior and had turned eighteen just before school started. And because the two-year-old Jeep that he had received for his sixteenth birthday was no longer new or good enough, his parents bought him a brand new, fully decked out, black Jeep Wrangler. Gavin had always been a pretty decent guy, at least as far as Becca was concerned, and she spent enough time with him and his family to know. But over the past year or so, something changed, and he went from a kind yet typical teenage boy to a hard partying jerk. Even Becca's mom, who'd always had a soft spot for Gavin, was appalled by his behavior. She no longer allowed Becca to be a passenger in his vehicle.

"That was close. Again. It's like he's trying to play real life *Grand Theft Auto*," Cooper stated, shaking his head.

"One day he's going to actually hit someone," Becca said, hopping off her bike and walking it the rest of the way up to the house.

They deposited their bikes in the grassy area next to the front door and walked up the wide front porch steps to the door. EJ's house was a Mediterranean style mansion with multiple large front windows and a massive archway over the front door. No matter how many times Becca had been here, and she was here a lot, this walk always made her feel small and a bit uncomfortable. She was allowed to walk straight in but always knocked before entering to alert whoever was there. Although now that she thought about it, she was uncertain if her knock was even heard in a house this big.

Just as she reached out to knock, the front door opened. Mr. Jones held a garment bag in one hand and was rolling a small suitcase with the other.

"Oh, hi you two. Off to the airport again. There's my car. EJ's in her room. Go on in," he said in quick sentences as he navigated the steps with his suitcase and made his way to the Uber. Becca and Cooper exchanged looks. Becca was almost certain that Mr. Jones had just returned from a trip this morning and she didn't remember EJ saying anything about him leaving again so soon.

"Bye, Mr. Jones," they said in unison and headed inside. Cooper decided not to navigate the stairs to EJ's room and went to the kitchen to grab a bottle of water and some food.

Typically, Ms. Elisabeth, EJ's mom, could be found in the kitchen surrounded by a plethora of snacks that she had assembled for the teenagers. But today, neither she nor the snacks were anywhere to be found. *So strange.*

Becca headed up the stairs. Xan was up in the loft playing multiplayer video games, the sound so loud that Becca could hear it through his massive headphones. That was one thing Becca never got into. Probably because her parents were pretty strict about that too. She thought about sneaking up behind him and grabbing the headphones off his head, both to turn down the sound and to scare him to death, but she thought better of it and walked down the hallway to EJ's room. Her door was shut so Becca politely knocked and announced her presence.

"EJ? It's me. Can I come in?"

"Yeah, hang on," EJ responded.

To Becca, it sounded as though EJ had been crying. Although, with the volume in which Xan was shouting into his microphone/headphones, it was difficult to tell. However, when EJ opened the door, Becca's thoughts were confirmed. EJ's mascara had started to run down the left side of her face.

"Hey, you ok? Have you been crying?" Becca asked.

EJ looked confused until Becca pointed to her own eye and said, "Mascara."

"Oh. Shoot," EJ said as she wiped her face with her hand. "Hang on." She disappeared into her bathroom, leaving Becca standing in the doorway. Becca walked in and over to the huge windows, pondering whether EJ's tears had to do with her dad leaving. Her gut told her yes.

EJ's bedroom overlooked the river, and Becca was always amazed at how beautiful the area looked from up here. Calm and peaceful too. The sun reflecting off the water somehow made the MasterCraft boat lodged at the end of their dock look bigger than its twenty-four feet. It was one of three boats that EJ's family owned, along with four jet skis that were currently in their boathouse. This knowledge, along with the incredible view, made a twinge of jealousy stir through Becca's brain. There were times when she wished it was her family that had all of this. Yes, they were well off, even had a boat that they kept at the marina, but it was nothing compared to EJ's family. Becca knew it was wrong to compare, and she was thankful for what she had, but every once in a while, the green-eyed monster reared its head. Luckily it didn't stay long. Becca turned away from both the window and the jealousy when she heard EJ come out of the bathroom.

"OK. Ready?" EJ asked, sounding as though nothing had happened. She walked toward her doorway.

"Yeah. Are you ok?" Becca asked in return.

"Of course. It's nothing. Honest. Come on, let's go. Cooper here?"

"Yeah, he's downstairs getting water," Becca answered tentatively, unsure of whether to press EJ.

"Ok, Maddie and Seb aren't coming over. They have to go out to eat with their grandparents. Lame."

Maddie Montgomery and her slightly younger brother Sebastian lived a few houses down from EJ. They were regulars at the Grove and were apparently Irish twins, or so Becca had been told. So, despite Seb being a full grade younger than the rest of them, they were all basically the same age and therefore did not discriminate. Plus, Cooper needed another guy around.

EJ clearly didn't want to discuss whatever it was that had caused her mascara to run, so Becca decided to let it go and followed EJ out of her room and down the stairs. Cooper was standing by the back door holding five water bottles.

"Hydration in hand," he said as Becca tried to catch his attention. He didn't see her and continued with, "Where's your dad off to? Didn't he just get home?"

EJ acted like she didn't hear the questions and merely said, "Maddie and Seb aren't coming so you can put two waters back."

Cooper stared at EJ, who wasn't looking at him, and then he looked over to Becca. Becca gave him a look of pure irritation, to which he shrugged his shoulders in innocence.

"Well, more for me then. I'll probably need it anyway. It's hot. By the way, that wonderful human being of a brother that you have almost ran me over with his Jeep."

Becca shot Cooper another look.

"Welcome to the club," EJ joked, her mood still as jovial as when she left the room. Although Becca read something else in her eyes. As they headed out the back door toward the mangroves, Becca nudged Cooper and whispered to him to keep it light. He nodded in agreement. And as per usual, Cooper came through.

"The banks of the river Broken," he said as he eased his way onto part of the damaged seawall. His gaze swept over the water from bank to bank, before settling back on Becca. He gave a little wink. "Do you know why it's named that?" he asked.

"Do we have to have a history lesson every time we come down here?" EJ complained as she climbed into her little perch of mangroves.

"Oh, come on, E. Humor me a little bit," Cooper said.

"Knock, knock," EJ said sarcastically.

"There she is," Cooper said. "So why is it called the Broken River?" he asked again.

"Because when the French, or whoever it was, found this place, they couldn't get through and when they did, it was a mess of broken trees and marshy land. And also, because it has so many little forks and splits that break off from the bigger sections and then the bigger sections end when you think they'd keep going. So, they said the river was broken," Becca replied in one very long breath. "Moving on."

"Thank you, Becca." EJ threw a disdainful look at Cooper before she leaned back, closed her eyes and laughed. Becca sighed in relief.

"And also,"

"COOPER!" Becca interrupted, concerned that he was going to add that they originally called it the River of Broken Hearts because so many people died when the river overflowed shortly after they settled. It had apparently continued to live up to its name throughout the years, although Becca didn't personally know anyone who had died from it.

"What? I was just going to tell you that it was the Spanish, not the French."

Becca rolled her eyes and walked silently down to the shoreline. She picked up a stone and flipped it over a few times in her hand. It was a bit oblong and not completely flat, but Becca thought she could make it work.

"This is a five," she said, holding up the stone for the group to see. She then kissed the stone and skipped it across the still water.

"One, two, three, four," Cooper called out, counting the skips. "Ooh, just short. Five was a bit ambitious for your first throw of the day. But nice try."

"She's been upping her game all week, trying to match Lindy," EJ said, eyes still closed and looking fully relaxed in the mangrove-made hammock. "Not sure I've ever seen someone dive all over the court trying to dig every single ball that she spiked over the net. But there was Becca, sprawled across the floor taking balls to the face, off the dome, missing them by a foot."

Becca laughed along with Cooper and EJ, and although she was slightly embarrassed, she was more annoyed at the fact that EJ could tell she was trying to one-up Lindy. She didn't want anyone to know how much Lindy's talent bothered her.

"Today I got to at least ten of them," Becca replied, quite proud of herself.

"But she had you by ten on kills," EJ said.

"Whoa, ten? Dang, Bec, you're slipping there," Cooper joked.

Becca could feel herself getting annoyed with the conversation and sighed loudly. Cooper seemed to get the hint.

"But to be fair, she's super tall and barely has to jump. She should have had a hundred more than you," he added.

"Not exactly helpful, but thanks for trying." Becca stated flatly.

Becca found another stone and tossed it across the water, this time getting six skips. She had tried really hard not to show that she was jealous of Lindy Stevens but apparently, she hadn't tried hard enough. Honestly, she didn't want to be jealous, but she was. And for the second time in the last ten minutes, she was having to deal with her resentment issues. She picked up another stone to skip.

"It's ok to be jealous of Lindy," EJ said, as if reading Becca's mind. "Shoot, I am. She gets to see Will every day!" EJ joked as she sat upright on the tree. She looked at Becca, held her gaze for a second, and then continued, "Seriously Bec, she's not going to take anything away from you. She makes the team better and if the two of you were in this thing together, well, we'd be fire for sure." EJ reclined back onto her natural hammock. "Now let's get to a much more important topic. Did anyone see Will today? That blue polo shirt really made his eyes pop. I wish I was staring into those beautiful eyes right now."

"Oh girl, don't I know it! That boy sure is easy on the eyes. Mm-hmm." Cooper teased, making his voice sound like a character from a southern chick flick.

"Becca, please throw that rock at Cooper," EJ commanded, obviously joking.

They all laughed again, and Becca was grateful for the change in subject. She wasn't sure how to handle Lindy and, quite honestly, didn't want to think about it. She didn't want to think about Lindy's brother either, because the run in from earlier this week was still fresh in her mind. Becca wasn't sure what it was about Will Stevens that seemed to captivate her, but she needed to make it go away quickly. Boys were not an area in which she wanted to be on EJ's bad side. That was a sure way to ruin a friendship. She tried to quiet her mind and quickly found herself immersed in the simplicity and tranquility of a late afternoon with friends. Any troubling thoughts of jealousy had vanished from Becca's mind as she found herself completely content being here with her friends. As the sun started to set out over the mouth of the river, Becca wished she could push the pause button and stay in this very moment forever.

CHAPTER 10

SADIE

*C*ollege was a different animal. To Sadie, it felt like a series of contradictions. On the one hand, she was greeted by a significant increase in independence but on the other hand, she found herself with significantly less responsibility. Longer classes but less overall work. Show up to class but there was never anything to turn in. One thing that almost everyone preached during her recruiting trips was time management. She was told that as an athlete, your time would be consumed by all the demands of your particular sport. Yet Sadie found herself with a substantial increase in her free time as compared to high school, where she was involved in multiple sports as well as a rigorous academic schedule, service clubs, church and travel ball. And she still found time to fish and hang out with friends. College kind of felt like a vacation to her. Then again, Sadie had always been an outlier, so maybe she shouldn't have been surprised by her boredom. And while school seemed easier, creating a social life seemed like an insurmountable peak. Not one who enjoyed large groups of people or parties or clubs, Sadie struggled, even within her team, to find people with whom to befriend. Sure, she got along with almost everyone, but she seemed unable to find people to really cultivate relationships with. She missed Kat immensely, for a multitude of reasons, but currently it was because Sadie longed to simply tag along while Kat did all the hard work of meeting people. Outwardly, Sadie hated all socializing, but internally, she was grateful that she could ride Kat's social coattails. Life seemed easier when Kat was around. And right now, she wasn't around much at all. At the beginning of the semester, they talked every day, and one or the other would try to visit on the weekends, but within a couple of months, Sadie could feel a separation between them that was more than just physical distance. Kat had a job and a seemingly active social life with JJ and his college friends. Even when JJ was busy with football, Sadie noticed that Kat still had a plethora of friends with whom to party, which appeared to be Kat's activity of choice these days. After a while, the phone calls became less frequent. One or the other would get busy and forget, or not answer, and then a couple of days would become a week or two. When Sadie returned home for the holidays, eager to see and finally catch up with Kat, she was greeted with the unwelcome news that Kat staying put. Work was the excuse, but Sadie suspected there was more to the story. The fact that she was no longer privy to that part of Kat's life put a pain in her heart that she couldn't completely define.

Sadie's first collegiate softball season went about the way that she had expected. Her position was blocked by a senior, who was an All-American, so playing time was minimal. She tried to get involved with a couple of on-campus church groups but her in-season schedule did not align with their meeting times. When May rolled around, Sadie found herself eager to return home to a summer of comfort and familiar living. She was out in the *Johnny Pesky* within an hour of driving back into town. It was out on the river that she realized that she hadn't seen Kat in over three months. Kat had popped onto campus during one of the early season tournaments to watch Sadie play. She stayed for a night and then headed back 'to work', or so she said. And Sadie hadn't seen her since. They hadn't spoken on the phone in a month. So, Sadie decided she would call her after she returned from the water. When Kat answered the phone, she sounded as though she had been crying.

"Hey stranger," Sadie said when Kat answered the phone, the sadness in Kat's "Hello?" not immediately registering in her brain. When it did, she followed up with, "Kat, is something wrong? Are you ok?"

Sadie heard a few sniffles on the other end of the phone but when Kat again spoke, her voice sounded a bit stronger.

"Hey Sade," she replied. "Yeah, no, I'm good. Just allergies or something."

Sadie felt herself roll her eyes at Kat's obvious lie, but she was unsure whether she wanted to push the issue right now. She opted to hold off.

"You sure?"

"Yeah, this pollen down here is the worst," she said, sniffling once more. "What's up, girly? No softball today?" Kat asked.

"Ah no," Sadie responded, somewhat surprised that Kat didn't know that her season had ended a week ago. "Season's over. I'm home for the summer."

"Wow, that was a pretty quick season, huh?"

"Not really. February to May, made it to regionals. Played almost seventy games."

"Geez. Ok, well then, consider me sorry for not knowing. How's the river? Any bites?"

Sadie almost asked how Kat knew she was out on the river but realized that it would be like asking why water was wet. Some things just were. "Got out too late this morning so I just cruised. I'll fish tomorrow. You coming home at all this summer?"

"About that," Kat said, and Sadie knew she was not going to like the next statement. "I can't really quit my job and come home for the summer."

"Kat, you wait tables and bartend at a college bar. It's summer, there can't be that many people around campus right now. Is this about JJ?"

Sadie heard, through the rumor mill that was her cousin Maggie, that JJ was spending his summer at his parents' beach house with some hot model whose name Sadie did not recognize. Nor did she care, but she knew that Kat must. And with the beach house being a mere ten miles up the coast on one of the county's barrier islands, she figured Kat may be hesitant to come back.

"JJ? No, everything is good with JJ," Kat lied, and Sadie could hear the pain in her voice.

"Kat, I may be naïve but I'm not dumb," Sadie responded.

"Everything is fine Sadie. Look, I have to get ready for work. I'll talk to you later."

"Kat, it's only. . ." Sadie heard the phone click in her ear. ". . .three thirty. Bar doesn't open until six," Sadie said to the silence on the other end of the line. She tossed the phone on her bed and sat down next to it. She looked at the ceiling and contemplated making the few hours' drive to check on Kat. If she left now, maybe she could get to the bar before Kat started her shift. Sadie grabbed her phone from her bed and her keys from the dresser, left a note for her parents and headed south in her SUV.

Sadie arrived at the Blue Lagoon, Kat's work, just after six p.m. As she walked in, she noticed a tall, burly, black guy behind the bar. *Well, that's definitely not Kat.* She walked over to him and asked if Kat was waiting tables or helping him behind the bar. Sadie was not anticipating his answer.

"Kat? Tall, skinny, blonde chick, Kat? She hasn't worked here since Christmas, man. Got herself fired for giving free drinks to the football team. Probably giving them more than free drinks too, if you catch my drift."

Sadie stared at him with a look of utter confusion that morphed into complete disgust at his accusation. She shook her head and left the building without thanking him for his help. Climbing back into her car, she called Kat and left a voicemail saying that she was in town. She then headed toward Kat's apartment. Sadie didn't see Kat's car in the parking lot but there was another lot on the opposite side of the building where Kat sometimes parked. She bounded up two flights of stairs to the third floor and knocked on Kat's door. Her roommate, a darkhaired Southern belle from Charleston named Emma Grace, answered.

"Hey Sadie," Emma Grace said in her southern twang that stretched the 'a' sound for an extra beat.

"Hey Em, Kat here?" Sadie asked.

"No," Emma Grace responded, sounding a little surprised. "Kat left a couple of days ago. She said she was going out of town with JJ for a week. She didn't tell you?"

Sadie sighed and shook her head. She hadn't seen JJ in town, as she'd only been home for a few hours, but she was fairly confident that the information provided by her cousin was accurate. Which meant that Kat had lied to her roommate too. That also meant that no one knew where Kat had run off to.

"I'm sorry Sadie. Do you want to come in?" Emma Grace asked, stepping aside to let Sadie enter.

"No that's ok. I'm just going to head back. Thanks though."

"Ok. Sorry Sadie. Drive safe."

"Thanks." Sadie paused, deciding to take a flyer and see if Emma Grace had any information about Kat and her current life status, since Sadie herself was obviously out of the loop. "Hey Em, is everything ok with her? I actually talked to her earlier this afternoon and she didn't sound right. And she obviously didn't tell me she was with JJ."

"Um, I think so. Honestly Sadie, she hasn't been around much. She was late on rent last month and hasn't paid yet this month. It's not like we're going to get evicted, since my dad pays our rent and she just pays him back, but he's not exactly happy either."

"I went to the bar where she was working. They said she hasn't worked there since Christmas. If she doesn't have another job, she doesn't have any money. Has she been staying with JJ?"

"I don't know. I see him around a lot but it's not always with Kat. He's pretty popular around here, if you know what I mean." Sadie chuckled. *Same old JJ.* "But she seemed her normal, happy self when she was packing the other day. I assumed they were back to 'on again' status," Emma Grace said.

Sadie sighed and shook her head slightly, willing her brain to process all she just heard. She thanked Emma Grace and asked to have Kat call her whenever she returned. Emma Grace said that she would pass along the message, and they parted ways. Sadie climbed into her SUV and sat there motionless for some time. She had it on good authority that Kat was not with JJ right now. She wasn't working, at least not at her former place of employment, and she wasn't at her apartment. *Where could she have gone?* Sadie truly did not know. She banged her fist on the steering wheel in frustration until her hand started to hurt. Then she turned on the car, put it in drive, and headed back home. Somewhere amid the emotional war between fear and anger, hope sprung up in the form of Grandpa Jack. Maybe he knew where Kat was. He always seemed to know everything.

CHAPTER 11

BECCA

*T*he next couple of weeks were relatively smooth for Becca. Eighth grade was hard but mostly because the amount of homework seemed to have doubled since the previous year. Becca had almost every class with Maddie, who was destined to be the class valedictorian, if such a thing were to exist in middle school. Maddie was a human Google search and seemed to remember literally everything that she read. Which was helpful when Becca didn't finish her English reading and need a cliff notes version before going into class. It didn't happen often, but sometimes the books they were required to read put Becca to sleep; occasionally even while she was in class. Debate was a breeze, especially with EJ. They both seemed to have a natural ability to argue their point and together were a near unstoppable force. She did dread the day that they had to square off against one another. And since EJ chose to follow a boy instead of an easy A, debate was the only class they had together. Aside from lunch, they rarely saw each other during the school day. And sometimes that was a good thing.

There had been no more literal run ins with Will, thank goodness. But he seemed destined to flash that incredible smile whenever he saw her in the hallway, which happened to be A LOT. And every time, her live-in butterflies would flit around in her stomach. It took all the willpower, no pun intended, she had to keep her cheeks from turning red with both embarrassment and excitement. She needed a distraction, especially with EJ still enamored with all things Will Stevens. Becca's algebra class was in the high school building, and she had to walk right by Weston Gold's locker to get to the room. *Gosh, he's so cute!* Maybe if she spent enough time thinking about Weston, she could get the butterflies that Will stirred up to die down. It was worth a try. After a few days, she noticed her spare thoughts drifting toward the wrong boy. *So much for that idea.*

Volleyball was another story altogether. Practice in and of itself was going well, however Becca could feel a growing animosity toward Will's sister Lindy. She was good, really good. Good enough to challenge Becca for the 'captain' role, which her coach routinely gave to the best player on the team. Normally, she would welcome a challenge, but in her eight-ish years in sports, no one had come close to matching Becca's ability. It was something that she would never brag about; her parents preached confident humility ad nauseum, but it was the truth. She was naturally athletic, so sports always came easy to her, and she played nearly all of them. Volleyball and lacrosse were her primary sports, if she had to choose, so to have her status contested here, on the court, well it was something she was completely unprepared for. So were the conflicting feelings of liking one twin while feuding with the other. Her brain was starting to hurt. Becca's immediate answer: try to forget the one while engaging in fierce competition with the other. *How hard could it be?* she had thought when her brain first concocted the idea. It was turning out to be much more difficult than imagined. On days when Lindy outperformed her, which was happening more than Becca wanted to admit, she'd finish practice angry and frustrated. Volleyball was suddenly becoming far less fun than it used to be. This part of the plan was not working well. Neither was the 'forgetting' the other twin since Will showed up in the gym every day after football practice, his sweaty golden hair sticking up in stray directions. His presence was also affecting EJ, as her sets became significantly more erratic upon his arrival. Which also wasn't helping Becca's mood, since she required at least a decent set to try to keep up with Lindy's kill rate. On one Friday afternoon, things came to a head.

Lindy was drilling every ball straight into the ground, looking every bit the superstar she seemed to be. Becca wasn't having a bad practice, but her performance was not on Lindy's level that day and her frustration was mounting. Will must have had a short practice because he walked in about thirty minutes into their practice and sat on the bleachers by the double doors.

"Look who just walked in," EJ said to Becca as they stood on the side of the court waiting on their turn to run a hitting drill. Becca glanced toward the door and happened to catch Will looking at them. Even from a distance, his blue eyes seemed to capture her soul. He flashed his signature smile, which elicited a flirty wave from EJ and an ever so slight head nod from Becca. She could already feel her cheeks heating up and prayed EJ wouldn't notice.

"His smile hits different, doesn't it?" EJ asked rhetorically. Becca rolled her eyes. This was the last thing she needed right now.

"Can we just focus on volleyball?" Becca said to EJ, her voice a little edgy.

EJ turned and gave her a look. "I am focused on volleyball. But I can multitask."

"Not well." Becca regretted her words as soon as they left her mouth.

"Excuse me?" EJ said, a little too loud. The coach glared at them and then told them to focus up and get on the court. Becca's cheeks were now legit red. Not only had her coach called her out, she'd done it in front of Will. And now EJ was mad at her. If the look of disdain on her face wasn't evidence enough, the really crappy sets that she was now shoving Becca's way, whenever she finally decided to set her, gave it away. *What a miserable day.*

The never-ending practice finally concluded with Lindy spiking a ball so hard off Becca's left shoulder that it flew all the way to where Will was sitting on the bleachers. *A miserable day with the worst possible ending.* After the coach finished her pep talk, which focused on their first game the following week, Becca tried to apologize to EJ but she cold-shouldered Becca and mumbled something about homework. Becca knew that EJ rarely did her homework, and definitely not on Friday afternoons.

"We still on for the Grove tonight?" Becca hollered after her.

EJ merely held up a hand and kept walking. *Oh boy.* Becca grabbed her water and decided to waste time in the gym while EJ was in the locker room.

"Good practice today," an overly cheerful voice called from behind her. Becca turned to see Lindy walking towards her. *I really don't want to do this right now.* But Lindy was still walking and talking. "And sorry for hitting that last one off your shoulder. I was trying to get it outside of you, but you move pretty quick." Becca had no idea how to respond. She could not have disagreed with Lindy more, but then Lindy had to throw in a compliment and muddle up her brain.

"Ah, thanks," she said cautiously. "And it was no big deal. It didn't hurt." *Oh geez, that sounded awful.* "I mean, you hit it hard, really hard. I'm just. . .ah," Becca stuttered.

Lindy just chuckled and said, "I know what you mean. So, what is this Grove that you were talking about? I've heard EJ talk about it too. Is it a restaurant or like, game room or something?"

Now it was Becca's turn to chuckle. "Oh no, it's nothing like that. It's just a piece of land next to EJ's house. We just call it the Grove because it's full of mangroves trees."

"Oh. OK. And EJ's house is on the water, right?" Lindy asked.

"Yeah, it's the mega mansion close to the boat ramp. In The Estates." Becca turned her head, confusion on her face, because she had not answered this question. And EJ hadn't returned to the gym from the locker room. Standing on the other side of her was none other than Will Stevens. Becca looked at him with a perplexed look. The town wasn't that big, but she was still somewhat shocked that Will knew where EJ's house was. Maybe EJ's crush was being reciprocated after all. Will seemed to understand the question her face was silently asking and answered, "My mom drove by there one day. We were driving around trying to figure out how to get to different places. She thought that road led to the boat ramp. It did not."

Makes sense.

"So how does one get an invite to the exclusive Grove club?" Will asked and Becca was now almost certain that the crush was reciprocated. She couldn't wait to inform EJ. That should be information that would forgive even the most heinous of offenses.

"I'll say something to EJ. It's her property. But I'm sure you'd be welcome. But maybe not tonight. I probably need to make amends first."

Will laughed and said, "Yeah, probably." Becca wondered how much of their scuffle he had seen. Or heard.

"Do you guys go out there every Friday?" Lindy inquired.

"Almost. Unless there's a football game."

Will looked down at the buzzing phone that was in his left hand. "Oh shoot, Lin, we have to go. Mom's in the car and J has an appointment at five o'clock." Becca looked at her watch. Seven minutes; she hoped the appointment was close. "See ya later, Becca." Will rushed out of the double doors but Lindy hung back a bit.

"Hey Becca, thanks for pushing me at practice," she said. "I appreciate the competition." At first, Becca thought she was being pointed and sarcastic, but both her tone and her facial expressions said that she was being sincere. Becca felt a twinge of guilt over her self-made, secret feud.

"You're welcome. It's making me better too."

Lindy smiled and said, "Have a great weekend," as she nearly skipped out of the gym.

Becca felt so confused and conflicted. She was both happy and a little sad that Will Stevens seemed to be reciprocating EJ's crush. And she was taken in by Lindy's kindness but also still feeling the competitor in her wanting to be the best. *Darn, these emotions. And probably hormones.* Becca had a lot to process but first, she needed to talk to EJ. And to someone else.

CHAPTER 12

"**H**ow was practice?" her mom asked. This was the other person that Becca needed to talk to. And Becca was glad her brothers weren't in the car with her. They could talk now, and she could get to EJ's ASAP.

Becca had a close relationship with her mom. Sure, there were times when her mom just didn't get it, like in her reasoning for not getting Becca a phone or with certain clothing, but for the most part, her mom was pretty cool. From a young age, Becca could remember her mom being an active participant in her life, asking questions and patiently awaiting the answers. Sometimes she would lose her temper, usually with the boys, but she was quick to apologize and bring things down to a more manageable level. But that did not mean she was a pushover by any stretch of the imagination. Both Becca's mom and dad were fairly strict, especially when it came to behavior, school and phones, or the lack thereof. It caused arguments for sure, but both parents tried to be patient and loving in explaining why they made decisions that they made. That mix of patience and unconditional love, along with the evidence of good counsel in the past, made her mother Becca's default person for advice and consultation when she couldn't figure it out herself. And between Lindy, Will and EJ, she was as lost as she'd ever been.

"Ah, it was ok. Mom, you played sports."

"Yes," her mom answered, confusion over the direction of the conversation evident in her voice.

"And you were good."

"Yes," she responded in the same tone.

"What did you do when you found someone that was better than you?"

"Well, I guess that depends. If they were on the opposing team, I wanted to beat them. Badly. And if they were on my team, well, I guess I was kind of like you in the sense that I didn't have a whole lot of competition until I got older. Not bragging, but like you, God blessed me with a decent amount of athleticism and sports was one of those things that just came easier to me than to others. Probably around high school, the gap closed and playing ability was much more on par. So, I just worked harder. Little secret for you; I didn't like to lose," her mom said playfully.

"Well, that hasn't changed," Becca laughed.

"Yeah, but now I don't get mad and go practice for hours until I can beat you," her mom joked back, although Becca had a feeling that statement wasn't entirely true. Her mom had been a college athlete and set a bunch of records at her high school. And she was still pretty competitive during family game nights.

"But did you ever get jealous of the other person? Like you wanted to beat them at everything because you didn't want to be second best?" She wasn't sure that she was asking what her heart wanted to say, because she wasn't really sure of that herself.

"Lindy Stevens, huh?"

Becca was stunned. How could her mom possibly know about Lindy? They'd only been practicing for a couple of weeks and Becca hadn't made mention of her until now. At least not that she could remember.

"Don't look so shocked, kiddo. Moms know everything." They were at a stoplight, so Becca's mom had taken the opportunity to peak over at her. "It's a small town and people talk. Also, I overheard you and EJ talking about her last week."

"Mom," Becca groaned.

"Not on purpose. You were both in the kitchen working on your homework and I was folding laundry. It's not like you guys are quiet. Anyway, do you know the verse in Proverbs, about iron sharpening iron?

Becca nodded, "Yeah, it's in the same chapter as "Let another praise you; and not your own mouth." The confident humility thing.

Her mom looked a bit surprised, in a good way, as she resumed driving and said, "Well, I'm glad you are both listening to me and reading your Bible. As you know, Proverbs is a wisdom book and gives godly advice for pursuing wisdom and living accordingly. This verse is no different. You sharpen a knife, or a sword, by rubbing it across a hard piece of iron, or another sword. If you don't, it's still a knife or a sword, albeit dull and not as useful. I read a commentary once about this verse relating to spending time in God's word and being around other believers who can help you grow spiritually as well as in the place where God has called you. It will help your effectiveness in glorifying God and strengthen your resolve when hard times come. Keep that in mind as I now take it out of its original context, but I think it can apply to this situation; surround yourself with people who will make you better and help you grow. In your case, right now, Lindy pushes you athletically. I also think this situation is challenging you mentally and spiritually. And as you grow in life, you are going to want people who challenge you to be better athletically, spiritually, in your work, as a spouse, as a woman of God."

Becca groaned. "But it's so hard. I like being the best."

"Remember when you played softball for like a hot minute and you thought you could knock anything down with your metal bat because you swung so hard?"

Becca nodded almost imperceptibly. She had a feeling she knew where this was going, and she wasn't going to like it.

"And you tried, very unsuccessfully, to knock down the wrought iron gate at EJ's house? Being humbled hurts," her mom countered.

Becca rolled her eyes and asked, "So practically speaking, what do I do?"

"What do you think you should do?" Both of her parents liked to turn their kids' questions back around on them. Her dad was the worst about it, but her mom had picked up on his little trick and had been doing it more often. It was dreadfully maddening.

Becca didn't even try to hide her annoyance. "Mom, I asked you. For advice. If I knew, I wouldn't have asked."

Her mom drove in silence. As they turned down their road, Becca acquiesced. "I should welcome the challenge with a good attitude."

"Not a bad idea," her mom responded. "And I will give you a bit of advice. Control the things that you can control."

"My attitude and my effort," Becca mumbled, her words overlapping her mom's as she said the same thing. Becca had heard that phrase on repeat for as long as she could remember. Her mom chuckled and then continued.

"And keep being you – kind, hardworking, a great teammate. Continue to let that light that God placed inside of you shine bright. And if you find yourself being pulled toward jealousy, pray about it. He will equip you with whatever you need to escape that temptation. And who knows, you and Lindy may end up being great friends."

"Maybe. But she's a little much. Even for me."

Her mom chuckled a little and said, "Yeah, but sometimes 'a little much' is just what we need."

As they pulled into the driveway, Becca remembered that she needed to talk to EJ. "Hey mom, can I do my homework tomorrow? I really need to go talk to EJ. I think I made her pretty upset at practice and need to apologize."

"Ok, but if you stay there, I really don't want you girls outside at the Grove late tonight. It's Friday. And there's no football game." Which meant that the Banks would be crazy tonight and the potential for overflow to the Grove was high.

"Yes ma'am. And Mom, thanks."

"Anytime, Becca girl."

Becca grabbed her backpack and lunchbox and dashed through the garage door. She needed to get to EJ's sooner rather than later.

CHAPTER 13

"**H**e said what?" EJ asked, unable to contain her excitement. Becca had biked over to EJ's, solo this time, and found EJ in the kitchen eating an orange. She had rolled her eyes when she saw Becca and started to turn to walk out of the room when Becca quickly apologized and spilled the tea about Will's request.

"He asked how he could get an invitation to the Grove," Becca repeated. "He's totally into you."

EJ squealed with delight and gave Becca an enormous hug. *All is forgiven, just as I thought.* Becca smiled as EJ continued hugging her, adding a bit of a bounce to the hug. But now Becca's arms were starting to hurt. EJ had come at her so fast with that hug that she had been unable to prepare, and her arms were pinned by her side.

"Can't move," Becca laughed.

EJ quickly released her arms and went running for her phone, which was plugged in on the kitchen island.

"You have his phone number?" Becca asked, surprised that she was even asking that question. Of course, EJ would already have his phone number.

"Technically, it's not his. Lindy and Will share it. I got it from Lindy earlier this week. I've already scouted for socials, but they don't have any, so I'll just have to send a text." EJ not only had her own phone but had access to nearly all social media sites. Becca knew that Ms. Elisabeth tried to restrict them whenever possible but EJ's dad pretty much let her do whatever she wanted. She'd been around for one of EJ's arguments with her mom and EJ's dad stepped in, saying that as long as it wasn't illegal, it was fine. That may be a slight exaggeration, but EJ definitely had a long leash as far as technology was concerned. And with pretty much everything else.

"Are you going to ask them to come over tonight?" Becca asked, suddenly concerned.

"Stop stressing. My mom already said that she didn't want us out there tonight. So, no. And Lindy's not that bad. You need to chill on that."

Becca didn't have the heart to tell her that, even though Will seemed like he was into EJ, she was more concerned about him and the way he made her feel.

EJ continued, "I'm just going to tell them to come over tomorrow. My dad is out of town again and Xan has soccer so we can all hang at the pool or something." EJ started texting on her phone.

The pool is even worse than the Grove. Becca was suddenly self-conscious and felt the need to get out of this real quick. *Xan and Bry play on the same team so maybe I can use that as an excuse.* "I have to go to the soccer game tomorrow. You know my parents aren't going to let me skip that."

EJ looked down at her phone as it buzzed. She showed Becca the response.

Cool. Who else? Becca gonna be there?

Of course. Prob Coop Maddie Seb 2, EJ responded, and then looked at Becca. "Now you're committed. And see, Lindy wants to hang with you. Told you she's not that bad."

Becca had a weird feeling in her stomach that told her it was not Lindy who was answering EJ's messages. Lindy would have already assumed that Becca would be there.

Waiting for parents, lyk tmrw, the phone buzzed back.

A huge smile crossed EJ's face and then she hollered, "MOM!!"

"Whoa, I'm right here," Ms. Elisabeth answered, walking out of her office that was on the far end of the kitchen. "Hi Becca, how are you? I was just on the phone with your mother. Are you ready for your first game next week?"

"Yes ma'am. . ." Becca started to answer before EJ interrupted.

"She's fine. I'm going to have some people come over tomorrow while you're at Xan's game. And Becca's going to stay the night."

Becca's eyes widened. This was new. She'd never heard EJ speak to her mother like that. They'd had some tenuous moments and since Becca was around quite a bit, she'd seen some of them. But EJ had never just told her mom what she was going to do, so matter of fact and without room for disagreement.

Ms. Elisabeth looked at EJ with sadness in her eyes. This, too, was shocking. She'd expected anger. Or, at the very least, frustration.

"That was unnecessary. Let's try that again, please." EJ's mom said.

"Why? At least I told you what I was doing. Gavin and Dad just leave and do whatever they want," EJ retorted, anger and annoyance dripping from every word. EJ cut her eyes hard at her mom and glared. Becca suddenly felt very uncomfortable in a place that had long been her second home.

"EJ," Ms. Elisabeth started. But Becca had already seen enough to know that she had no desire to be here any longer, let alone stay the night.

"I actually can't stay tonight. My mom said I had to come back and finish my homework. And I should get going before it gets too dark," Becca said.

"Oh, just stay Becca. You can blow off your homework for one night. It's not going to hurt your GPA," EJ replied, the annoyance still in her voice.

Becca stared, mouth agape, at EJ, who was busy on her phone, and then glanced at Ms. Elisabeth. Her eyes asked the unspoken question to which Ms. Elisabeth mouthed, "It's ok." Becca was still very unsure of what was transpiring, but decided to leave before things got any worse.

"I'll call you tomorrow, EJ. Bye, Ms. Elisabeth." Becca hightailed it to the front door, hearing EJ groan and moan behind her in the kitchen. As she was shutting the front door behind her, she heard Ms. Elisabeth say,

"Don't ever speak to me like that again. I don't care what your father does. He's not in charge here anymore."

What in the world is going on? Becca pedaled home as fast as she could, the awakened butterflies in her stomach giving her an extra boost of urgency and possibly speed.

CHAPTER 14

"**S**o that's Lindy Stevens," Becca's mom said as she pulled into the gym parking lot, referencing the tall blonde walking along the sidewalk in front of the gym. Lindy waved as she made her way toward the double doors. Becca realized that this was probably the first time her mom had seen Lindy, since her dad generally handled drop off in the morning and Lindy was gone by the time Becca left the gym after practice.

"Yep," Becca replied as she waved back, hoping that Lindy wouldn't wait for her. Tonight was their first game and Becca could feel the butterflies acting up. She always felt a little nervous before a game but today the butterflies seemed to have hit hyperdrive. She needed to sit in the car for a minute and catch her breath. Much to her delight, Lindy didn't wait. Becca took a deep breath and exhaled it slowly. She turned to say something to her mom and caught her staring at Lindy as she walked through the gym doors.

"I thought you wanted me to get along with Lindy," Becca said, grateful for the distraction from her flittering friends.

"I do," her mom replied, looking over at her with a questioning look.

"Then why the stare down?" Becca asked.

"Stare down?" her mom asked in confusion. Becca pointed toward the door. "Oh, no stare down," her mom answered. "Lindy just reminds me of someone that I used to know."

"Oh, well, that's fun," Becca said sarcastically. Eager to avoid a trip down memory lane, and moderately aware that her butterflies had temporarily settled, she reached out to grab the door handle with one hand and grabbed her bag with the other. "Ok, gotta go," she said.

"Becca," her mom said as Becca climbed out of the SUV. "Have fun tonight. Play hard. And smile."

Becca gave her mom a little smile and said, "I will."

"Love you, Bec."

"Love you too."

As she jogged through the parking lot toward the gym, Becca saw EJ coming around the far corner of the high school.

"Hey, E," she said, the excitement of the first game apparent in her voice.

EJ gave a little wave and stopped to wait for another teammate who was walking up behind her. EJ had been acting a little strange since the weekend, when Becca bailed on spending the night. She did end up going back over there on Saturday after Bryson's soccer game. She and Cooper arrived to find Will, Lindy, EJ, Maddie and Sebastian already in the pool. EJ quickly said "Hi," but her attention was focused on Will. This surprised Becca not at all, since EJ had been vying for his attention since the first day of school. What was strange, however, was that after Will and Lindy left, EJ continued to ignore her. Becca wasn't sure if it was because of the previous night or because Will kept sneaking peeks at her throughout the afternoon. Becca had done her best to ignore him. Not only because he was the current object of EJ's affection but also because, despite her best efforts, his attention still made her butterflies mingle. A lot.

Becca decided not to wait for EJ and headed into the locker room. It had received a fresh coat of paint over the summer and the royal blue lockers that lined three sides really popped in contrast to the crisp white of the walls. There was a thick, red, belt high stripe running along the fourth wall with the word EAGLES painted in blue and red above it. Lindy was sitting on one of the red benches tying her shoes, her white uniform looking almost exactly like the fourth wall. Fresh, clean, new; how Becca was starting to feel about both the season and her relationship with Lindy. Saturday's pool party had helped ease some of Becca's concerns about her. She still felt a twinge of on-court jealousy, but Lindy's niceness turned out to be genuine. She was beginning to rival Cooper for 'the nicest person in the world' status. And she was funny. She and Cooper had the group in fits of laughter all afternoon.

"Hey Becca!" Lindy said in the overly enthusiastic tone that turned out to be her normal voice.

"Hey," Becca said in reply, trying to focus her mind on something other than EJ's irritation with her.

"You ready?" Lindy asked, hopping up from the bench. "I'm pumped. It's been a year since I played a game and I'm so ready!"

"For sure," Becca replied. "Wait, it's been a year? I thought you played all the time."

"I did when we lived in Germany. Volleyball is big over there. But we were in Colorado this past spring as my dad finished up his Air Force stuff. And my mom was flying back and forth to Frankfurt for my little brother. There were some issues with the adoption, and he had to stay in Germany when we moved back to the States. So, I couldn't play."

"I didn't know you had a little brother," Becca said.

"Yeah, he just turned two. And he has some issues. He freaks out with lots of people and loud noises, so my mom has to stay home with him a lot."

"Oh. Dang," Becca said. She didn't know how to respond to that, so she just found some commonality to talk about to fill the void. Which, as it turned out, wasn't that difficult.

"My dad was in the military too. Navy though. But he got out a long time ago. Before I was born, I think."

"It was a pretty cool life, but I'm kind of glad we're done with that. I didn't really like all the moving. It's nice to make friends knowing that I'm not going to have to say goodbye to them in a couple of years."

Becca hadn't thought about that before. Lindy's extremely extroverted personality was starting to make sense. She was used to having to step in to the 'new girl' role and make friends. She seemed pretty good at it, and Becca was surprised at how easy Lindy was to talk to. And at how quickly her jealousy had subsided.

"Volleyball was a constant. I could always find people who played," Lindy continued. "Speaking of," she said as she walked over to the rolling basket full of volleyballs, "let's go!" Lindy started pushing the basket out of the locker room doors, nearly hitting the group of girls now entering, EJ included.

The group dodged out of the way and ribbed at Lindy for her enthusiasm as she headed down the hallway to the gym. Becca laughed and tossed her stuff into her locker. She walked around the room fist-bumping her teammates as they danced to the music that was playing over EJ's Bluetooth speaker. The butterflies that were so active earlier settled down and were nearly dormant. She was ready to go. Becca walked over to talk to EJ but as she approached, EJ looked at her and then said that she had forgotten something. She ran out of the locker room before Becca could get to her. Becca looked around. EJ's knee pads and court shoes lay under the bench next to her bag. Her phone and speaker were lying inside of her locker. And she had her uniform on when she bolted. *That's weird.* Becca shook off her concerns and bounced out of the locker room doors. Today was the culmination of all those long practice sessions. The season started now, and she was more than ready. And nothing was going to bring her down.

*****

The set was wide. EJ had clearly avoided setting Becca all night and would have continued had the coach not called a timeout and all but demanded EJ set her. When she was hitting from the outside, Becca had a clear advantage over the opposing player, and they should have been capitalizing on that. But they were halfway through the second game and Becca had yet to receive a ball. Until now. She took her approach and as she went to jump, she realized the ball was further out than she'd anticipated. She could handle it; she'd just have to reach more directly over her head to compensate, as opposed to up over her right shoulder. Becca contacted the ball and sent it well over the blocker's outstretched arms. It hit squarely in front of the back row defender. Becca, on the other hand, did not hit the ground as evenly as the ball. As she came down, her weight was shifted too much over her left side and her leg was not prepared for it. She felt a pop as her knee buckled backwards, and she collapsed in a heap.

The sound that escaped her lips was unnatural. Becca grabbed at her leg as the tears rolled uninhibited down her cheeks. The intensity of the pain told her something was wrong. When she saw her mother standing over her, she knew it was bad. Her mom was not one to overreact, especially when her kids were hurt, so her presence caused Becca to cry even more. There were other people standing around her, but the tears clouded her vision so much that she had no idea who was there. She could hear her mom saying something, trying to calm her down, but her ears seemed to be just as murky as her eyes. Becca's only thought was that her volleyball season was over before the first match was. The assistant coach helped Becca's mom stand her up and nearly carried Becca to the locker room. They sat her down on the same bench on which Lindy was sitting earlier, and her mom carefully lifted her leg so that it joined her. Becca lay all the way back on the bench, both hands covering her face. Her mom said something to the coach and then Becca heard the door to the locker room shut behind him. She felt one of her hands being lifted from her face and her mom wipe away a straggling tear.

"Bec, it's going to be ok. But I need to check out your knee."

Becca felt her eyes starting to well up again. She didn't really want her mom, or anyone for that matter, to touch her leg. Part of her was afraid of the physical pain that it would cause. The other part was afraid of the emotional pain that would come from her biggest fears being confirmed. Becca merely nodded her head in affirmation. Her mom moved down by her leg but before she reached for it, Becca said,

"Mom, wait." She sniffled and wiped her eyes with the back of her hand. "Mom, how bad?"

"It'll hurt a little bit," she answered honestly.

"No, I mean, yeah, I know. But, how bad?"

Her mom took a deep breath before answering. "Looked like your ACL. Possibly MCL."

Becca picked her head up from the bench and looked at her mom. "How. Bad?" she repeated.

Her mom finally understood and said, "If it's torn, surgery. And no sports for nine to twelve months."

Becca dropped her head back down on the bench and started crying once again.

CHAPTER 15

SADIE

*T*hree tortuous days had passed before Kat had finally answered her phone. Sadie had driven straight to her grandfather's house, certain that he knew exactly where Kat was, only to be told that he hadn't spoken to her in at least a month. Sadie had called everyone she could think of to ask if they had heard from her and even accepted her cousin's invitation to a ridiculous party at JJ's beach house to see if Kat happened to show up. She hadn't. Sadie had been contemplating a call to the police when Kat had happily answered her phone as if nothing at all was amiss. Sadie lost it, to which Kat responded with an absurd 'chill out' and then proceeded to tell Sadie that she was with her mom soaking up the sun on a beach somewhere. Exactly where, Kat never did disclose, and Sadie questioned the veracity of that statement. Partially because Kat had already lied about having to work all summer and partially because Kat's relationship with her mother was tenuous at best. Sadie's irritation had not been allayed by the end of the conversation and as a result, she hadn't tried to call Kat for nearly a month. Kat hadn't called her either, and before Sadie knew it, she was headed back to school without having spoken to Kat for more than five total minutes.

The summer heat had lingered into October and then quickly morphed into a dreary, cold winter, completely excluding fall from the party. Spring wasn't much better, less regarding the weather and more related to, well, everything else. Sadie found herself playing a little bit more than in the previous season but was learning that playing time was not always based on merit. There were far more politics involved than she would have ever imagined. And she had no clue how to handle that. Add that to her nonexistent social life and Sadie just felt like a hot mess. She didn't feel as though she fit anywhere, or with anyone. Her team liked to party, but that had never been her thing. She would occasionally attend but always abstained from drinking anything other than soda. Being sober around the inebriated got old real quick. The search for on-campus Christian groups continued to prove fruitless as her softball schedule tended to interfere with their meeting times. On the few occasions she was able to attend, she found athletes, or even the athletically inclined, to be in the minority. The lack of commonality and her inconsistent attendance made cultivating friendships nearly impossible. There was no river or lake nearby in which to fish, so Sadie often found herself alone at a neighborhood park, kicking the soccer ball around to clear her mind. Well, at least trying to clear her mind. She missed Kat and wished that she was around, even if it was just to talk. She'd know how to keep Sadie from being inside her head all the time. It would probably involve doing something ridiculous that Sadie would have never done on her own, like talking or throwing her own party. Sadie would outwardly resist and endlessly complain, but in the end, her mind would be a little bit clearer. She wished that Kat would roll on into town and do just that. On more than one occasion, she thought about calling and asking her to, but the drifting that started in summer had left them oceans apart. To be honest, neither really made a significant attempt to negate that change. Sadie knew that she should, but she was still holding on to some anger and bitterness from Kat's ice-cold shoulder. She pridefully, and probably selfishly, chose to lean into that and push away as well.

They did speak occasionally, but it was all very superficial, more like the obligatory call to mom every week to tell her you're ok. Kat would assure Sadie that all was going well. She had a new job, had enrolled in the local community college to take a few classes and that, despite the on-again, off-again thing with JJ, she was happy. Sadie would say that things were going okay with softball and that she was trying to 'put herself out there' as Kat recommended. It wasn't a lie, but it certainly wasn't the truth either. Sadie would hang up the phone and wish things weren't this way, but she could never seem to push aside the hubris that blocked her from being completely honest. She was sure that part of it was because Kat wasn't being forthcoming with her, nor was she making much of an effort at anything else. Why should Sadie be the only one fighting for this friendship?

That season ended rather abruptly, and to Sadie it was bittersweet. She still hated to lose, but she was hopeful that the mental turmoil the season brought would finally fade away. She'd matured in her ability to handle losing but struggled mightily with the fact that her hard work and good choices were not paying off in the form of playing time. Or anything else. It went against all that she had been taught, and it was causing her to question everything. By the end, she was caught in a web of wondering if anything was worth it. Literally anything. She quietly headed back home to the solace of the river, hoping that the water would wash away the mess. And wishing that she could put aside her pride and call Kat. Neither would happen.

CHAPTER 16

BECCA

The last month had been difficult for Becca. More mentally than physically but there was still a challenge there as well. With her mom's history of working with the orthopedic doctors, Becca was able to get an MRI the next day. As a shock to no one, her mom was right; a tear of the anterior cruciate ligament. Becca's mom had the surgery scheduled for a week later, so that she could get the swelling down and move her knee or something. Whatever the reasoning, Becca was not happy. Pushing the surgery meant more time away from sports. Volleyball season was a bust, as was soccer. But there was an outside chance that she could be back for the end of lacrosse season. At least that's what the internet told her. Her mom said the chance wasn't outside at all: it was a complete zero.

Surgery had gone as well as Becca could have expected, although she hadn't really known what to expect. The pain was bearable, until the awful physical therapist got ahold of her and tried straightening her leg. Becca had buried her face in her hands and tried like heck not to cry. She was unsuccessful. But every visit was a little easier and she was walking without crutches within a week, albeit with a limp. She and Cooper could have been twins if he hadn't been busting his rear in therapy. But now he was out of the wheelchair, and she was the one taking the elevator to get to the second floor.

After a month, her walking was almost completely normal, and she could maneuver her leg through nearly its full range of motion. The last bit of bending was a struggle but that was it. She was still weak, but otherwise, things were moving in the right direction. Mentally though, she found it difficult to cope. Right after her injury and surgery, people were checking on her, giving her words of encouragement and telling her how much they would miss her on the volleyball court. But now, the attention was on Lindy and how great both she and the team were. Becca found that she was both happy and annoyed that the team was playing so well without her. A small part of her wanted them to struggle and to realize just how important Becca was to the team. But that was clearly not happening. At first, she wanted to be mad at Lindy for it all, but Lindy made it very difficult for her to do so. She made and delivered chocolate chip cookies to Becca right after the surgery, (they were delicious), and was easily the most present and helpful friend. Will was also more than willing to help, but after seeing EJ's look of disdain when he carried her backpack to lunch one day, Becca had been declining all his subsequent offers.

Speaking of EJ, Becca wasn't sure what exactly was going on there. EJ had come over to see her the day after she got hurt but was still a bit standoffish and quiet, which was completely out of the ordinary for her. And then for the past month, EJ had been making herself scarce. She'd been avoiding Becca at school, spending her time trying to get Will's attention or with Quinn Gold and the rest of the cheerleaders. That, in and of itself, was suspect, because EJ never previously would have been seen hanging out with Quinn. Mostly because Becca would have never been seen hanging out with Quinn. And not just because she was Weston's younger sister. Becca and Quinn had been near mortal enemies for years. No one knew why; they just didn't like each other. And by default, EJ didn't like Quinn either. Until now. And EJ had neither come over to hang out with her, nor invited Becca over to her house. She thought it might be because her lack of mobility precluded her from getting to the Grove, but Cooper said that neither he nor Maddie and Seb had been out there either. EJ seemed to have transformed into a different person overnight and Becca couldn't even get near her to ask what happened.

Five weeks to the day after her injury, Becca finally returned to the gym to watch her team play. They only had three games left in their season and the final two were away, so it was her last chance to watch her friends and teammates play. The butterflies that she felt on that first game day were little babies compared to the monarchs that were flying around today. She was confused as to why she was more nervous to watch than to play. Becca's mom came with her, and they found a seat next to EJ's mom. Becca found herself looking around the gym to see if Will happened to be there. *Why do I care? I don't like Will, I like Weston. Stop thinking about Will.* That had been her mantra since the pool party, but it was turning out to be easier said than done. She saw Mr. Stevens enter the gym solo and then remembered that Will had a football game today over in Sheffield. *Ok, see, nothing to see. Focus on the game.* Becca watched as the team finished their warmups and half listened to the conversation between her mom and Ms. Elisabeth.

"Still in Europe. There's no timetable," Becca heard EJ's mom say. Becca thought that they must be talking about EJ's dad, since he spent quite a bit of time in Europe for business. Becca's mom was turned away from her, so she had some difficulty making out what she said next, but Becca thought she heard Gavin's name.

"Not good," was the response from Ms. Elisabeth. "He's spending far too much time at the Banks and thinks that because he's eighteen he has a right to act in whatever manner that he sees fit."

Now Becca was certain that they were talking about Gavin. For as long as she could remember, her mom had been pretty close with EJ's older brother. She said it was all that time she spent with him, between the church nursery and as his soccer coach when he was five. That paved the way for Becca's mom and Ms. Elisabeth to become fast friends and they had an easy friendship, not unlike Becca and EJ. At least the one she used to have with EJ.

"Wonder where he gets that idea," Becca heard her mom say in a sarcastic tone. "I'm not sure I have any type of sway with him anymore, but I'll try something. Life was much less complicated before they became teenagers," Becca's mom said, loud enough for Becca to hear clearly. She must have known that Becca was attempting to listen in on the conversation. She didn't know how, but her mom knew about everything. Becca gave her mom a look of mock irritation and focused her attention on the match that was now starting.

By the end of the first game, the butterflies that Becca had felt upon entering the gym had completely disappeared. The team, her team, had won the first game in dominant fashion. Lindy was clearly the best player on the court and her effort and intensity seemed to have made everyone else around her better. Becca found herself torn between excitement for the win and depression at not being on the court too. Or maybe it was at the realization that the team didn't need her to win. She already knew that; they'd won every game thus far and it was already something that Becca was struggling with. But seeing it in person pricked her heart with a hurt that she was not at all prepared for. Becca felt her mom calmly stroke her ponytail, as if knowing that Becca was internally grappling with conflicting emotions. She remembered her mother's words from way back at the beginning of the season when she was wrestling with the tension caused by Lindy's ability. *Ask God to help you; He will equip you with what you need to get through it.* And that's exactly what she did. By the middle of game two, the unease had lessened. She couldn't say that she was overjoyed, but at least she didn't feel as though she was going to fall apart. At least not right now.

After the game, she made her way to the court to see her team. They all seemed excited to have her there and allowed her to join them in celebrating yet another win. All, that is, except EJ. She said a quick "hey," and then walked away. Lindy saw the encounter and gave Becca a puzzled look as she walked over to her. Becca's friendship with Lindy had started to bloom over the past few weeks. Lindy's overwhelming kindness and friendliness quashed the animosity Becca had originally felt. And since things seemed to be going sideways with EJ, she was grateful for another friend.

"Is something going on with you and EJ?" Lindy asked as they walked toward the locker room together.

"I don't know. I guess. She's been acting strange and pretty much avoiding me lately."

Lindy looked at her with concern. "Do you think she thinks I'm trying to take you away from her? Because I'm not. I can be friends with everyone. In fact, I want to. Oh gosh."

Becca chuckled and shook her head. "No, EJ's not like that. Plus, she started acting like this a while ago. Like, before I got hurt. It's just been worse lately."

"Oh," Lindy said, dragging out the sound a few extra beats. Her voice and her face both portrayed a realization that Becca was not privy to.

"What's that supposed to mean?" Becca asked.

Lindy stopped at the door to the locker room but instead of entering, she nearly dragged Becca down the hallway and away from potential listening ears.

"Whoa, knee, knee," Becca said, cautiously moving behind Lindy.

"Well, it's no secret that EJ likes Will," Lindy started. Becca was slightly surprised that Lindy knew what she thought was privileged information but given the way EJ had been acting since the beginning of the school year, she realized that EJ's feelings were obvious. "Will pretty much told her that he wasn't interested. Politely, but he likes someone else."

Becca was stunned. In her lifetime of friendship with EJ, she'd never once seen a boy reject her. EJ was the girl that every boy liked. Literally, every boy. Even Gavin's friends, who were clearly much older. Becca was also surprised because EJ still seemed to be everywhere that Will was. She thought it was because the feelings between the two of them were mutual, but maybe it was because EJ, too, was shocked at his revelation and was being a little extra to get his attention. Becca had so many questions.

"When did this happen? Because she still hangs around him. Did he tell her who he likes? And what does this have to do with me?" Becca's inquiries came rapid fire.

"That day at EJ's house when we were all at the pool. When we were leaving, she said something to him and he said, 'Thank you, but you're not really my type.'"

"Wow, I don't think anyone has ever said that to her. But still, why would she be mad at me for that?" Understanding crept over her face as she asked the question. "Oh no."

Lindy nodded her head but then added, "He will never admit it to anyone, and he certainly didn't tell EJ that, but he's also not great at hiding it. I think that's why EJ may be acting the way that she is."

"Nope. Absolutely not. I cannot get between EJ and Will. That can't happen. Can it? No, no. Not happening." Becca's voice started out resolutely, but as she kept talking, she became less sure of herself. There was a part of her that liked the fact that she beat out EJ for the affection of a boy. And if she were honest with herself, she liked him too. Maybe even more than Weston. Maybe. But no, she couldn't.

Just then, EJ came through the doors of the gym on her way to the locker room. She glared at Becca and Lindy and then turned into the locker room without a word. Becca's eyes widened at the hostility she saw from EJ.

"You need to talk to her," Lindy said.

Becca inhaled deeply. She was grateful for the new friendship she had with Lindy, but she missed EJ. It felt as though part of her was missing. Well, two parts, since sports were temporarily gone. That, she couldn't do anything about. EJ, hopefully she could.

"I hope she'll listen," Becca replied, sounding hopeful but once again feeling as though she was going to break apart.

CHAPTER 17

Becca's attempts to talk with EJ were fruitless. Not having her own phone was a clear inhibition, as she couldn't simply text her whenever she liked. She had an iPad that she used for homework and her mom would let her FaceTime certain people, EJ being one, however EJ never picked up. Becca even tried the old-fashioned method of simply calling EJ on her mom's cell phone but to no avail. Talking at school also seemed nearly impossible. They did plenty of talking in their debate class but not directly to each other. And since that was their only class together, the opportunities for such conversation were scarce. Also, EJ had seemingly found herself a new set of friends with which to roam the halls and eat lunch: the cheerleaders. Becca wasn't about to entangle herself in that group. EJ was also noticeably absent from church and youth group. Ms. Elisabeth and Xan still made it on Sunday mornings, but they were always by themselves. Becca went over to EJ's house with her mom one Sunday after church, as her mom was having lunch with Ms. Elisabeth, figuring the element of surprise might work, but was quickly disappointed when Ms. Elisabeth informed her that EJ was out of town for club soccer. Becca was so disconnected from EJ that she didn't even realize that club season had started. Ms. Elisabeth seemed equally surprised that Becca had no idea. Things may be fractured worse than Becca thought. And for something that she didn't do and couldn't control.

Her mom had asked a few times if she wanted to talk about EJ and the apparent tiff that they were having, but she had declined. Not because she didn't want to, but because Becca didn't know what to talk about. She hadn't done anything to warrant EJ's behavior toward her. She couldn't help the fact that Will liked her. And even though he made her butterflies dance, she did her best to limit any interactions with him, for EJ's sake. If anything, EJ should be overjoyed with Becca's behavior. All of it was so mind blowing and confusing that there wasn't anything to say. Her mom didn't push the issue but did caution her to give EJ some grace because not everything was as it seemed. And that was even more confusing.

Soccer season at school was in full swing and missing yet another sport season was beginning to mess with Becca's mind almost as much as the EJ situation. She felt as though she was losing part of who she was. As a result, Becca submerged herself in her rehab. She pushed herself harder than she probably should have, but the knee didn't hurt, and she didn't have anything else to do. Although, she felt like the entire process was taking way too long. With her patience wearing thin, her identity slipping away and her best friend legit ghosting her, Becca found herself depressed. Not even Lindy's constant optimism could pull her out of her misery.

On a Saturday in early November, things got really bad. Becca had ridden her bike over to the county park to watch Lindy play a pick-up game of beach volleyball. She got there early and thought about navigating the Grove to EJ's house to take another stab at talking to her. But Will happened to be at the park as well, and Becca would have to walk right past him to get to the path that led into the trees. She decided it was better to avoid any potential interaction with him, so she parked her bike by the courts and chatted with Lindy. At least she had that friendship. As the game started, Becca found that she was still struggling mightily with the 'only watching' stuff. She longed to get up and go play. Part of her felt like she could, but she knew better. And it affected her mood. So did the fact that Will had moseyed over to her side of the court and was standing right next to her. He said hi and asked how her knee was. She didn't want to be rude but also didn't really want to be engaging in this conversation either. She opted for politeness, thinking that a quick exchange wouldn't hurt. She returned his smile with one of her own and then told him that her knee was doing well. But, as the saying goes, no good deed goes unpunished.

As Becca turned her head back toward the court, she caught a glimpse of a boat that had pulled up to one of the docks by the boat ramps. And staring back at her, hand on hip and lips pursed together in anger, was none other than EJ. She looked as if she wanted to jump out and strangle Becca. Without saying goodbye to either Will or Lindy, Becca grabbed her bike from the rack and pedaled furiously back home. She threw her bike in the side garage, knocking down both of her brothers' bikes and a set of her father's old golf clubs in the process. Becca neither cared nor stopped to pick them up. She headed straight to her room and slammed the door behind her.

CHAPTER 18

*B*ecca knew she would be in trouble for the slamming of her door. But she honestly could not have cared less. Her life was crashing down around her and for all she cared, she could stay in her room forever. In fact, that may be the best option all together. She curled up in the corner of her bed with a pillow and waited for the inevitable. It took all of two minutes for the knock, and then the door opened.

"I'll pick them up later," she said, working hard to hold back the tears. "And I know I'm grounded. So can you just leave me alone?"

"In a minute." Becca was surprised to hear her dad's voice. She had been expecting her mom, thinking that her dad was out somewhere with the boys, and since it was typically her mom who handled her emotional outbursts. At least since she'd hit the teenage years.

Her dad sat down on the bed next to her and pulled her out of the corner. She tried to resist but knew she was virtually powerless against her father's muscled arms. He then wrapped them around her and the strength she initially resisted became the comfort that she desperately needed. They sat there in silence as the tears began to stream down Becca's face. Her dad spoke first.

"I know you are going through a tough spot right now. I just want you to know that I love you."

That turned the silent tears into muffled sobs. He squeezed her tight and kissed the top of her head. They sat there together for a while, until his grip became soft enough for Becca to wipe her face on his shirt. It was something she had done since she was a child, and he always made some crazy remark or movement that caused her to laugh. Maybe her subconscious was hoping for that same reaction. As usual, her dad came through in the clutch.

"I didn't realize Kleenex made clothing," he quipped.

Becca did the obligatory teenage eyeroll but also chuckled and smiled at her father. He smiled back and gave a little wink as he walked out of her door.

"I'll pick up the garage, but you're still grounded," he hollered behind him, leaving the door open for her mother.

"He's a good one," Becca's mom said as she took over the spot on her bed that her dad had just vacated. "Make sure you find one like him."

Becca rolled her eyes again and wiped her eyes with her hands. "Getting the double dose today, huh?" she asked.

"I'd let your dad handle it, but you know what he says about teenage girls."

"They're weird and mysterious and I've never been one, so it's all you," they both said in sync.

They sat silently for a few moments before Becca's mom asked if she wanted to start. Becca shook her head in the negative, so her mom went first.

"First things first, I want to say how proud we are of you for how focused you've been on school and in your rehab. Injuries are difficult, and to this point, you've handled it well."

"Blew that today," Becca mumbled under her breath.

"Yeah kinda," her mom said but Becca could tell that she was joking with her. "But seriously, I know that it's tough. Injuries ended my entire playing career."

"Yeah, but that was your senior year of college."

"Didn't make it any easier," Becca's mom admitted. "In fact, it may have been worse. I didn't really get a say in how my career ended. It just did. When you get injured earlier in your career, the opportunity to return is still there."

"I didn't really think about that," Becca replied. "But you also were starting the rest of your life. You knew what you wanted to do and had something to fill that void. I have nothing right now. No sports, no friends, nothing. I feel like I don't even know who I am anymore." Becca's eyes started to well up with tears again.

Her mom put her arm around Becca's shoulder and pulled her close.

"I know you've heard me, and your father, say this before, and I'm sure to you they are just words, but I need you to try to understand the truth behind them. Because it took me a very long time to do so, and it caused me a lot of pain and struggle. I don't want you to go through that too. Volleyball, lacrosse, your grades, your future job; those are just things that you do. They are not indicative of who you are. Your friends, your family, your future spouse and kids, they do not define you. The only person that can define you is God himself. Because He created you. And He calls you His child. Loved, redeemed, cherished. He made you bold. And beautiful. And athletic. Intelligent. Witty. Kind. Caring, A natural born leader. A wonderful friend."

Becca sighed. She'd heard this spiel before. And while she understood, it didn't really help her feel any better right now. And she certainly didn't feel like a wonderful friend since EJ literally avoided her very presence.

"I hear you, but none of that makes me feel better," Becca said. "I feel so lost and lonely. And this thing with EJ, Mom, she hates me, and I didn't even do anything. She won't talk to me at all. In fact, she goes out of her way to avoid me. So yeah, I hear you. But my best friend in the world hates me so that says something about me. And it can't be good."

"Honestly, I think it says more about her. And I'll admit that her actions are a bit much but try to give her some grace. And a little more time. She'll come around. But going back to what I said before. Your feelings also don't define you. Feelings change and fluctuate and for at least one week of every month are completely irrational." Her mom chuckled at her own comment, but Becca merely rolled her eyes in irritation. "I know, I'm not as funny as your father. But a courtesy chuckle every now and again would be nice," she joked.

"Ha. Ha," Becca responded.

"Thank you," her mom joked again and then continued, "How'd the volleyball team do this season?"

"Seriously? You know the answer." Becca's mom sat silently, awaiting a response. "Undefeated," Becca finally answered, although not happily.

"They had a great season. And they had a great season, even without you. And I'm sure that made you a little frustrated. Maybe even a little mad. But their success doesn't take away your contributions to the team or negate your athletic ability. It shows that a team is bigger than one person. Just like this life is bigger than what you do or what you feel. You're more than someone's opinion of you or than who your friends are. God gave all of that stuff to you, and he can take it away too. That doesn't mean you've done something wrong or that those things and those people are bad or that He's not good. He's God, and he knows what is best for us and wants what's best for us. And what's best for us is Him."

Becca thought for a moment about what her mom said. It made sense and followed the lines of what she'd been taught in church, but the taking away of sports and of her best friend hurt. A lot.

"Why does it hurt so much? And if it's not bad, why does He take it away?"

Her mom took a deep breath before answering. "That goes back to original sin and sanctification, and we can have a whole theological discussion on that if you'd like, but I can tell from the look on your face that now is not the time. So, I'll try to go with more practical advice. Something that I've learned, and have learned the hard way, is that it's good to enjoy the things that God has given us and love the people that He has placed in our lives. And it's good to dream and to plan, but we need to try to hold all of that with an open hand. There are going to be things, and dreams and even people, that God asks us to give up: to transform us, to help us grow or to help us draw closer to Him. And it's going to be a hard thing to do no matter what, but it hurts a heck of a lot more when it's pulled out of a closed fist. The open hand also allows you to more readily accept whatever new thing He has planned for you. Like Lindy. I don't think your friendship with her would be as strong if you and EJ weren't in the middle of whatever this is."

"I get what you're saying but I don't think you really understand. You've never lost a best friend. You don't know how it feels."

Becca felt her mom flinch at her statement. She figured her mom must be getting frustrated with her, especially for saying that she didn't understand. Becca steeled herself for her mom's rebuttal, but her mom's response was soft. In both words and tone.

"Honestly kiddo, I'm not great at these talks. I can't even pretend to know or understand it all. But what I do know is that in the moments of greatest need, when I've leaned into Him the most, He's been there. God has been stronger and more capable than everything I've thrown at Him. And I've thrown a lot. It's taken me a long time, but I've come to realize that only He gets to say who I am and that He really is all that I need."

Her mom gave her one more quick hug before getting up from her bed. Becca watched as her mom paused at her doorway, seemingly contemplating her next move. She leaned her head against the doorframe and then whispered,

"And I do understand. More than you know." Becca watched her walk out of the door without even looking back.

CHAPTER 19

SADIE

After another far too short summer of fishing and boating, Sadie headed back for her junior year. Her mind was moderately less muddled than when she left in May. Over the summer she had decided that she would push herself out of her comfort zone and would try to be a little more involved with both her teammates and within the Fellowship of Christian Athletes group that was starting up on campus. She wasn't going to change who she was, neither in her work ethic nor in her moral code, but she was going to try to allow herself room to grow in all areas of her life. She'd also decided that she was no longer going to sit around and wait for Kat to come back into her life. Sadie had tried to call a few times over the summer, but only one call was answered, and the rest were never returned. The uncertainty hurt too much. It was time to move on. She hoped that was possible.

Sadie jumped straight into the deep end, putting in extra work in the batting cages, working with her younger teammates on everything from time management to the proper way to run a double cutoff, and even volunteered to help with FCA, on her very first visit. For her, sink or swim was the best way to move forward. Mostly because she knew that if she waded gently into the shallow end, she'd turn around and run back out. Quickly. For her very uncomfortable efforts, she was rewarded with a few nagging injuries which required daily visits to the training room as well as a decrease in playing time during the fall season. But also, with the respect of her teammates, who had named her co-captain of the team, and a new group of friends. One of whom became something more than just a friend.

Christian became a constant in her life almost immediately, and his outgoing personality most certainly aided in her social growth. He played on the soccer team at school and was one of the driving forces behind getting the FCA group started on campus. He was cute and kind and funny and for reasons unbeknownst to her, very much liked Sadie. He invited her to every social event that FCA sponsored, of both the formal and informal type, as well as to his soccer games and dinner with his team. By the end of September, Sadie was officially his girlfriend, and she didn't think she could be happier. Except there was still that one little Kat-sized hole that she could feel in her heart. Sadie wanted to call her on the night that Christian formally declared their status, to tell her all about him and about everything else, but the months of not answering phone calls had taken their toll on Sadie's psyche. So, she pushed the thought, and the person, from her mind. Again.

With the added extracurriculars on top of an already intense school schedule, Sadie gave her brain little time to think. Which was exactly what she needed. The little bit of free time she did have was spent attempting to rehab the ever-persistent injuries or with Christian. Her plate was full. There was no room for anything else in her overactive brain. Which was why it was early December when Sadie was made aware that she hadn't even thought about Kat in months. And that was only because, completely out of the clear blue winter sky, Kat showed up at Sadie's school. At the softball field to be exact.

The team was finishing up their last conditioning session before heading out for winter break. Sadie grabbed her water bottle from the basket, took a swallow and sprayed some water on her face, trying to cool herself down. It may have been winter, but it was still quite warm outside. As she dropped the bottle back into the basket, a figure caught her peripheral vision. She did a double take, as the figure was well back from the field but had the distinguishable messy bun atop its head. *There's no way.* Sadie racked her brain for the last time she had talked to Kat, let alone had seen her. It had been a very long while for both. But there she was, leaning against a fence, messy bun and all, waiting for Sadie. Sadie felt a weird flutter in her belly; a rush of excitement mixed with unexpected nervousness. The feeling surprised her and triggered the realization that it had been over a year since she had seen Kat. And at least four months since she spoke with her. The nervousness started to grow in the pit of Sadie's stomach as she contemplated the possible reasons for this surprise visit. She hoped and prayed that nothing had happened to Kat's family. Or her own. And that thought made the pit of her stomach fly to the middle of her throat. She needed to find out what was going on, and now.

Grabbing her things, she said a quick goodbye to her teammates and walked toward Kat. As Sadie approached her, she realized how much she had missed her friend. There was still a little hurt in her soul for the way that Sadie perceived Kat's avoidance but mostly she felt a strange mix of anticipation and nervous energy. This is what her heart had longed for over the past few years; her best friend being here with her. But her overly logical brain kept its iron thumb pressed firmly down on her heart. *Hopefully, she doesn't have any bad news. And even if she doesn't, this could still go badly.*

Sadie saw Kat push off the fence in anticipation of her arrival. She found herself searching Kat's face for some sort of clue as to her reason for being there, but all Sadie saw was a smile. Sadie felt her body relax, if only a little bit, and returned Kat's smile.

"Don't remember you sweating this much," Kat joked as Sadie approached, clearly in response to how wet Sadie's head and face were.

"I'm surprised you even remember what I look like," Sadie teased in reply.

Kat stretched her arms out for a hug, to which Sadie obliged. *So far, so good.*

"It's good to see you, Sade."

"Good to see you too, Kat. Been way too long."

Kat leaned back and pushed a wet piece of hair out of Sadie's face. "You look like crap," she said, in her typical blunt fashion. "Smell like it too." She crinkled her nose and waved her hand in front of her face in mock disgust.

"Well, I did just run three million sprints," Sadie defended. "I'm going to assume that since you are smiling and joking, this isn't a visit to break some bad news about your mom or my family?" Sadie questioned.

"Wow, jumping straight to the point, aren't we? No, your family is fine. Your mom actually called me yesterday to check in. As for my own mother, I haven't spoken to her in who knows how long. Since I haven't had any first responders show up on my door pronouncing her dead, I'm going to assume she's alive and around somewhere with some guy."

Interesting. Guess that summer rendezvous with your mom wasn't all that great after all. If it even was with your mom. Stop it, Sadie. She internally admonished herself for her thoughts and tried to refocus on the conversation.

"Then why are you here?"

Sadie saw Kat's eyes widen to the size of basketballs at her words.

"Sorry, sorry, that came out way wrong. I'm glad you are here. It's just completely unexpected. We haven't even talked in a while. So, forgive my shock at actually seeing you. At the softball field, no less."

"I would have waited at your apartment, but since you didn't tell me that you moved," Kat put significant emphasis on the word 'moved,' "I would have been waiting for a very long time with some very strange individuals. I knew that if you weren't currently at the field, you'd show up eventually. So here I am."

"You could have called."

Kat held up a broken cell phone. "Not really."

"Dang, Kat. I thought I was the violent one."

Kat merely laughed in response. She put her arm around Sadie's shoulder and led her out toward the parking lot. "It's been a long drive and I'm starving. What's good around here?"

"It's like four o'clock in the afternoon. I don't think you qualify for the senior citizens discount quite yet. And if you want anything other than fast food, I'm going to need to shower."

"Yeah, you are," Kat joked with a smirk, although Sadie noticed that the smile didn't quite make it to Kat's eyes. *She's hiding something.*

"Well?" Sadie asked.

"Fast food is fine. We can take it to your apartment."

"Do you want to drop your car off at my apartment first?"

"Um," Kat hesitated. "About that."

"Please tell me you didn't hitchhike all the way here," Sadie replied, slowing her pace to a stop while turning to face Kat.

"Seriously, Sade? Me, hitch a ride with a stranger?" Kat threw a hand to her hip, in faux offense.

"Wouldn't be the first time."

"True," she admitted, "But no. Well, sort of no. Maybe kind of. My car broke down just before I got to Edgewater, so I had to get it towed. The only place I knew to send it was Cunningham's Auto Shop, so I rode with the tow truck guy over there. Miles, do you remember Miles Cunningham? He was like two years older."

"Yes, I know Miles. And all the other seventeen Cunningham siblings."

"I think it's eight but yeah, it's a lot. Anyway, Miles is helping his dad out at the shop right now, so he offered to drive me home. Since I don't really have a home there anymore, at least I don't think I do, I asked him if he would drive me here. Since I was on my way here anyway. He dropped me off at your old apartment. But you obviously don't live there anymore, so I walked over here."

"That's like a four hour round trip for Miles! Good grief, Kat. Although now that I think about it, he probably thoroughly enjoyed the ride. He's always had a thing for you."

Sadie caught Kat's eyeroll but continued, "And you know that you could have gone to my parents' house. It was basically like your home anyway."

"I know. But I wanted to see you and I had no idea when you were going to be home for break."

"You could have called."

Kat once again held up her smashed cell phone.

"Right." Sadie paused and again looked at her friend. "Then how did you call a tow truck?"

"That's where the kind of, sort of hitchhiking comes in. I had to wave down a passing car and ask to borrow a phone. Fortunately, the driver knew the number for a tow company and called for me."

"I bet he was more than happy to call for you. And even wait with you," Sadie said somewhat sarcastically.

"What makes you think it was a guy?" Kat asked innocently, although Sadie could see a bit of a smile playing at the corners of her mouth.

"Oh, I don't know. Beautiful damsel in distress on the side of the road, waving down drivers. I bet the very first car that drove up stopped for you."

"No!" Kat said indignantly. "It was the second," she followed up sheepishly. "The first was a school bus."

Sadie rolled her eyes as they both started to laugh. That was such a typical Kat O'Malley story. There was never a shortage of guys, boys or men, willing to lend her a hand. Or a ride.

"Not sure I've met a guy that would say no to you," Sadie teased.

Sadie caught a flicker of something in Kat's eyes before she turned her gaze away and started to walk again toward the parking lot.

"Hey, my car is in the other lot," Sadie called out after her, pointing off to her right. Kat cut a hard ninety degree turn and continued walking. Sadie thought she could see tears on Kat's cheek but the speed at which Kat was walking made it difficult to see her face clearly. Maybe it was just the angle of the sun casting weird shadows on her face. But Sadie didn't think so.

"Hey, Kat, what's wrong?" she asked.

"I forgot that molasses moves faster than you walk. C'mon, let's go."

Kat's voice held no tension in it, so maybe it was the sun. Although she didn't slow down for Sadie either. As she continued to get further away, Sadie realized that Kat looked different than she remembered. Still tall and thin but gone was the grace and confidence with which Kat used to move and exude. She walked as though she literally had the weight of the world on her shoulders – head down, shoulders slouched, body curled inward like she was bracing against the wind. Except there was no wind. *What happened, Kat?* Sadie pondered the circumstances that could have created such a rapid and dramatic transformation. And then it occurred to her that maybe it wasn't so rapid after all. Maybe this had been years in the making. And Sadie wouldn't have known because she'd let their divergent currents of selfishness slowly push them apart. In that instant, Sadie realized that the pride of self-preservation had been her biggest mistake. The person she was watching walk away felt like more of a stranger than a best friend. And that broke her heart.

CHAPTER 20

"**S**orry for the mess," Sadie said as she unlocked the door to the apartment that she shared with two of her teammates. "I'd say that we would have cleaned up if I knew you were coming but I can't guarantee that it would look much different. We're not the cleanest." She pushed a pair of her own tennis shoes out of the entry way and did a quick survey of the living area. It wasn't too bad. A stray sweatshirt on the couch and a couple of dishes in the sink but otherwise it was decently clean. Maybe it was a product of the impending Christmas break or maybe they weren't quite as messy as Sadie initially thought. Either way, she breathed a quick sigh of relief.

"If this is what you consider a mess, please don't come visit me," Kat said.

"Says the girl who cleans for fun," Sadie replied, knowing full well that no matter where Kat lived, it always sparkled with cleanliness. "You used to clean up my room, in my house, remember."

Kat chuckled at the memory as she took her coat off and looked for a place to hang it. Sadie put her backpack and the bag of food down on the coffee table and grabbed Kat's jacket from her. She walked over to the small kitchen counter with two mismatched bar chairs and laid the coat over one of them.

"It's a college apartment. No fancy coat closets or anything like that."

Kat nodded her head in response as she took in the modest three-bedroom apartment. The furniture in the living area was a mishmash of cheaply made end tables, a brown and black coffee table that wobbled with any significant weight, a thrift store television stand, a borrowed kitchen table with four chairs, and two secondhand couches, nothing of which matched any of the other furniture. However, to Sadie, it was a perfect blend of the three personalities that shared the space. The only new item was a big screen television that they had purchased together and were going to have a hard time splitting up in a couple of years.

Sadie watched Kat closely, wondering what she was thinking. The short car ride back to the apartment had been full of chatter as they had tried to catch each other up on life but Sadie could tell that Kat was holding something back. There was something different in her voice, a perceived distance in her tone and in her words. She decided to allow Kat to control the conversation, since it was Kat who had taken the time and initiative to come see her.

"I'm gonna hop in the shower really quick," Sadie said, pointing towards her room and the bathroom beyond. "Make yourself at home, please. And don't feel like you have to wait for me to eat. You can sit on the couch and just eat at the coffee table. Water and Gatorade are in the fridge. Cups are over the sink if you want one." Sadie started toward her room but then stopped when she heard Kat call her name.

"Hey Sadie."

Sadie turned around warily, thinking that she detected a hint of pain in Kat's voice. She caught Kat's eyes from across the room and tried desperately to read whatever was going on behind them.

"Is there a bathroom I can use?" Kat asked.

"Oh, yeah, sorry. You can use the one at the end of the hall. On the right."

"Thanks," Kat said, flashing a half-smile as she walked past Sadie and gave her a little shove into her room. "Shower. You stink."

Sadie shook her head and walked through her room into her bathroom. Maybe she was making things up; extracting something that wasn't there. Maybe the time apart had caused her to lose touch with the ability to read Kat. *Maybe, but maybe not, right Kat?*

Five minutes later, Sadie was showered, dressed and sitting on the couch next to Kat. She opened her turkey and cheese sub and devoured the entire thing in about ten seconds. Running sprints always made her feel famished. She looked over at the grilled chicken sub that Kat was picking at and was half tempted to ask her if she was going to finish it. Without even looking at her, Kat pushed the remainder of her sandwich in front of Sadie. Obviously, Kat hadn't lost the ability to read Sadie.

"You sure?" Sadie asked. "You barely ate any of it. And if I remember correctly, you were the one who said you were starving."

"Take it. I ate the chips. They're more filling than you'd expect."

Sadie stared at Kat, racking her brain to think of a time in which Kat hadn't finished a meal. She couldn't think of one.

"Are you sick or something?" Sadie asked. Kat turned and looked questioningly at Sadie, her eyes full of both fear and affirmation at the question. "Oh crap. That's why you're here. You're sick." So much for letting Kat control the conversation. "Are you dying? Please tell me you're not dying." Sadie left no time for Kat to answer before continuing her spiral. "Oh my gosh, you are dying. What is it? How long do you..."

"I'm not dying. I'm pregnant," Kat interrupted, her voice barely above a whisper. Her head was turned slightly away from Sadie, and her eyes were averted as well. Because of that, Sadie was certain that she had heard her wrong.

"What?" Sadie asked. Her question was met with silence.

Sadie leaned forward on the couch, trying to get Kat's attention. More specifically, trying to look her in the eyes. Her brow furrowed as she tried to both wait for Kat to answer her and to figure out what exactly Kat had said. There's no way she said what Sadie thought she heard.

"Kat. . .what's wrong?"

Kat swung her head back around to face Sadie and answered in anger, face full of tears.

"I'm pregnant. Preg. Nant. As in with child." Kat turned her face away from Sadie again as Sadie just sat there, mouth agape. Sadie was unsure how much time had passed before she found her voice. When she did, what came out of it made her wish she still hadn't.

"Wha. . ., I. ., wha. . .how?" Sadie stuttered.

"How? Really, Sade? I know you're naïve but that's a ridiculous question," Kat returned, the anger in her voice only slightly diminished. Sadie watched as Kat wiped her face with the back of her hand, eyes still avoiding her own. Sadie looked away and put her own face in her hands, trying desperately to make her brain think before her mouth said something stupid yet again.

I don't even know how to process this, let alone what to say. She methodically rubbed her hands over her face as she willed herself to make sense of what Kat just unloaded. The anger in her own soul was beginning to bubble and she wanted to yell out all sorts of 'ridiculous questions'. *How in the world could Kat have done something so dumb? She knows better than this. She went to church with me almost every week. Why would she even put herself in this kind of situation? What was she thinking? How is she going to care for a kid when she is still a kid herself? And has no family to help. I can't believe she got herself into this situation. Does JJ know? Assuming it is his. Is it his? Of course it's his. His parents are going to lose their crap. God, please help me. I don't know what to do right now.* A shift on the couch next to her pulled Sadie out of her internal Q&A session. Lifting her head out of her hands, she saw Kat looking at her, body wrecked with fear, eyes full of shame. As she looked at the pain written all over the face of her childhood best friend, Sadie immediately felt the anger fire within her extinguish. In that moment, her heart ached for the person closest to her in the entire world, despite the physical and emotional distance of the past few years. It had to have been an answer to prayer because she knew she could never have reached that point of compassion on her own. Even if it was Kat.

"I know what you're thinking," Kat started, her voice cracking slightly, tears still rolling slowly down her face. "And I'm sor. . ."

Before Kat could finish, Sadie threw her arms around her and enveloped her in the biggest hug she'd ever given. She held on tight to Kat, hoping by some slight chance she could remove all the distance between them with one embrace. Sadie could feel the tears starting to build up in her own eyes. She could also feel Kat's body beginning to tremble as she started to sob. Sadie tightened her hug and let her own tears fall. After a few minutes, Kat's body quieted, and Sadie loosened her hug to allow for a free hand to wipe the wetness from her face. Kat sniffled and looked over at Sadie, her face wet and red from all the crying.

"At least you're not dying," Sadie said. She didn't necessarily mean it as a joke, but Kat started laughing anyway.

Sadie rolled her eyes and smirked as she got up to grab a few paper towels from the kitchen. She and her roommates always forgot to get tissues for the apartment so paper towels would have to suffice. Sadie handed Kat a few sheets as she sat back down on the couch. Kat leaned her head against Sadie's and Sadie put her arm around Kat's shoulders.

"Wanna talk about it?" Sadie asked, although she herself was undecided on whether she wanted to talk about it. The logical and moral side of her brain was still judging Kat's actions and decisions while the emotional part of her brain was attempting to be a sympathetic friend. She wasn't exactly sure which side would win out in the conversation. She would defer to her friend and pray for the best. After all, this was Kat's situation, not Sadie's.

"Later."

"Ok," Sadie said, silently thanking God for giving her more time to prepare for what was to come. She allowed the silence to linger for a bit and then said, "Hey Kat."

"Yeah?"

"I'm still here. Always. Forever. You're not going to have to do this alone."

"I know," Kat responded.

CHAPTER 21

*T*hey talked first about Sadie's life, with Sadie giving surprisingly little push back when Kat asked her about things. At this point, Sadie couldn't figure out how to comprehend Kat's news, so she was grateful for the opportunity to talk about literally anything else. Sadie filled Kat in on her boyfriend, Christian, who was the complete antithesis of JJ in nearly every way. He was kind, caring, almost annoyingly attentive, and very strong in his faith. Kat seemed genuinely overjoyed for her. Sadie gave a quick rundown of her very tedious schoolwork and merely brushed the surface when it came to softball, not wanting to tumble back down the rabbit hole that had swallowed her up the past two years. Part of her wanted to tell Kat everything, to get her advice and feel as though she had another person in this fight, but there was a larger elephant in the room that required attention. And it was Kat's. It was about to be addressed.

Kat and JJ had been "on again, off again" for years, as Sadie well knew. Recently, it was more off than on. Kat was his fall back and she knew it, but she couldn't seem to let him go and move on. She tried, or at least that's what she said, but nothing worked. There had been no one else so there was no doubt that it was his child, but he did not yet know. Kat said that she hadn't seen JJ since that night, nor had she spoken to him. She admitted that she was monumentally afraid of his reaction. And even more fearful of his parents. It was common knowledge that his family had a particular disdain for those of a different socioeconomic class. And they had an outright hatred of Kat, for reasons that no one could quite figure out. An illegitimate child, in general, would have been a travesty for a family of their pedigree but one with Kat O'Malley would be a humiliation of epic proportions. Sadie understood why Kat was terrified.

As Sadie digested all that Kat had to say, she found her brain swirling with questions, none of which would sound anything but judgmental, no matter how nicely she asked them. It would be better to save them for another time when the landing would be a little softer. Or maybe it was best to disregard the voices in her head altogether. Sadie tried to refocus and be a supportive friend who merely listened and consoled. She succeeded for a while but when Kat finished speaking, the silence was not at all quiet. As she lay in bed staring at the ceiling, Sadie pondered the unanswerable and chided herself for not being more proactive in their friendship. *How could this possibly happen? Could I have done something to prevent this? Maybe if I had visited her or made time to call her more often, she wouldn't be in this situation.* Logically, that line of questioning made little sense, but all manner of logic disappeared when Sadie felt even the least bit responsible for something. In softball and in life. As usual, Kat interrupted her thoughts by asking about them.

"What are you thinking about over there? And don't say 'nothing' because I still know you way better than that," she said.

Sadie contemplated how to best answer that question without giving herself away and stepping into waters she didn't want to be in just yet. She settled on a very vague, although very true, answer.

"Lots of things. You know me, my mind never shuts off. It's a problem."

"Wanna know what I'm thinking?" Kat asked and then answered without waiting for a response. "Thinking about old times. Softball games, late night fishing trips, summer days out on the *Sweet Carolina*. Staying up way too late talking and giggling about everything and nothing. Your mom's cooking."

Sadie laughed as she replied, "Yeah, good times." She let her mind momentarily drift to the days when life was simpler.

"I miss that. I miss this." Kat was silent for a while. "This, you and me spending the day together, talking and laughing and crying, it feels like home. It's the only thing that has ever felt like home."

Sadie missed this too, missed Kat and the closeness of their friendship. She tried to forget about the distance that had developed between them and the growing regret she was feeling for not doing a better job of being a friend.

"The difference between now and then is that there are now three of us laying in your bed," Kat stated flatly.

Sadie felt her eyes widen in shock at Kat's statement. What was she supposed to do with that? Laugh? Cry? Pretend she didn't hear? She slowly took her eyes off the ceiling to sneak a peek at Kat, who happened to be staring at her with a sly smile, stifling a laugh. Sadie relaxed, rolled her eyes, and said,

"Geez, Kat, way to make it weird."

They both laughed until their faces hurt, and Kat said she had to use the restroom.

"I already pee more. And puke a lot."

Sadie had no idea what to say in response to statements like that. She was still wrestling with the mere fact that Kat was pregnant and all the implications thereafter. She lay there, rubbing her jaw, thinking again. *I cannot believe that she's pregnant. Why would she put herself in that position? She knows better than to do that. Especially with her mom and her background. Why would she do something so irresponsible? How is she going to take care of a child with no one to support her?* As her mind mulled over the questions, she already knew the answer to the last one. She would help; her parents would help. Kat really was family, even if there was no blood relation. And, although Sadie felt as if this was one of the most monumental mistakes a person could make, she would never stop being Kat's best friend. All the whys and hows could wait.

Kat came out of the bathroom and plopped back down on the edge of Sadie's bed. She sat there, very still, for a few moments before lying back down. As she did, Sadie could see a small tear leak from the corner of her eye.

"I'm scared, Sadie. Scared of telling him, scared of his reaction. Scared of being pregnant and having a kid." It was as if Kat had been reading her mind and decided to answer the unspoken questions. Sadie remained quiet, wondering if she would continue, hoping she would so that it wouldn't be up to her to fill the silence. Kat took a deep breath and began again. "I didn't plan on this. I wasn't trying to get pregnant. And please don't give me a lecture, believe me, I know," she added quickly.

Sadie rolled over and propped herself up on an elbow. "I wasn't planning on it."

Kat put her hands over her belly. "What am I going to do? I've been able to handle a lot of what life has thrown at me. But this? I can't do this alone."

"You don't have to. You have me. You've always had me. And you have my family. What's the line that you like to use? 'Just accept it.'" Sadie sat up and nudged Kat, giving her a little smirk and then continued. "My family loves you like you are one of us. Because you are. This isn't going to change that. Shoot, my mom called you yesterday and I haven't even talked to her since last weekend! But speaking of shoot, my dad and brother may want to kill JJ for doing this to you."

"Your parents will kill me for letting this happen. I should have known better. But nothing I can do about that now," Kat despaired. "And I can't ask them to be the support system for their daughter's friend and her illegitimate child. I won't do that."

"I will. And they'll do it. They may be strict but they're not going to throw you or anyone else out just because they made a mistake. Unless it's me on the softball field. Then it's 'see you later, have fun walking home.'" Sadie laughed at her joke but got zero response out of Kat, so she quickly quieted down and tried to focus. She was so much better at sarcasm and stupid jokes than serious conversation, but she was going to have to buck up and figure it out for Kat's sake. She silently sent up a quick prayer for help. "Kat, I'm serious. You are not going to have to do this alone. No matter what JJ's reaction is or how much he will invest in this child, you will always have me. You will always have my parents. They love you more than me anyway."

There she went again, making stupid sarcastic comments that continued to fall flat. It was seemingly uncontrollable. Although, there were times in which Sadie thought there might be some truth to that previous statement. But now wasn't the time or the place. *Get it together, Sadie.* She shook her head and continued,

"I was planning on going home sometime tomorrow or the next day so just come home with me. You can spend the holidays with us, and we will figure out a way to tell my parents. Speaking of parents, are you going to tell your mom?"

Kat rolled her eyes and gave Sadie a look that clearly indicated Sadie had lost her mind.

"Guessing that's a no," Sadie commented.

"Good guess," Kat responded as she looked back at a particular spot on the ceiling that had held her attention for the past few minutes. "I don't know, Sadie," she said, returning to Sadie's prior suggestion. "I don't really want this to become public knowledge. You know how gossip spreads back home. And I really don't want JJ to hear it from anyone other than me. And I certainly don't want his parents to find out. And I haven't exactly been back home in a while. That might spark some unwanted conversation."

"We can keep it quiet. You spending the holidays with us isn't going to raise any eyebrows. You basically lived with us throughout high school so it's just normal. Plus, your car is there, and you need to get your phone fixed so you can call JJ and tell him. Just don't go puking everywhere," Sadie quipped.

Kat sighed audibly. "Ok. But we only tell your parents when I'm ready. And no promises on the puking; I can't control it at all."

"Deal."

Sadie pulled Kat up into another hug before lying back down, already knowing that her mind wasn't going to allow her to sleep. She wondered if Kat would have the same problem but then heard gentle snoring coming from the other side of the bed. *That was quick. At least one of us will get some rest tonight.* Sadie inhaled as much air as she possibly could, held it for a second, and then exhaled prayers for Kat, for the baby growing inside of Kat, and for herself. Because it would take God's intervention to help her understand why Kat would do something like this, and to keep her from saying something really hurtful in the process. Her mind then contemplated a number of different scenarios. How her parents would react, how JJ would react, what the fall out would be when his parents found out. The mental pinball game kept Sadie wide awake for hours until finally her body succumbed to fatigue sometime after four in the morning.

CHAPTER 22

BECCA

*B*ecca's punishment for destroying both the garage and bedroom door was three weeks of being confined to school, therapy, church and her house. In that time, her Bible class at school assigned her a book of the Bible to read and summarize within the context of the 'whole story' of the Bible. She was secretly hoping for Jude, since it was the shortest book, but was instead given Ephesians. It's funny how God works sometimes. Ephesians is a letter from Paul to the Christian church at a city called Ephesus. It's about the gospel: our desperate need for a Savior because of sin, God's forgiveness and grace, and our redemption because God's love for us, shown through the death, burial and resurrection of Jesus. It teaches who we are and how we are to live out our lives faithfully and fulfill our purpose of glorifying God. It's also about the spiritual conflicts and battles that we will face along the way and how God gives us the tools, or in this case the armor, to face those battles. There's a whole lot more but that's the gist of it, and it seemed to be echoing the things that her mother had been saying over the past few months. Sometimes they were crazy and stuck in their ways, but life kept proving that maybe her parents did know what they were talking about. A little.

Becca felt as though these last few weeks of reading her Bible had her ready for anything. So, now equipped with a purposeful peace, a complement of God's armor and a bolstered confidence, thanks also to Lindy's incessant pep talks, Becca decided once again to try to talk to EJ. It had been almost three months since that absurd week in September when everything seemed to have unraveled, and Becca was really missing her best friend. Lindy was great, but they did not have the history she had with EJ.

It was the Friday before Christmas break. Becca had heard a rumor that EJ was going to France for two weeks so she decided that would be a great conversation starter. Becca and EJ had their second period classes in the high school building, with EJ in French and Becca in her math class. Becca typically went out of the back doors after class but EJ's class was in the front of the building so she decided that she would try to catch EJ in the front hallway between the two buildings. She remembered reading about the armor of God and thought that since she'd been reading her Bible and trying to do the right thing, she'd be protected from anything EJ could throw at her. She found out real fast how misinformed she was.

As she quickly rounded the corner, she saw something that brought her to a screeching halt. There, leaning against his locker, flipping his brown hair back, was Weston Gold. But that wasn't what caused her to stop. Nestled up right next to him, with her arm around his waist, and his around hers, was EJ. At first glance, Becca thought maybe they were just being exceptionally friendly but when Weston leaned down and kissed EJ, on the lips no less, all thoughts of friendship immediately disappeared. Between Weston and EJ and between Becca and EJ.

Becca was hot as she turned on her heels and stormed out of the back door. How could EJ do that to her? Weston was her crush, not EJ's. And Becca had gone to special lengths to avoid EJ's crush, even though he liked Becca, and Becca kind of liked him. She refused to even look at EJ during debate and spent the rest of the day in complete silence, certain that her face was a particular shade of red and that steam was blowing out of her ears like all those cartoon characters. At one point, both Lindy and Maddie cornered her to get her to calm down and talk but she just stared at the floor in silence. Eventually they acquiesced, and Becca was free to resume her fuming in solitude. But not for long.

Seeing EJ cuddled up next to Weston again after school caused Becca to forget everything she'd recently read and nearly blow a gasket. The frustration of the last few months probably aided in her rapid descent into anger, but it was not something she was capable of thinking about right now. When EJ started walking through the parking lot towards Gavin's Jeep, Becca decided it was the perfect time to release the steam. It didn't matter that her mom was waiting for her in the front pick up circle. Or that half of the school was still around and would be front row spectators to the confrontation.

"What are you doing?" EJ asked when Becca stepped right in front of her, causing EJ to abruptly stop.

"I could ask you the same thing," Becca spat back at her.

EJ rolled her eyes and tried to step around Becca. Becca moved quickly back in front of her.

"Get out of the way, Becca," EJ said, clearly irritated but her voice remained somewhat quiet. She tried to step back in the other direction, but Becca again beat her to the spot, thankful that she'd been working on her lateral movements for the past two weeks.

"Why? Why Weston? You could have any boy in this school, but you chose him."

"What does it matter? You were never going to act on that schoolgirl crush. Besides, he doesn't even know you exist."

"It matters because you don't do that to a friend. Especially your best friend."

"Exactly," EJ said, her voice starting to rise. "You don't do that to your best friend, but you did. So, I'm just following your lead."

"I didn't do anything!" Becca shouted. "I can't help that Will likes me! But I didn't do anything about it. In fact, I've been trying to completely avoid him! So much so, that I'm sure he thinks I'm the rudest person to ever walk this Earth. All for you! And what do you do? You go steal Weston!"

"It's not stealing if you don't have it, Becca." EJ said flatly. "And you'll never have him."

"And you'll never have Will," Becca spat back. EJ rolled her eyes in disgust, but Becca knew that she'd hit the mark. "My gosh, EJ. I can't believe that you're this bent out of shape at the fact that someone you like doesn't like you back. Or maybe it's because he likes me instead. That's it, isn't it? You can't handle me winning for once."

EJ took a step forward so that her face was now nearly touching Becca's. "For once? Really Becca? Try all the time. I'm so sick of you winning. Thank God for Lindy. Or maybe I should say thank God for your busted knee."

EJ's words were sharp, and they pierced Becca like a serrated knife. They seemed to hit something deep inside that unleashed a pain far greater than the physical pain caused by her knee. Out of that, Becca responded in a way that she would eventually wish she hadn't. She reached out with both hands and pushed EJ across half of a parking space and pinned her up against the car that was parked there. Her eyes narrowed as EJ's widened.

"You gave me that trash set on purpose. You did this to me." The words that emanated from Becca's mouth were laced with a near poisonous anger. Words that she didn't even know were there.

EJ was momentarily stunned, but the fire quickly returned to her eyes. She shook off the shock and spat back at Becca, "If only I was that good. It wasn't on purpose, but I can't say I'm upset about the outcome."

Now it was Becca's turn to be surprised. She took her hands off EJ and just stared at her. The rage that she initially felt tumbled quickly down a cavern of hurt, hitting every ledge on the way down, each impact sending a bit of anger flying, only to be replaced with heartache. Accusing EJ of causing her injury had not been a thought in her conscious brain and she was every bit as surprised as EJ. But EJ's response was even more unexpected, and it left her completely staggered. Becca, feeling her eyes fill with salty tears, did the only thing she could think to do.

"I'm done," she said quietly and turned to walk away.

EJ, still clearly consumed with anger, yelled after her. "Fine. I'm over it anyway. Becca the superstar athlete. Becca the brainiac. Becca the perfect little Christian girl from the perfect little family. You have freaking everything and I'm tired of it. I could use the break."

These words also hit Becca hard, but she didn't have the energy to reengage. Nor did she have the wherewithal to realize that some of the other middle school kids had their phones out and filmed the entire encounter. Social media would be abuzz for about forty-eight hours. It didn't matter. She wouldn't need social media to replay the fight; her brain would take care of that for her.

CHAPTER 23

"**I** get that, but she deliberately took the guy she knows I've had a crush on for years!"

Becca and her mom were in the car on the way home from dinner. Her mom, like the rest of the school and countless Snapchat and TikTok users, saw her encounter with EJ earlier that afternoon. When Becca had gotten in the car, her mom gave her a look, noticed the pain on her face and proceeded to silence the mounting questions from her brothers. Becca had gone straight to her room and lain face down on her bed for hours. She hadn't even picked her head up when her mom came in and announced that the two of them were going out to dinner. Becca had no idea why. She figured she'd be grounded for life, not rewarded with a dinner without her annoying brothers. Becca picked at her spaghetti and allowed her mom to carry the conversation, which was about nothing in particular. But when she heard EJ's name, the anger from this afternoon was rekindled and she couldn't contain her words. She freely divulged every bit of information, emotion and frustration that had been suppressed for the past few months. Including how she felt about both Weston Gold and Will Stevens. Her mom had waited until they got in the car to point out that while she understood the ire, Becca's actions were a bit extreme.

"First of all, you don't own people so no one can take them," her mom said in response.

"You sound like EJ."

"And your injury was just an accident. Very few people get through a sports career without some sort of injury. Hopefully, this was the big one, but if you play long enough, there may be more. It's just part of the game."

"That set was absolute trash."

"Maybe, but it was not on purpose. Also, that boy is bad news."

"Mom," Becca huffed, irritated at her response. There was a part of her that believed her mom's words, not about Weston, of course. But if truth be told, Becca was unsure what to truly believe and what any of it meant. EJ didn't club her leg, or run into her, and even if she gave her a purposefully terrible set, she could not have envisioned that Becca would blow out her knee. But the fact that EJ was happy about the outcome? And that she was tired of a 'perfect' Becca always winning? What in the world was that supposed to mean? If anyone was the picture of perfection, it was EJ. She was beautiful, athletic, rich. She had everything anyone could want and had already traveled nearly everywhere in the world by the age of fourteen. Becca stared out of the window, her mind running in circles and her emotions following closely behind. As they approached her neighborhood, Becca broke the minutes long silence.

"Let's say you're right about my injury, that still doesn't explain why EJ said she's tired of me and my perfect life."

Her mom paused for a second and then said, "Just because things appear smooth on the surface, doesn't mean they are. It's like the river."

Becca's mom had a thing about the river. She gave her kids moderate amounts of freedom on the water but not before monotonous lectures about the respect the water commanded and the countless swirling tides and downed branches lurking underneath the surface. 'Don't know what you don't know. Or can't see,' she'd say. Her mom sighed and continued,

"I'm going to tell you something that is not public information and does not need to be discussed outside of this car. Especially not in front of your brothers. EJ's parents are getting a divorce."

Becca started at the words and snapped her head towards her mom so hard that her neck popped. "They what?" Becca said, completely shocked. Her hand rubbed at the back of her neck as she watched her mom's head confirm her previous words.

"I was hoping that EJ would come to you herself but that seems highly unlikely at this point."

"A divorce? Since when?" Becca asked.

"Around the start of the school year. Actually, I think EJ and her brothers found out right before volleyball season started. Well, that's when Mr. James left," her mom answered.

Becca began to think back to the start of the season. The house being quiet that Friday night. EJ's running mascara. Gavin barreling down the road nearly hitting her and Cooper on their bikes. Mr. James leaving in a hurry. Then the awkward encounter between EJ and her mother followed by EJ's weird behavior at the pool party the next day. Everything changed from that point forward. Becca thought it had to do with her and Will, and maybe some of it did. But apparently not all of it. Now that she was thinking about it, Becca couldn't remember seeing EJ's dad since that night. Granted, she and EJ were not on the best of terms, but Becca couldn't remember seeing him around town or even at school soccer games. And since she had to spend her time in the bleachers this season, Becca would have noticed him. EJ was easily Mr. James' favorite child and he rarely, if ever, missed a soccer game. He had high hopes for her in that arena. And EJ did not disappoint; she was a phenomenal soccer player. So, despite his frenzied work schedule, he always tried to make it to as many of EJ's games as possible. And he hadn't been there. At all.

"What happened? Why would they get divorced? They have everything." Becca was stunned. "And why wouldn't she tell me?"

They pulled into the garage and her mom turned off the car but neither made a move to exit the vehicle. Her mom sighed again and seemed to be contemplating her response. When she spoke, her voice was soft and compassionate.

"The first two questions, I'm not going to answer. I will leave that up to EJ to tell you whatever she finds appropriate, whenever she feels the time is right. As for why she hasn't said anything yet, I can only speculate. I can only imagine the pain, hurt and possibly embarrassment that EJ must be feeling. I know that divorce is an unfortunately common thing these days, but that knowledge doesn't make it any easier when it's your parents. It also happened right before your injury. I would think that the timing made it nearly impossible for EJ to process what was happening and seek you out before you got hurt. And to be honest, I'm not sure anything was official at that point in time. And then, your focus was on your rehab. You dove in headfirst, which is not a bad thing and I'm not insinuating that you were a bad friend. But for the first time in both of your lives, you were not a constant presence in the life of the other. You'll find that as you grow up, you will grow apart from the people in your life. Because every person is different, with different likes and dislikes, goals, circumstances. Different plans for their lives. Even when you try, life happens, and you grow apart. Sometimes you're forced apart and there's no way to bring it back together. It's not the. . ."

"Mom," Becca interrupted. "I have no idea what you're talking about. I just want to know why she didn't tell me."

"Right. Sorry. Yes, all those things."

Becca remembered looking out of the window of EJ's room on the night that Mr. James left. She remembered thinking about how beautiful it was; calm and peaceful, perfect in every way. She'd been completely oblivious to the tension looming just below, in the water or in the house. *I guess life really is like the river,* Becca thought as she laid her head against the glass of the passenger's side window.

"I guess I just figured that with as rich as they are and all the stuff that they have and the trips that they take, nothing could ever be wrong. I get that money doesn't buy happiness but it's gotta help. And they always seemed really happy. It doesn't really make sense. Not much makes sense anymore."

"'All that glitters is not gold,' 'Don't judge a book by its cover,' 'The surface can be mislead...'"

"I get it, I get it," Becca interrupted, getting irritated by the idioms her mother was conveying.

"Do you? It's not just about the divorce. Think about everything that EJ must be keeping below the surface. Her perception of life has just been dramatically shifted. Maybe even shattered. Do you think that EJ's actions over the past few months may be a byproduct of the hurt she's feeling? Like your actions today?"

Becca tapped her head against the car window, letting her mother's words rattle around in her brain. She thought about the betrayal she felt by EJ's actions with Weston. And then she tried to allow herself to feel the emotions that would come if it were her parents getting divorced. It was so next level that she had to force herself to stop thinking about it or risk being distraught over something that wasn't happening. She was so caught up in her thoughts that the hand on her shoulder made her jump.

Becca's mom leaned over and looked Becca in the eyes. "I know you're putting yourself into EJ's shoes, and I hope you know that you will never have to deal with that. And you don't really need to go there. You can be compassionate without feeling all her feelings. But also keep in mind that hurt people hurt people. It's not right, and I certainly don't mean to excuse her behavior, or yours for that matter, but it happens. That's why I asked you a few weeks ago to give EJ some grace. I really did think that she would realize her need to talk about what is going on, and for someone to walk through it with her. But I also know that it's hard and probably a bit embarrassing to admit that things aren't what they seem. Especially when they seem better than most. I know it's going to be difficult, but I hope you find it in your heart to forgive EJ and pray for another opportunity to reconcile your friendship. She's an important part of your life, as you are in hers. And life changes too fast to put off important things."

There was an intensity in her mother's eyes that Becca rarely saw. It was generally reserved for the most significant issues, so the importance of her mother's words was not lost on her. However, Becca could see something else in her mother's eyes. Sadness. It was almost as if her mother could feel the pain that she was going through. Or maybe that EJ's family was going through. Becca wasn't sure. But it added to the sense of urgency that her mother seemed to be pushing. Regardless, Becca didn't know if she was ready to forgive EJ quite yet. Both her words and her actions hurt Becca to the core and the fact that there was some underlying reason for it all didn't take away that pain nor repair the damage. And she highly doubted that EJ would be in a forgiving mood given the fact that she basically assaulted her in the parking lot. Becca broke eye contact with her mom, looked out of the front windshield and stared at everything and nothing at the same time.

"I'll try. But I don't think it's going to be easy. She really hurt me, Mom. And up until today, I hadn't done anything to deserve that from her."

"I know it won't. Just pray for her and for her family. And remember what you've been reading in Ephesians. Try to live it out."

"That armor certainly didn't protect me today," Becca admitted frustratingly.

Her mom chuckled and reached her arm around Becca's shoulder to pull her closer. "That's not exactly how it works, kiddo."

Becca sighed. She knew her mom was right. Everything about life was so confusing right now. Becca missed the simple days. Like at the Grove or on the boat, when the only care she had was when the sun was going down. She had a feeling that those days were behind her for good.

CHAPTER 24

SADIE

Kat had called JJ a couple of days before Christmas, told him she was in town and that they needed to talk. They had met down at the Banks the next day, under the cover of mangroves and tall grass, and Kat had broken the news. It did not go well. Sadie could hear JJ's loud and angry yell from the car where she was waiting. Granted, she had rolled down the windows, despite the cold air, so she could hear Kat in case she was the one yelling, but it was still loud. Kat had come back to the car crying and shaking her head. When they talked about it later, Kat only said that JJ was completely shocked, yelled a bunch of stuff and then left. That was two days ago. Today was Christmas Eve and whatever cold front had been present earlier was now long gone. It was unseasonably warm; a perfect day to be outside and away from people. And from phones that weren't ringing.

They walked out to her grandfather's dock, stopping to unlock the shed and grab a couple of poles. Sadie wanted to take out the boat, but Kat didn't think her stomach could handle the bouncing, even if the speed was kept to a minimum. Sadie was more concerned about the fish smell bothering Kat but that would also mean they would have to catch one, something that was a rarity around this dock, for reasons unbeknownst to her. Kat was once again wiping her eyes because they couldn't come to her grandfather's dock without first making a pit stop at her grandfather's house. And, again for reasons unknown to Sadie, Kat told Grandpa Jack everything. Sadie and her grandfather had always had a close relationship, but he and Kat seemed to have some sort of higher bond, despite not actually being related. It was weird, to be honest, but Kat also had a way of captivating people. And Grandpa Jack had a way of making everyone feel at ease. That was probably one of the many reasons why he was such a well-respected doctor. Good ole Jack had wrapped Kat in a bear hug and told her not to worry about a thing. He would make sure that she saw the best physicians around and would handle all the bills, no arguments. He said to 'consider it a Christmas gift for being an extraordinary person and a wonderful friend to his granddaughter.' That statement seemed to be the correct lever to open the floodgates because Kat wept nearly uncontrollably which, in turn, caused both Sadie and Grandpa Jack to cry as well. Now here they were, Sadie baiting up the hook and Kat sitting herself down on the edge of the dock, toes in the water, like always. With everything that was going on in their lives, the water, this dock, was the perfect place of quiet refuge. Sadie cast the line a few times and slowly reeled it in. The mid-morning sun warmed the side of her face and produced a glittery gleam on the water that made it difficult for Sadie to see much below the surface, even with her polarized sunglasses. She turned her head slightly to avoid the sun and caught a glimpse of Kat gently kicking the water with her feet. Sadie chuckled internally.

"This is familiar," she said, breaking the silence.

"What?" Kat asked, more in a 'what did you say' tone rather than a 'what is familiar' tone.

"This is familiar," Sadie repeated, casting the line once again. "Me fishing or bringing the boat back in. You, sitting on the dock, kicking at the water. Only difference is usually I'm the one we're waiting on to start talking."

"So, start talking," Kat quipped.

"There she is. After the last few days, I was wondering if you'd ever return."

"Here I am. Here I am," Kat said, although her voice sounded very dejected.

Sadie reeled the line in and set the pole down on the dock. She walked over and sat down next to Kat. She kicked at the water as well, though it was more like toeing the water as she still had her deck shoes and didn't want to soak them.

"Softball's been a bit of a struggle if I'm being honest," she started. "I'm learning the hard way that meritocracy isn't always the basis for playing time. It's got my brain all messed up." Kat turned and stared at her with a confused look on her face. Sadie kept going. "Shoulder's been a bit of a pain lately but that's probably just fatigue. Working extra on both my defense and my swing."

"What are you doing?"

"You told me to start talking, so I am."

Kat rolled her eyes and shook her head. "I wish it was always this easy to get you to talk."

"Yeah, me too," Sadie admitted. She nudged Kat with her elbow. "Your turn."

Kat sighed and Sadie wondered if that meant she would remain in her current silent, solitary, disheartened state or if she would enlighten Sadie as to what she was thinking. After a few silent seconds Sadie said,

"Is this what it feels like to be on this side of the non-conversation? If so, I'm sorry. This is pretty awful."

Kat gave a half smile that lasted half a second so Sadie decided to reenter the silence. Sadie watched a flock of seagulls fly across the cloudless sky, no doubt making their way toward the marina where they could feast on the discarded shiners and shrimp left behind from early morning fishermen. She could hear their squawks as they alerted others to the scraps of food. The warmer temperature brought out a few more boats than one would normally expect this time of year as both the locals and the tourists attempted to take advantage of the weather and the holiday. Luckily, they were far enough away to be seen yet not heard. The stillness of the water was occasionally broken by a jumping fish, which in turn caused the water to gently lap against the side of the dock. The result was a tender sway and a peaceful drum. Other birds that Sadie could never name chirped their beautiful songs in the surrounding trees. Sadie leaned back and closed her eyes, trying to quiet her mind and just enjoy nature's symphony.

"I wish life was as peaceful as this," Kat said after a few minutes.

"Me too."

After what seemed like forever but was probably five minutes, Sadie realized that Kat still had no interest in talking. She stood up, grabbed her fishing pole and spent the rest of the morning casting and reeling. Her success in that arena was only slightly more fruitful than getting Kat to talk; she caught only puffer fish, which seemed to be mocking her as it alternated between puffed and relaxed. Finally, Kat spoke, but it was only to say that she was feeling sick and needed to get back home. Sadie quickly dumped the bait bucket into the river and put away the fishing poles. *Here's to another day of awkward silence and terrible fishing. I'm not sure I can do this much longer.* She hoped Kat's reticence would soon end and they could get back to happier times. These eggshells were hurting her feet.

CHAPTER 25

BECCA

*E*J had indeed jetted off to France for the entirety of Christmas break. Her father was currently living in Paris so, according to Becca's mom, EJ and Xan were splitting the holidays between there, with him, and Stockholm with their mother. Becca would catch herself thinking that divorce couldn't be that bad if it still included holidays in Europe. But then she had to remember that it was about as atypical of a holiday as she could imagine. Gavin had refused to go with them and spent his Christmas doing who knows what. Becca occasionally saw his Jeep around town, going way too fast, as usual. *I can't imagine Christmas with my family scattered in three different countries.*

Becca tried not to think about EJ too much because she was afraid that if she did, she would accidentally reveal information that she was not supposed to know. Or maybe accidentally on purpose. She couldn't control what happened when she gave into the hurt that she still felt. So, she spent her break doing the same thing that she had done for the previous three months, rehabbing her knee. She was almost four months post-surgery and was hoping to get the ok to start running within the next week. The benefits of having a physical therapist as a mother, which included access to exercises and advanced equipment that most did not have, only slightly outweighed the detriments of having someone make you slow down because they knew you were moving too fast. It was creating some tension in their relationship that Becca didn't really like.

Becca also found herself spending quite a bit of time with Lindy. She still kept a bit of distance from Will, but after EJ's betrayal with Weston, she no longer actively avoided him. The butterflies had settled a bit, but Becca still found herself getting slightly 'flushed,' to use Cooper's word, whenever he smiled at her. After the pool party at EJ's, both Will and Lindy had started spending more time around Becca's core group of friends, which also included going to youth group on Sundays. On the Sunday after Christmas, Becca's mom suggested that Becca invite Lindy over to spend the night. Since her injury and the subsequent fall out with her best friend, Becca hadn't been going out or spending much time with anyone other than at school and church, so her mom thought this would be a good way to start moving forward. Becca thought that her mom might have secondary motives of both getting to know Lindy better and finally meeting her mother. But either way, she was getting some much-needed friend time, even if her family was sort of involved.

If Becca's mom's goal was to meet Lindy's mother, she hid her disappointment well. Lindy's dad had taken both her and Will to the youth party that afternoon and then dropped Lindy at Becca's. As her parents chatted with Lindy's dad, Becca took Lindy up to her room to put her stuff down. Wasting no time, Lindy said.

"Saw you blush when Will walked in behind me. I knew you still liked him."

"No, I didn't," Becca said, although her defense was not very strong, as she was blushing once again. Lindy said everything she needed to with just a look.

"Ok fine," Becca conceded. "I think he's cute. And nice. And funny. And he's got great hair. And I think I daydream about him."

"Ok, ok, ok. Girl talk isn't the same when it's about my brother. Yuck."

They both laughed and Becca had to admit that it was weird liking her friend's twin brother.

"I guess I should have realized a while ago that the likelihood of one of my friends dating my brother was pretty high. Not really sure how I feel about it. I wouldn't want to have to choose sides, if it came to that," Lindy admitted.

"Nothing will happen here. My parents are super strict on the not dating thing. So, no worries," Becca said, a small hint of disappointment in her voice.

"I'd be lying if I said that I'm upset about that," Lindy admitted. Becca gave her a look of confusion and Lindy explained her reasoning. "I value our friendship and enjoy hanging out with you. Selfishly, I don't want to share you with my brother. Or lose you because of my brother. But, on the other hand, most of the girls in school are terrible options and I don't really want him dating them either. So if it came down to you or say, Quinn, I don't know what I'd do. Probably beg him to never date."

"Will likes Quinn?" Becca asked incredulously. First EJ, now Will. Becca could feel the heat rising in her face.

"No, not at all. Gosh, no," Lindy said. "That would be awful. I was just giving an example of a bad option."

"Phew," Becca blew out a huge sigh of relief. Lindy gave her a sly smile to which Becca responded, "It's because it was Quinn, nothing else."

"Uh huh," Lindy replied sarcastically.

Becca's dad called up the stairs to say that Mr. Stevens was leaving, and both girls popped their heads over the stairwell to holler a farewell. Becca also said goodbye to Will, which prompted another round of teasing from Lindy.

Becca's mom then told them that they were going to watch a movie and that there was popcorn, snacks and ice cream if the girls would like to come down. Becca wasn't sure that she wanted to deal with her brothers, or the thousand questions that her parents were likely to ask Lindy, but she really wanted ice cream and Lindy said she "loved movie nights." They headed downstairs and Becca immediately groaned when she entered the living room and saw the movie choice. *Jack Ryan, Shadow Recruit.*

Lindy looked at her with a bit of confusion and said, "What? This is a good movie. It's old, but good."

"Old?" Becca's dad asked with a chuckle.

"They're fourteen," her mom reminded him. "Everything is old to them."

"Fair point," her dad admitted.

"Do we have to?" Becca asked, her voice a little whiny, and for a reason.

"Do you really not like this movie?" Lindy asked. "We don't have to watch it. I can grab some popcorn, and we can go back upstairs. If it's ok to eat upstairs, that is."

Bryson thudded down the stairs, Xbox controller in hand, and provided an answer to Lindy's question. "She's tired of hearing about how they met. We all are." He popped a handful of popcorn into his mouth and grabbed a Gatorade.

"I don't. . ." Lindy seemed genuinely confused and the look on her face caused Becca to temporarily forget her irritation at the movie choice and burst out in laughter. She could tell that Lindy was trying to do the math but that the movie wasn't old enough for what she was thinking.

"Not at the movie. In the movie," she said.

"You were in the movie?" Lindy asked, the confusion on her face even more apparent.

"No," Becca's mom responded with a chuckle. "We met in a similar fashion as the two main characters."

"Oh," Lindy said, realization spreading over her face. "Becca told me you were in the Navy, and you were a physiotherapist," she said, looking toward the couch where Becca's parents were sitting. "I didn't know you were his rehab person. That's kind of cool."

"She wasn't," Becca said. "My dad's best friend was her patient. He got hurt in a helicopter crash, just like Jack Ryan. My dad came to visit him at the VA, and it just so happened to correspond with his therapy time. And the rest is history."

"I wish it would have been that easy," her dad joked, eliciting an elbow in the side from her mother.

"It was love at first sight for him. I'm not so easily swayed by emotions," Becca's mom quipped. "And Bry," she said turning her attention to Becca's brother who was heading back up the stairs. "You get 90 minutes. And who are you playing with?"

"That's it?" he complained and then stopped when he saw the look on his mother's face and realized this was a battle he was destined to lose. "Fine. Xan's still up in, wherever he is right now, so I'm playing with him. Fortnite." He quickly bounded the rest of the way up the steps to avoid any more questioning.

Becca poured out a big bowl of popcorn for Lindy and scooped some ice cream out for herself as the inevitable questions about Lindy's family commenced. Her dad was career Air Force, mom was a teacher turned stay at home mom. Dad was from Tennessee, mom from Colorado. They met during his last year at the academy. They had lived all over, but mainly in Europe. Her dad was currently finishing up his last year of service at the base about thirty minutes from Edgewater. Lindy said that her parents chose the base because of the civilian opportunities there after her dad's military retirement and picked Edgewater because it reminded them of the towns that they grew up in. Becca's mom, as expected, asked about Lindy's mom and why she wasn't around much. Lindy explained that they had adopted a little boy from Germany right before they left but that there were complications surrounding his adoption and he had to stay in an orphanage for almost a year. He had some medical problems that weren't properly attended to while there, and they had left some significant lingering issues that her mom was helping him work through. They spent a lot of time at the hospital and the rest of the time at home because her brother had a hard time being around people. Hearing Lindy talk about her brother only served to reignite Becca's butterflies and daydreams, even though it wasn't the brother they were talking about. She had obviously stopped listening because the next thing she knew, her mom was calling her name, asking her to bring over the rest of the popcorn.

As much as Becca would have liked to get back at EJ for the whole Weston ordeal by becoming Will's girlfriend, she knew it was a bad idea on multiple levels. First, that was a terrible reason to get into a relationship. Then there was the whole no dating until sixteen thing that her parents seemed pretty non-negotiable about. And most importantly, she really liked Lindy and likewise valued their newfound friendship. Mixing it up with Will would only serve to jeopardize that friendship. This was one situation in which she wanted to avoid the daily double.

CHAPTER 26

SADIE

"**I** don't care that he wants nothing to do with it and is willing to pay, you cannot get rid of the baby! It's a human being!" Sadie shouted into the phone.

"I know that, Sadie! But I'm struggling to take care of myself. I have no idea how I'm going to manage with a baby. Especially if JJ doesn't help."

"Well, you should have thought about that before you decided to sleep with him!" Sadie said spitefully.

The silence on the other end of the phone was deafening. Sadie internally chastised herself.

"Kat, I'm sorry. I didn't mean. . ."

"Yeah, yeah you did. I'm honestly surprised you waited this long to throw that in my face," Kat responded, a mixture of shame and resentment evident in her voice.

It was January. Both girls were back at their respective schools; Sadie managing classes, softball and various other extracurriculars, Kat trying to manage work, a few classes and a pregnancy. Sadie was keeping up with her promise to check in with Kat daily but the conversations over the past couple of weeks had done nothing but frustrate her. According to Kat, her discussions with JJ had ranged from overjoyed excitement at having a child to ultimatums to terminate the pregnancy. And everything in between. Sadie had tried her best to keep her mouth shut and allow Kat to talk or vent or work through things aloud. But this was the third time that this particular subject had been broached, and Sadie could no longer hold her tongue. It was one thing to get pregnant outside of wedlock, and to her, that was bad enough. It was another thing altogether when talking about ending a life. And Kat knew that. The fact that it was anything less than an absolute 'no' from Kat made Sadie burn with anger. And when she was angry, she tended to throw knives with her words without thinking about it first.

"Kat," Sadie started.

"It's not that simple. Not everything in life is black and white, even though you may think it is.

"'Thou shall not murder' is pretty black and white."

"That's not fair," Kat said, her voice pained but not defensive. *Because she knows I'm right,* Sadie thought.

"Kat, I've said this a thousand times, and I will continue to say it for however long I have to – you're not going to have to do this by yourself. Not the pregnancy, not the birth, not the raising of a child. Regardless of whatever JJ eventually decides, no matter if you decide to find your mom or not, you are not alone. If you decide you don't want to keep the kid and give it up for adoption, I will be with you through that as well. But under no circumstances can you terminate this pregnancy. It's wrong on every level. And you know that. You can't justify that. I will not be a part of that." Her voice was still tinged with frustration.

If it weren't for the heavy breathing on the other end of the phone, Sadie would have thought that Kat had hung up on her. She couldn't tell if Kat was angry and trying to control her breaths or crying and trying to catch them. Eventually Kat murmured something unintelligible, and Sadie knew it was the latter.

"I didn't catch that," Sadie said, trying to calm her voice.

"I said 'you don't understand.'" Kat sounded as though she was about to choke on her words. "His parents told him to 'take care' of this or he. . ." Kat gulped, fighting the tears and trying yet again to catch her breath. She was crying so hard it sounded as if she was heaving. On her end, Sadie sat in utter shock, not only at the revelation that JJ told his parents about the pregnancy, but also at the fact that they were actively pushing to end it. Kat continued before Sadie could respond. "They'll cut him off. No money, no job, no nothing."

And when you're Richy Rich and the heir to a fortune, that's basically like death, Sadie thought. She already had a disdain for JJ and his parents because of their gossipy, elitist attitudes but she would have never thought that they would pull something like this. She wished that JJ had the guts to stand up to his parents, but she knew that would never happen. And she seriously doubted that JJ wanted a kid anyway. That would put a serious damper on his lifestyle. A thought popped in her head.

"Maybe by 'take care of this' they just meant make sure that he was supporting you financially even if he didn't want to be an active part in it. Or push you toward adoption."

"Not according to him."

Sadie sighed audibly as her watch buzzed. Her thirty-minute alarm for practice. Shoot. This was a conversation that needed to continue but obviously not right now.

"Hey, Kat, I've got practice in thirty minutes, but I'll be done around five. It'll take me about three to four hours to get to you, but I'll be there tonight. We can talk about this more then, ok?"

"Don't do that," Kat replied, her voice wavering.

"Why not?"

"Because I won't be there," she said quietly.

"Kat! What? Where will you be? Oh, please don't do anything stupid!" Sadie was shouting again, this time out of concern instead of anger.

"I'm on my way to you. If that's ok. That's really the reason I called: to ask if I can come by tonight because there's a lot I need to tell you. I was going to save most of this for then."

Sadie breathed another audible sigh, of relief this time, and answered, "Of course it's ok. I'll leave my key under the mat for you. Let yourself in and I'll be back as soon as I possibly can."

When Sadie returned home from practice, Kat was sitting on her bed with a very large, very full duffel bag and a backpack next to her. Sadie had spoken to her roommates just before practice started and confirmed with them that it was alright for Kat to be there and to stay the night so that she wouldn't have to drive the four hours back at a late hour. She had sent a text to Kat to let her know. Apparently, by the appearance of the duffel, Kat had already planned to stay the night. And maybe a few more. Sadie walked over and wrapped Kat in a hug, grateful that she had the forethought to shower and change in the locker room. Although she was not yet showing, Sadie could definitely see a difference in Kat's appearance in comparison to when they left each other after Christmas. And it wasn't the stereotypical pregnancy glow. Kat looked even thinner than before, sickly almost, with dark circles under her eyes. If Sadie hadn't known better, she would have thought Kat had started using drugs. Even with her grandfather being a doctor and she herself majoring in the medical professions, Sadie didn't know enough about pregnancy to know how a body was supposed to react to creating another human, but she didn't think this was it. Kat was no longer crying but her face was still a little pink. Maybe from the cold but it was more likely that it was from the tears. Sadie sat down next to Kat on the bed and in her typical style, led off with a sarcastic statement.

"Moving in?" she said, pointing toward the duffel. Immediately, the tears began to roll down Kat's face once again. *Wow, pregnancy hormones are no joke.* "Um. . .I'm sorry. . .," she said aloud, more as a question than a statement. "It was just a joke."

Kat dropped her face into her hands, her entire body shaking with each sob. Sadie sat wide-eyed and perfectly still, not having a clue what to say or do. Eventually, Kat turned her head and through tears said, "I got kicked out of my apartment. Well, it was more a room than an apartment. But still, I don't have it anymore."

"Good grief, Kat. What happened?"

Kat took a deep breath, composed herself a bit and answered. "I don't have any money. I haven't worked in almost two months because every smell in the restaurant made me throw up. I don't have any savings or fallback money because nearly everything I made went to rent or tuition. The little bit of extra money that I had went into fixing my stupid, old car and getting a new phone. And it's not like I can call my mom for money."

"Why didn't you say anything?" Sadie inquired, a little irritated that this was the first she was hearing of any of this.

"How exactly was I supposed to do that? Hey Sadie, your former best friend, who you rarely see anymore, needs saving once again?" The antagonism in Kat's voice caught Sadie off guard. But the word 'former,' coupled with the apparent accusation of neglect, set her off. All the frustration of the past few weeks came pouring out of her mouth without a filter.

"So, this is my fault now? Because I wasn't around enough? I didn't see you clamoring to come visit me either. You haven't even been to one of my games in the last two years. So wrapped up in stupid JJ. Look where that got you. Well, obviously you know," Sadie replied curtly, hand gesturing toward Kat and her pregnant, messed up self. "And 'former best friend,'" Sadie included the air quotes, "What on God's green Earth is that supposed to mean? I didn't choose this. You did!" Sadie's voice had risen multiple decibels in a few sentences and continued to climb. "You chose a narcissistic, rich kid who cares nothing for you and did nothing but knock you up. And he can't even man up and take responsibility for it! That's not on me!"

The sadness that once filled Kat's eyes had now turned to hurt and then changed to something Sadie had rarely seen in Kat: actual anger. "Well, c'mon Sadie, tell me how you really feel," she retorted. "First of all, that's not at all what I meant. I'm well aware of whose fault it is. And I didn't choose JJ over you. I haven't been around as much for the same reasons you haven't been around – life. It happens and lately

I've been thinking that it sucks because I missed you and I missed our friendship. But now maybe I'm wrong. Yeah, I made a mistake. Yeah, I've got decisions to make that are going to drastically change my life forever. I thought you'd be there for me, with me. Not to save me; I truly don't need you or anyone else to save me. I never have, despite what it probably looked like to you." Kat paused and shook her head before continuing. "I should have known that you'd be like this. Completely unable to understand anything other than that black and white, right and wrong standard you have in your mind. And you judge anyone who would do something that you deem wrong. You think you're better than everyone else because you don't do anything wrong. Well, not everyone can be perfect like you, Sadie." Kat stood up, grabbed her bags and headed toward the door.

Sadie had half a mind to just let her go but the daggers that Kat just threw hit their mark. The hurt combined with her ridiculous need to have the last word in any argument caused her mouth to open and stupidity to exit.

"Where you gonna go, Kat? To your apartment? To JJ's?" Sadie knew her words were cutting deep.

Kat looked at Sadie with an expression that could not conceal her hurt. Her blue eyes filled with glassy tears and her features dropped. Her chest retracted as if she'd been hit directly in the sternum. Sadie was immediately filled with regret, but her pride refused to apologize. She sat there motionless; her own hurt reflected in her hard stare. Kat allowed her tears to fall and then silently turned toward the door and left the room and the apartment altogether. Sadie fell back onto her bed and yelled in vain at the ceiling. She had no idea where Kat might be headed and that had a part of her worried. But that part wasn't big enough to overcome the prideful portion that could not have cared less.

"Just don't do anything stupid," she said to the empty doorway.

CHAPTER 27

*I*t took Sadie almost two weeks to put aside her hurt and her pride and call Kat to apologize. During that time, she'd given considerable thought to what Kat had decided to do, but her hubris would not allow for any action. Finally, after a convicting church service on forgiveness, she made her first attempt. The call went straight to voice mail. It took two more days and five unanswered voicemails before Sadie decided to call her mom. She had no intentions of spilling her guts about what had transpired between them, only planning to ask if her mom had talked to Kat, but when her mom answered the phone with a 'What happened with you and Kat?' greeting, she did not have much of a choice. Her mom then informed her that Kat had been staying with Grandpa Jack. *Of course she was. I should have known.* Sadie bypassed Kat's cell phone and dialed her grandfather directly. After a pleasant conversation in which he did no berating whatsoever, Grandpa Jack turned the phone over to Kat.

"I am so sorry," Sadie said as soon as she heard Kat's voice on the other side of the phone. "For what I said. For basically throwing you out."

"You didn't throw me out," Kat said softly. "I left on my own accord."

"But I should have never let you leave. You should have never been in that position anyway because I should have never said those things to you."

"You meant what you said, Sadie. Maybe your tone was off, but your words weren't." There was a pause and then Kat continued, "I realize the position that I'm in, what I've done. I also realize that the way that you are wired makes certain things difficult for you to understand."

"Please, Kat. Please don't tell me. . ."

"I didn't," Kat interrupted, already knowing what Sadie was asking. "I'm keeping the baby."

Sadie breathed an enormous sigh of relief. Before she could respond further, Kat started talking again.

"Now that you know, you can go back to your life. I won't bother you any more with this. You have a softball season to focus on, school, a boyfriend. Your own life to live." Kat's voice was quiet, but there was a hardness there. Sadie was taken so aback by the content that she didn't have time to assess whether Kat was still angry or steeling herself for the potential fallout of her words.

"I don't understand. I said I'm sorry and I meant it. Every word of it." Sadie was beyond confused.

"I know and I accept your apology, and I'm sorry too. For the things I said. And for bringing you into all of this. It's a lot for anyone. And it wasn't fair to you to involve you."

"Kat, stop. Please stop. You're my best friend and you always have been. You always will be, no matter what has happened or what will happen. I want to be involved in this, and in everything. Don't push me away, Kat. Please. We had almost three years of drifting apart, and yeah, the circumstances that brought us back together may not be ideal, but it brought us back together. I don't want to go back." Sadie was pleading like her life depended on it. And it might. She hadn't realized just how lacking the last two and a half years had been until Kat came back into her life.

"I'm not pushing you away. I just think you need more time."

"More time for what?" Sadie didn't think her level of confusion could get any higher, but Kat kept surprising her.

"To accept all of this."

"KAT!" Sadie yelled into the phone. She breathed in and out, trying to calm herself. Her confusion had turned into frustration and if she wasn't careful, the frustration would turn once again to anger. "I don't understand what you are talking about," Sadie said through gritted teeth. "You're pregnant. And you're keeping the baby, thank goodness. I don't know what else there is to accept."

"I'm a flawed person, Sadie. You're a flawed person. We are all flawed."

Sadie took the phone away from her ear and banged her head against the wall. She had no idea where Kat was going with any of this. She put the phone back up to her ear and spoke, quietly and evenly.

"I know all of this, Kat. You know how well I know all of this."

"I do. And it messes with your brain. That's what I mean. It only affects your brain, not so much your actions. But for most people, it affects their actions. And that also affects your brain."

"Right now, you are hurting my brain."

Sadie thought she heard a chuckle on Kat's end of the line.

"I accept your apology. I do," Kat said sincerely. "I'm staying with Grandpa Jack for a while until I can find a job that doesn't elicit my gag reflex. Just think about what I said. You can call me tomorrow. I've gotta go."

And the line clicked dead. Sadie threw up her hands in frustration and the phone went flying across the room. Fortunately for her, it landed safely on the bed. She closed her eyes and rubbed her face with her hands, trying desperately to figure out anything about the conversation. But the only thing she was getting was a headache. Sadie looked at her watch and realized that she still had an hour before she had to be at practice. She grabbed her shoes from the entryway and decided to go for a run, hoping for some runner's high epiphany that would bring some clarity to this situation. Or at the very least, provide an outlet for the anger that she could feel welling up inside of her.

When she returned, she was just as confused as when she left, albeit sweatier and slightly less angry. She had left her phone on her bed, and when she picked it up, she saw that she had a text from Grandpa Jack. It read: **SUBTEXT.**

Seriously? She didn't have time for this. Sadie shot back a quick text without thinking about what she was writing.

You know I don't read between the lines very well. Clarity would be helpful.

She stared at her phone as the words suddenly seemed to jump off the screen. **Read between the lines.** Sadie began to replay the conversation in her head. Kat's subdued tone; the edge in her voice. Taking the blame for something that she shouldn't have. *Kat's acting strange. Being vague and standoffish like I do when I can't reconcile things and shake the.* . . And suddenly it all became clear. *She's not talking about me. She's talking about herself.*

CHAPTER 28

BECCA

January quickly melted into February, figuratively. It never snowed where they lived. But February meant the start of lacrosse season; yet another season watching from the sidelines. Becca's knee felt great, but the doctor said she wasn't ready to return to sports yet. Which made sense from a physical standpoint as she hadn't started cutting yet. And maybe even from a mental standpoint because she was honestly a little nervous when doing the light jumping in rehab. But still, watching was difficult. She kept herself busy by being the team manager, which basically just meant putting up the goals before and after each game and practice. Occasionally, she'd grab her stick and toss with a teammate until the coach decided that she was moving around too much for her liking. Becca knew her knee was stable enough for the very little bit of movement that she was doing but Coach was the coach, and she had the final say. It was annoying, but at least she got to be around the team. Lindy was playing on the school's beach volleyball team, so during moments of downtime during lacrosse practice, Becca tended to ease over to the sand courts to watch. And Becca had a lot of downtime. The sand courts also gave a direct view of the baseball diamond through the right field fence so she got to watch Will too. Double bonus.

Things with EJ hadn't changed a lot, but there was a little bit of improvement. Becca had spent a decent amount of the break talking to her mom and praying about the situation with EJ. She felt her heart soften a bit and it seemed as though the hurt was subsiding. She got the opportunity to apologize for her behavior when school resumed, but EJ didn't return the sentiment. Which kind of made Becca want to renege on her own apology. But she didn't because she truly was sorry for her actions. The forgiving EJ part, well, she was getting there. EJ was still dating Weston, which continued to rub Becca the wrong way, but she was learning to deal with it. She and EJ weren't hanging out and what little talking they did was very superficial, but at least they weren't actively avoiding each other anymore. During a few of their conversations, Becca tried to intimate that she knew what was going on with EJ's parents, but if EJ caught on to her subtle hints, she didn't show it. Becca's mom had suggested waiting until things settled down, both with the return from Europe sans her father and with EJ's absurd soccer schedule, before trying to sit down and have a hard talk with her. Becca acquiesced, mostly because she still didn't know what to say.

And then the rumors started. EJ at the Banks on the weekend. EJ on the boat with the Golds. EJ getting hammered at the Banks and on the boat. EJ doing things that were so anti-EJ that Becca questioned the validity of it all. She would never have gone to the Banks and involved herself in all the same things that she despised Gavin for. But then again, EJ had changed. A lot. So maybe there was some truth to it all. Becca decided that she needed to have that talk sooner rather than later. And she would employ Cooper to be the much-needed buffer. Cooper would be more than willing, and he was the perfect person to do it. He knew their history better than anyone else and he was completely non-threatening. But that also meant that she'd have to tell him about the divorce. And get him to be ok with her plan. Oh boy.

Becca walked over to Cooper's house one Saturday morning and found him outside playing hockey. His leg was finally strong enough to get back on both roller blades and ice skates and he'd been working hard to get back to the sport he loved. When he saw her, he skated off his driveway and down the road to meet her.

"What's up, stranger?" he called as he neared her.

"Stranger?" Becca repeated.

"Yeah, we only ever see each other in class now."

144

"Cooper, we just had a big thing with youth group like last week. Remember?"

"Yeah, I remember. Just feels weird without EJ and the Grove I guess."

"Well, that's what I'm here to talk about," Becca said, taking a deep breath. "I need to talk to her, and I need you to come with me."

Cooper nodded his head as he thought about what Becca was asking. "Buffer boy, huh?"

Here we go, Becca thought. "No, well, ok, yeah." She thought it best to just be honest. "I can't talk to her by myself. She doesn't exactly want to be near me right now. But if all these rumors are true, or even a little bit true, we have to talk to her. This isn't EJ."

"Agreed. We don't need another Gavin."

"Exactly. And she's not Gavin. Not even close. She's always hated the way he changed and became, well, whatever he is now. So, we need to figure out what is going on. Please help me."

"I shouldn't be telling you this, but I know what's going on," Cooper admitted. "Her parents are getting divorced."

Becca looked at Cooper in complete and utter astonishment. "Crazy, right?" he said.

"How did you know?" Becca asked.

"Wait, you know? How did you know?"

"My mom. She and Ms. Elisabeth are like best friends, or whatever parents call themselves. But she said that it was completely lowkey. So, I will ask again, how did you know?"

Cooper suddenly looked very uneasy. He stared at the ground and began hitting road pebbles with his hockey stick. And he didn't say a word, which was a clear sign that something was up. Cooper Cunningham had never been quiet a day in his life.

"Cooper," Becca said, her voice conveying her growing vexation. "What are you not telling me?"

Cooper's mouth moved but Becca heard nothing. She threw up her arms in a frustrated shrug and glared at him. He glanced at her and then fixed his eyes back on the ground.

"I still talk to EJ a lot. She told me," Cooper whispered and then shrank back as if afraid of Becca's reaction.

Becca's eyes widened at Cooper's revelation. And then it was her turn to be silent. She had no idea what to think, let alone say. She felt like Alice tumbling down the rabbit hole, with everything upside down and backwards. Except she didn't think she was going to land so comfortably. Her two best friends in the world had both betrayed her. For reasons that she could not understand. She backed away from Cooper as her eyes started to fill with water. He was talking but everything sounded like she was underwater. It was just noise. She turned and ran back toward her house but as she neared her driveway, her legs didn't turn. They kept propelling her forward as her eyes began to leak tears. She ran until her knee started to hurt. And then she kept going because she really didn't care if she hurt herself again. It would just make her knee feel like the rest of her: broken.

CHAPTER 29

When she could absolutely go no further, Becca allowed her body to collapse. Somehow, she was on the soft sand of the beach courts at the county park. She had no idea why she came here, of all places, especially when it was so close to EJ's house. Yet here she was, face salty and wet from the mixture of sweat and tears, legs shaking on the sand underneath her. Becca looked around and to her great relief, the park was completely deserted. There were a few trucks with trailers, but all occupants and their boats were out on the water. She sucked in deep breaths of air to replenish her oxygen. It was only a mile from her house to the park, but it had been well over five months since she'd run this far. Her lungs hurt almost as much as her legs. But neither could hold a candle to her heart.

When her lungs had their fill of air and her legs recovered some semblance of strength, she pushed herself up off the sand and walked gingerly over the boat ramps. There was definitely some pain in her knee, but she didn't think it was anything major. At this point, she was more concerned with the sand that had adhered to her legs thanks to the sweat. They were starting to itch, and she needed to clean them off. *Maybe the water can wash away some of this pain too.*

Becca walked down the boat ramp until the water was midway up her calves. The water was still chilly but after her run, it felt reinvigorating. She scooped some of it over the remainder of her exposed skin and rubbed the sand away. As she stood back up, she allowed her eyes to roam the river. There were only a few visible boats and little activity around the marina and yacht club, despite the relative warmth. At least by February standards. She thought it was odd, but then felt the wind whip her hair around her head and realized that any water excursion would be both cold and stomach churning. She could see some white caps closer to the river's mouth. Becca let her eyes traverse the river with its many forks and split. She thought she saw some people out on a dock down by where the main arm of the river turned left and underneath the old bridge but otherwise, the entire area was quiet. Becca reached back down into the cool liquid and splashed some on her face, trying to rinse away both the sweat and the memory of twenty minutes ago. Her mind didn't miss the irony of trying to wash away the broken with the Broken.

Becca wasn't sure what she had expected as far as EJ's relationships with the rest of the friend group but the fact that EJ was confiding in Cooper made her burn with rage. At EJ for replacing her so easily and at Cooper for taking sides. If she were honest about it, Cooper had been playing both sides because, like a genuine politician, he was a people pleaser and tried to always steer clear of conflict. But her brain wasn't going to be honest about it right now. And given the fact that Cooper was aware of both her years-long affection for Weston and the way EJ had been treating her lately, Becca figured he would be teetering more to her side of the fence.

"Becca?"

A familiar voice called out from behind her and forced her to withdraw from her thoughts. It was Lindy and her voice also brought forth a realization of why she was here. Becca's subconscious had longed for Lindy because, right now, she seemed to be the only person that she could trust. And this is where Lindy could normally be found. Becca turned around and started walking back up the boat ramp.

"Is the water, like, freezing?" Lindy asked, her tone as peppy and optimistic as ever. It amazed Becca that the same voice that annoyed her at the beginning of the school year was the very one that seemed to bring the most comfort right now.

Becca forced a smile and said, "It actually feels pretty good."

Lindy gave her a look of uncertainty and proceeded to shrug her shoulders and reply, "Whatever you say." Becca watched as Lindy's facial features began to change the closer she got to her.

"Are you ok, Becca? Your face is really, really red. Wait, have you been crying?"

Becca tried with all of her might to maintain her composure and lie to Lindy, but she couldn't. Her eyes welled up with tears again and she could only nod her head in the affirmative. Becca walked over to the seawall and sat down, allowing her legs to dangle off the side. Lindy rolled her volleyball to the side and followed Becca, sitting down next to her but keeping her long legs folded up underneath her. It was probably a good thing considering that Lindy's legs were a good three inches longer than Becca's and her feet would have been submerged into the chilly water.

They sat silently for a few minutes until Becca found control of both her tear glands and her vocal cords. And when she started talking, she didn't stop. She told Lindy everything, from the beginning. About Weston, about EJ, about Cooper and his absolute betrayal. Lindy proved to be a more than capable listener, especially since she had heard or seen most of what had occurred over the past few months. And while she was most certainly on Becca's side regarding EJ, her advice and reasoning for Cooper's actions were less than ideal. At least as far as Becca was concerned. Lindy made the observation that Cooper was caught between a rock and a hard place. As were Maddie and Seb, although neither seemed to be as close to EJ as Cooper was. He had been close friends with both Becca and EJ for so long that it really wasn't fair to ask him to choose. And that if EJ was confiding in Cooper, as opposed to say Quinn Gold or the other cheerleaders, that was a good sign, right? It meant she was still tied to her original group of friends and hadn't been completely lost to the dark side. Lindy had a point, although Becca's current emotional state would not allow her to admit it. She wanted her hurt to be justified and her anger to be reciprocated. But honesty and perspective were what she needed.

Lindy continued to stand firm on her stance that Becca needed to talk to EJ. Becca wasn't sure that she agreed. Especially since it would probably end up being more yelling than talking. Becca had considered herself relatively levelheaded until all of this, and she was realizing that she herself had an angry side that she didn't really care for. Lindy gave her best pep talk and put her arm around Becca's shoulders, telling her that it was all going to work out. The butterflies in Becca's stomach told a different story but she was grateful for the optimism. Lindy then asked a question that Becca hadn't been expecting.

"How did you get here, by the way? I would assume that your mom didn't drop your sad self here and leave you. And I didn't see your bike."

Becca chuckled. "I ran."

"You ran here?" Lindy asked in both shock and concern. "From where? From your house?"

Becca nodded.

"Geez, Becca. What about your knee?"

"Still attached." Becca's wise crack didn't relieve Lindy's concern. She sighed and then said, "I didn't really think about it. My body just took over my brain at that point and time. It's fine though. A little sore but that's probably because I haven't run that much in a while. I'm fine."

Lindy just stared at her. "Ok, my knee is fine. And I will be. Eventually," Becca admitted.

"Just call me next time. Instead of jeopardizing your future in sports. I would really like to play volleyball with you at some point."

Becca pursed her lips and nodded in agreement. "Me too," she said. "Can you tell my mom to get me a phone?"

Lindy took her arm off Becca's shoulders and slapped both hands against the seawall.

"Done," she said. "Your mom likes me. And you need to get with the times."

"Facts."

They both laughed and Lindy handed Becca her phone so that she could text her mom and let her know that she was at the park and that Lindy would bring her home later. And then she decided to test her knee a little more by bumping the volleyball with Lindy. What started out as a completely miserable day ended on a more positive note. Becca was still unsure about a lot of things, but this friendship was not one of them. Of that, she was grateful.

CHAPTER 30

SADIE

"**Y**ou said I could call you today," Sadie said in response to Kat's perfunctory greeting when she answered the phone.

"I did," Kat acknowledged and then let silence overtake the conversation. Sadie waited a moment or two and then broke it.

"How are you?" she inquired, not really sure what to say.

"Still pregnant." Kat replied.

Sadie was a bit miffed by the snappishness that she could hear in Kat's voice but then remembered that she herself answered questions in the same manner when she was in stressful situations.

"Well, that's good," Sadie responded, and really meant it, given their previous conversations.

"What do you want, Sadie?"

Sadie took a deep breath and tried to channel her inner Kat. She was used to being on the other end of these chats and had little experience being the optimistic, sane one.

"I don't think you need any more time," she said.

"Pretty sure you got that wrong. I said that you need more time," Kat retorted.

"Oh, I heard you. I also heard what you meant. And you don't need more time to decide if I can handle it. Or if you want me to handle it. I'm here and I'm not going anywhere. At least not for a couple of hours."

Sadie could almost hear the gears turning in Kat's mind. She gave her three beats and then said,

"I'm on the dock."

Sadie heard Kat sigh and then the phone clicked off. After figuring out her grandfather's cryptic message and noticing that she had a rare day off, Sadie decided to make the drive home and talk to Kat face to face. In preparation,

152

she had spent a considerable amount of time reading her Bible and talking to God. She figured she could use all the help she could get since Kat was obviously still upset with her and trying to push her away. And Sadie also had it on good authority that Kat was mired in the guilt of her actions and the confusion of how to handle her situation. Mainly because that's what her grandfather said when she spoke with him late last night. He had called after Kat had gone to bed.

She sat on the edge of the dock, allowing the brisk morning breeze to cool her body. The temperature was mild for February but there was a moderate wind blowing out of the north which gave the air a little bite. The river was choppy and occasionally a rogue wave would hit the side of the dock, spewing mists of water onto Sadie's legs. Even though she was just a few hours away, she missed this place. The peace, the serenity, the way the river seemed to wash away her stresses and clear her mind. It was exactly what she needed. The softball field had become more a quagmire than a haven but this place; she'd always have this place. It was her sanctuary.

Sadie felt the dock move when Kat stepped onto it. Without turning her head, she said,

"Thanks for coming out."

"Least I could do given that your grandfather is housing me, feeding me and paying for my medical bills. And he told me to."

"Smartest person I know," Sadie said and patted the wood next to her.

She could tell that Kat was complying begrudgingly because she sighed loudly as she walked to the end of the dock. Sadie kept her shaded eyes fixed on the mangroves on the opposite riverbank and said a quiet prayer. She was surprised at how nervous she was about having a conversation with her best friend. This was their normal and right now it felt very unnatural. Maybe because she was generally on the receiving end of the advice. Or maybe because, despite the daily calls over the last month, their divergent currents left them too far apart. She inhaled the crisp air and blew it out slowly.

"Kat, I am really sorry for the things that I said to you. I know that there are times that I seem judgmental in my statements or reactions, but you know as well as I do that it's not from a place of judgment, it's from an inability to understand. But that does not excuse anything. So, I'm sorry. And I hope you can forgive me."

"I already told you that I did," Kat replied, her eyes looking down at her feet, which were gently kicking the top of the water.

"Thanks. I appreciate that. You also need to know that this changes nothing between us."

"This changes everything, Sadie," Kat said, swinging her head around to look at her. Sadie's eyes were shaded with her sunglasses, as per usual, but Kat's eyes were uninhibited, and Sadie felt as though she could see right through them to Kat's soul. And she looked dead inside. Sadie merely stared back at her, awaiting an explanation.

"I'm about to be a single parent at twenty years old. I have no family to help me, no college degree, no finances to speak of. I was forced to fend for myself at a young age and I was very fortunate to have found a family as great as yours to take some of that burden off of me. But now I really have to grow up. It's no longer just me. I have to figure all of this out and I don't have time to deal with your issues too."

"My issues too?" Sadie repeated. "What are you talking about?"

"C'mon Sadie. I know you. Your head is spinning. You're trying to figure out how I could be so careless, why I would do something so immoral, what you should have done better and how you can fix it. And I have neither the time nor the energy to deal with those questions. I can't keep focusing on the past. Or on you."

Kat turned her head back towards the opposite bank. Her words stung and Sadie found herself unsure of how to respond. Of course, Sadie had questions, and yes, she did tend to linger in the past, trying to figure out how to fix things that probably couldn't be fixed. It did affect her mood, and Kat was typically the person to pull her back into the present. But this was different. How, Sadie wasn't sure. But it was. She turned her head so that she was facing away from Kat as she contemplated what to say next. Her blood was boiling, and Kat's stiff arm hurt, but she knew that if she responded in anger, Kat would walk away. And that would hurt far more than the pain she was feeling now. Sadie willed herself to calm down, tried to say a silent prayer but no words formulated in her brain. The only thing that registered was the word breathe. So, she did. A lot. And when she felt like she could speak without her voice increasing in decibel level, she turned back toward Kat.

"I'm going to say this as calmly as I can, and I hope you will do me the favor of listening to everything that I have to say." Sadie paused, awaiting a response from Kat but she continued to stare into the void across from them. Sadie took a deep breath and continued.

"I haven't asked you to deal with my issues in a long time and I didn't come here today to do that either. I'd be lying if I said that I haven't wanted to talk to you about all the stuff in my life and in my brain, but we haven't exactly had that kind of relationship over the past year or two. And I'm sorry for that too but I'm not going to dwell on it."

"Why did you come here today?" Kat asked as she turned back to face Sadie, heavy emphasis on the second word of that question.

"I came to ask you not to push me away. I came to tell you that whatever guilt or shame you might be feeling, it's ok. I'm not judging. It doesn't change who you are. It doesn't change the fact that you are my best friend and I'm going to walk through all of this with you. If you let me. And if you don't, I'm still going to be here. I'm not going anywhere."

Kat's face had been nearly unreadable throughout the duration of the conversation, but now her expressionless features began to slowly morph into the hardened face of a defiant teenager. Sadie braced herself for the worst. And then Kat's features softened. She had always been much better than Sadie at negotiating herself down from the emotional ledge and returning to a state of saneness. Sadie exhaled in relief.

Kat turned her gaze back across the river. "Even if I were feeling guilt and shame, that's for me to process on my own and I really don't need your constant reminders of my failures. And you say that you aren't judging, and consciously, you're probably not. But I know that the 'why' questions are there. They are always there. It's your inability to see life any other way than in black and white. It's not your fault; it's just the way that you are wired. It's one of the things that makes you so great; you don't get mixed up in stuff that you know you shouldn't, and you're not swayed by people or emotions. But it also hinders your ability to be gracious and forgive when you don't understand why someone would make a different choice than what may be morally right. And where you see the why questions as a way to try to understand something that you never will, everyone else sees it as being judgmental. As you thinking that you are better than everyone else because you would never be dumb enough to make the mistakes that we've made."

Sadie didn't think she could be any more peeved than she was earlier, but Kat's words just proved her wrong. She could feel her face heating up as she responded.

"You know that's not true. We've had this conversation before. I don't think that I'm better than anyone else!" Sadie insisted. She shook her head and took a very deep breath. The last thing that she wanted to do right now was to lose her head. *C'mon Sadie, don't get defensive. Breathe.* Self-talk on the softball field was generally a conscious, controlled thing. Right now, Sadie had zero control over her brain. It was just churning on its own, seemingly uncontrollable. *God, I need you right now because I don't have a clue as to what to say and I don't want to screw this up any more than I already have.* Another deep breath. Sadie closed her eyes. She so desperately wanted to plead her case as to why Kat was wrong in her assessment. And then she realized, again, that this wasn't about her. Sadie decided on the opposite approach.

"I'm sorry that my reactions to things come off as judgmental. That is never my intention. I will work on that. But again, please don't push me away. I'm here for you, Kat. I want to be here for you. With you. What do you need me to do to prove to you that I'm not passing any judgment and that, to me, you are the same Kat you've always been?"

"I need you to back off," Kat responded without hesitation.

Sadie stiffened at Kat's words and Kat seemed to notice because she sighed and softened her body language and her tone.

"I just. . ." Kat paused, appearing to struggle for the right words like Sadie had earlier. "Just please don't push me on this, ok? I'm not saying don't talk to me, just don't, I don't know."

With that, Kat unseated herself and walked off the dock in the general direction of the house. Sadie assumed she made it back inside although she didn't turn around to look. She just sat motionless, biting her lip in frustration. Her heart felt as though it was fracturing. Sadie pleaded with it to hold together, but pleading didn't seem to be enough. She slapped at the water as hard as she could, spraying water droplets all over herself and the dock.

"Why can't you have a name like, 'Peace' or something? Or at the very least, not live up to your name so darn well!"

The river answered with a smack of a wave against the dock, water once again spewing all over her. The splash caused Sadie to turn her head to her right and there she saw the old, beat-up boat tied to the cleats. Instantly, she knew what she needed to do. She pushed herself up from the dock and climbed into the boat. She untied the lines and instead of cranking the motor, she just shoved hard off the dock and laid down across the two seats, allowing the tide full control. The dichotomy of the river was something she wasn't sure she'd ever grasp but she hoped that somewhere in the drift she could find at least a modicum of peace for her troubled heart and mind.

CHAPTER 31

BECCA

"**H**ey EJ," Becca said, after she had cornered EJ in the locker room after school one day. Becca had convinced her mom to let her stay at school for the lacrosse game, instead of going home and doing her homework first. Since she was allowed to leave her last period class early to set up the lacrosse field, (the perks of having her coach as her teacher), Becca's remaining responsibilities as team manager usually didn't require her to be there until close to game time. Her reasons for staying at school were twofold; she wanted to hang with the team before the game, and she knew that EJ would be cleaning out her locker from soccer that afternoon. Since her county park conversation with Lindy, she'd been working her channels for ways to get EJ in a situation in which she would have to talk. At least a little bit. She had gone over to Cooper's house the day after talking with Lindy and apologized for her reaction. They had a good chat, and both felt as though it was past time for Becca and EJ to start talking to each other again. Together, they decided on a plan to basically corner EJ. With the help of both Maddie and Sebastian, Becca and Cooper were able to piece together tidbits of information and figure out that EJ had planned on staying after school on this particular afternoon to clean out her locker. Becca was honest with her mom when she requested to stay after and, although her mom wasn't thrilled with the 'cornering' aspect of the plan, she agreed with the talking part and was resigned to the fact that this was probably the only way it was going to happen.

EJ looked around the room for either an escape route or another person. Becca knew that she couldn't keep other people from walking in, especially with the lacrosse game starting in an hour, so the goal was to walk out with EJ to a waiting Cooper, who would serve as mediator for a courtyard conversation. With Becca standing directly in front of the door, EJ seemed to realize rather quickly that there was no path for a clean getaway. She turned back to her locker, gathered the remainder of her gear and said,

"What do you want, Becca?"

"I just want to talk. That's it."

"So, talk," EJ replied curtly.

Becca rolled her eyes. This was going to be harder than she thought. "Rephrase. I want to have a conversation. With you."

"I don't really want to do this here," EJ admitted, slamming her locker shut and turning to face Becca. Becca stared hard into EJ's brown eyes but was having trouble reading them. Or maybe having trouble reconciling the anger in EJ's voice and actions with the perceived sadness she saw in her eyes.

"Well, that's good because I wasn't planning on doing this here. Cooper's waiting for us. He's. . ."

"So now you're partnering with Cooper to gang up on me. Real sketch, Becca," EJ interrupted.

"It's not like that at all," Becca said, hoping this wasn't going to blow up in her face.

"I can just stay in here and wait you out," EJ said, crossing her arms over her chest, her face defiant.

"I've got nowhere to be," Becca said, leaning up against the wall next to the door.

A stare down commenced; Becca looking hopeful and carefree at EJ, and EJ spitting fiery darts with her eyes in Becca's general direction. After a few minutes, EJ decided to yield, albeit with a heavy sigh and a massive eye roll.

"Fine. Let's get this over with."

She walked toward the door and Becca pushed herself off the wall, following closely behind EJ so that she couldn't turn and bolt. As they opened the door, Becca saw Cooper waiting patiently for them. She was grateful that he had been working so hard on his leg strength because EJ turned to run, and Cooper was able to step right in front of her and absorb her momentum with ease.

"You need to do this," Cooper said as he gently grabbed EJ's arms and directed her toward the courtyard. "You both do."

The three friends walked to the empty courtyard and found a table in the corner away from the prying eyes of teenagers walking into the gymnasium or to the athletic fields. Becca sat down opposite EJ while Cooper occupied the spot on the bench next to EJ, to prevent another escape attempt. EJ glared at him before resuming her defensive position of arms crossed over her chest and hard eyes fixed on Becca.

"You wanted to do this, so let's do this," EJ said, her words biting like an artic wind.

Becca shot Cooper a look of concern which he responded to with a look of uncertainty. It was not helpful at all. Becca took a deep breath and laid her forearms on the blue tabletop. It was one of those standard commercial picnic tables, the ones with holes in the top and on the benches, that could be found in probably every school in the country. There was a smattering of red, white and blue tables around the courtyard. The double doors closest to them led into the lunchroom and on good weather days, they ate lunch outside. Most days in Edgewater could be considered good, so this area got a lot of use, as evidenced by the Jackson Pollock-like ketchup and mustard stains on the concrete. Becca tapped her fingers on the holes in the table. EJ huffed and looked away, annoyed. It was Cooper's turn to shoot a look toward Becca, although it was more than just a look because he mouthed 'Say something.' Becca's fingers now gripped the table through the holes, and she opened her mouth.

"How's soccer going?" Becca asked, still unsure how to go about getting to her point.

"Fine."

"Your mom said that you got a tryout with the junior national team."

"Yeah. Is this what you went through all this trouble to talk to me about? Because it seems like a waste."

"She's concerned about you," Cooper said, talking to EJ but staring at Becca. "We both are."

"He's right. There've been a lot of rumors going around about you at the Banks. It doesn't seem like stuff you would do but I've, we've, heard about it from a lot of people. Normally, I wouldn't think twice about them being anything more than dumb rumors but since we don't really talk or hang out anymore, I don't really know what to believe." Becca said.

EJ continued to stare into space, her eyes narrowing so much that Becca wondered if they were still open. When she decided to speak, her eyes stayed focused on whatever it was that she was looking at.

"It makes me pretty heated that the two of you would swallow those rumors and stage an intervention. Y'all should know me better than that," she said, her voice even, eyes still looking elsewhere.

Cooper answered before Becca had a chance to finish processing. "Five months ago, I would have agreed with you. And even though you and I still talk, we don't hang any more. Things have changed. You've changed."

EJ caramel skin was starting to redden, and she looked both angry and uncomfortable. She turned her eyes back to Becca and angrily said,

"If I've changed, it's your fault! You knew I liked Will, and you couldn't just stay away. You had to go and ruin everything. Everything was perfect until you ruined it. It's all your fault!"

EJ was shouting by the end of her diatribe and Becca was very grateful that no one was around to witness it. And even though EJ was both staring at and talking to her, Becca somehow knew that she wasn't talking about her. She kept her composure, only by the grace of God, and calmly replied,

"I know about the divorce."

Becca watched EJ's eyes pop open in disbelief and then narrow again as she whipped her head in Cooper's direction.

"It wasn't me!" Cooper said, holding his hands up in surrender and leaning away from EJ. "She already knew!"

"My mom told me," Becca admitted. "The night of our parking lot fight."

"She had no right," EJ said, her eyes starting to fill with tears.

"She wasn't planning on it. She said that she was waiting on you to tell me but after that incident, she felt as though I should know that there was more going on than just Weston and Will."

"There's nothing else going on. You betrayed me. That's it," EJ said, trying to portray anger and ferocity, but her voice quivered, and the tears began to overflow their rightful boundaries. Becca thought she looked more like a scared child than a perturbed teenager and her heart began to ache for EJ. Despite their current situation, EJ was still an important part of Becca's life, and she wanted more than anything to restore their friendship. Becca stood from her seat and walked around the table towards EJ. She sat down next to EJ and put her arms around her.

"I'm sorry, EJ. I'm sorry you're going through this," Becca said quietly.

EJ consented to the hug, even leaned into it, for about as long as it took Becca to finish her sentence. And then, like a light switch flipped, she pushed back against Becca and swung her legs around the bench, nearly knocking Cooper off his seat. She stood up quickly, grabbed her stuff and walked away, saying absolutely nothing. Becca and Cooper simply watched her leave, both recognizing that going after her would be pointless. Becca signed loudly as she watched EJ turn the corner without looking back and then she put her head on the table. She really thought there was a breakthrough right there. And maybe there was a small one. EJ didn't push her away immediately; she did accept the hug, at least for a second or two. Cooper was the first to break the silence, as silence seemed to be uncomfortable for him.

"You've known since Christmas Break?" he asked. Becca nodded her head without picking it up from the table. "She just told me at the end of January. I thought it happened when they went to Europe. How long has this been going on for?" Cooper asked, more to the universe than to Becca. But Becca answered.

"Remember the last time we were all at the Grove? The Friday that Gavin almost ran us over and Mr. Jones was. . ."

"Leaving." Cooper said, finishing Becca's sentence. "Dang." They both returned to their state of silence, Becca still resting her head on the table. The buzzing of Cooper's phone interrupted both of their thoughts.

"Oh shoot, it's three forty-five. Gotta run. Call me later?" he said as he arduously unfolded himself from the picnic table. Cooper's strength may have returned but his flexibility was still suspect.

Becca slowly picked her head up from the table and murmured an assent. She needed to get up and get moving too. The game started at four and she needed to make sure that all the water bottles were filled, and they had extra lacrosse balls. But she didn't move immediately. Both her brain and her heart hurt. EJ didn't address the rumors at all, except to say that she was surprised they believed them. Although the way she said that, along with her body language, suggested something else. She clearly didn't want to talk about the divorce, but the sadness in her eyes and the way she accepted Becca's hug, even if only for a second, made Becca think that EJ really needed someone to be there for her. She didn't know what to do now. She felt more confused than she did a month ago. *Zero for two today, genius. Failed with EJ and missed the team. Winning,* she thought, sarcastically. Becca walked sullenly to the locker room to fulfill her managerial duties, wishing she would have heeded her mother's advice and waited to talk to EJ.

Although, she wasn't sure it would have made a difference. She wasn't sure about anything anymore.

CHAPTER 32

SADIE

*I*t was spring break, although the only break Sadie got was from attending classes. Softball season was in full swing, and she had practice Monday and Tuesday, games Wednesday and Thursday and was leaving Friday for a weekend series out of town. Such was the life of a college athlete. As a team, they were warned about showing up to anything red with sunburn, and, although her beigy skin tended instead to tan, Sadie tried to limit her time by the pool. But since it was a rare week of low humidity, lots of sun, and temperatures in the seventies, Sadie found herself outside more than not. There were two oak trees behind their apartment building to which her downstairs neighbors had tied a hammock. The trees gave off a moderate amount of shade and since there was nothing behind them except a makeshift preserve, which was just an area of tall grass that had yet to be developed, the area was also very quiet. Sadie had a decent relationship with her neighbors and knew that all three of them were out of town for the break, so she assumed the responsibility of ensuring that the hammock was operational for their return. She took up temporary residence there and either read a book or took a nap. She was on said hammock, taking a mid-morning power nap, when her phone rang.

Sadie opened one eye and tried to focus on the caller ID. When she saw the name, both eyes bolted open, and she nearly fell out of the hammock trying to sit up. It was Kat. Sadie had done her part in backing off, sending intermittent text messages for Kat to respond to as she wished, and making a weekly phone call to check in. She was trying to balance respecting Kat's wishes and still proving that she was going to be there no matter what. It was a tricky line to traverse, and Sadie often wondered if she was doing it wrong. But she was going to keep that concern to herself, since it was one of Kat's complaints. Kat had been decent about returning text messages, but the phone calls were always one way. Except for right now. The feeling in Sadie's stomach was reminiscent of December when Kat randomly showed up at the softball field. Was it good news or bad news on the other end of the line? Sadie yearned for the former and hoped that she had successfully navigated the last few weeks. She wanted things to return to normal, whatever that was. She took a deep breath. There was only one way to find out.

"Hey Kat," Sadie said, trying not to sound too excited.

"Hey, how's your break going?" Kat asked.

Sadie read nothing in the tone of her voice so answered honestly, "It's good. Taking a nap on a hammock right now."

"No practice today?" Kat asked.

"No. Doubleheader starting at four. Have to be at the training room at two."

"Ok. What about tomorrow?" Kat inquired.

"Same schedule," Sadie responded, wondering where the line of questioning was leading.

"Do you mind if I come to your games?" Kat asked.

"Seriously?" Kat hadn't seen Sadie play since her freshman season.

"Don't sound so shocked," Kat replied. "Ok, you can sound shocked. I know it's been a while. But yes, I'm going to hitch a ride with your parents."

"That's awesome!" Sadie was overjoyed, not just because Kat was coming but also because there was humor in her voice. It was something that Sadie hadn't heard in a while. "I won't have a whole lot of time between games, but my parents usually take me out to eat after the games so, oh crap. My brother has a game tonight so they're only coming up for the first game. Shoot, I won't even really get to see you." The realization instantly made Sadie lose her earlier joy.

"Wanted to ask you about that too," Kat said. "Grandpa Jack is contemplating coming tomorrow so I was wondering if I could stay the night, and we could hang out tomorrow morning. I didn't know what your schedule was. . ."

"Of course you can!" Sadie interrupted, her joy returning and causing her to nearly shout into the phone.

On the other end of the line, she heard Kat laugh in response. Sadie couldn't remember the last time she had heard a real laugh coming from Kat's lips and a smile crossed her face that would have made a clown proud.

"Ok, I'll see you tonight then. Good luck."

"Thanks. And thanks for coming up. I'm excited."

"So am I," Kat admitted. "See ya later."

Sadie hung up her phone and flopped back into the hammock, once again almost flipping both herself and the fabric upside down. This was good, right? Kat coming to visit her, sounding happy and joyful again. Yeah, this was good. Really good.

CHAPTER 33

$\mathcal{S}$adie played the first game of the doubleheader and had probably the best game of her college career. She honestly thought that she would be incredibly nervous, with everything that had been going on between her and Kat, but Kat being there made it feel like old times. She hadn't felt this confident on the softball field since high school.

After the second game, Sadie bounded out of the dugout, a huge smile on her face. Kat walked up to her and gave her a quick hug. Sadie took the opportunity to give Kat a once over and saw that she was starting to look like Kat again. The gaunt look from the beginning of the year was gone and she looked healthy. And there was maybe a hint of glow. She still wasn't really showing, although the shirt she was wearing was a little baggy and would have hidden any small bump. They walked together to the locker room, where Sadie quickly changed and grabbed a bag of ice for her shoulder, and then they walked to Sadie's car. The conversation was light, a general Q&A about school, softball, Grandpa Jack and Christian, who Kat had apparently met during the first game and told Sadie that he was a keeper.

They decided on take-out from a local diner for dinner. Kat went healthy with a chicken salad and vinegarette dressing and Sadie opted for the complete opposite: a messy cheeseburger with fries and a chocolate shake. They made their way to Sadie's apartment to eat, where her roommates had just arrived with their own takeout. Together, they all had a nice dinner and found themselves playing card games until the wee hours of the morning. By the time they all went to bed it was nearly two a.m., but the laughter and joy that Kat was expressing was worth any lost sleep. And although Sadie was eager to find out if she was out of whatever doghouse Kat had put her in, she was going to allow Kat to dictate any conversation around the topic. She had thoroughly enjoyed the night and had no intention of ruining it by bringing up a sore topic. But as the sun rose later that morning, Kat had yet to discuss the events of the recent past. Sadie had almost resigned herself to the fact that it was a topic which would never be broached.

They slept in, well, Sadie slept in. Kat said she was up at eight, and maybe she was, but Sadie didn't roll out of bed until almost ten. She had a protein shake for breakfast and then both girls headed for the pool. Her roommates declined to join because they both had spent the past two days there and could feel their skin starting to sizzle. Kat and Sadie alternated between basking in the sun and cooling themselves in the crisp pool water for almost an hour. They had just returned to their pool loungers when Kat said,

"I'm sorry, Sadie."

The comment caught Sadie off guard, and she responded with, "For what?"

Kat simply stared at her behind her large sunglasses until the realization crept over Sadie's face. Then she nodded and turned her face back toward the pool. There were only three other people in the pool area, and they were all on the far end of the pool deck, yet Kat's voice was as soft as a whisper. Sadie had to strain to hear her.

"I could blame it on the hormones, and maybe that did play a part in it, but really that's just an excuse," Kat said. She paused for a second and Sadie mentally told herself not to say a word until Kat was completely finished with whatever she wanted to say.

"I'm scared," she continued. "Still. Of being a mom. Of being a single mom. Of trying to support myself and a child." Pause and deep breath. Kat was still looking towards the opposite side of the pool, but Sadie was staring straight at Kat's face. Kat had her full attention.

"And I'm ashamed. I'm ashamed that I let JJ dictate my life. That I put myself in this situation. That I even thought for a second about terminating the pregnancy. After our fight, I was incredibly angry. At you, yes, but mostly at myself, even though I wouldn't admit it. In that anger, and in my guilt and shame, I pushed you away. I blamed you for something that you weren't even doing because it was easier than admitting that it was me who I was angry at."

Kat was quiet for a while. Sadie thought that maybe she was finished but was hesitant to break the silence on the chance that she wasn't. She was also silently praying for God to give her the words to say. Her mental and emotional feet were sore from walking on eggshells for the past couple of weeks and Sadie was eager to say what was in her heart and move on. But she also feared that one wrong word would result in the utter destruction of the trust she was trying to rebuild. Fortunately, Kat started talking again, and any gut-wrenching decision was delayed for at least a few more minutes.

"Your Grandpa Jack has to be the closest thing to God on this earth. He has been so generous with his money and his house and his food. And even with his time. He works a ton, and I mean a ton, but he sits with me every night. Mostly it was him watching TV or reading a book, and me fighting through my tears in silence, but he is so patient. He never pushed me to talk or to stop my blubbering and deal with the consequences of my actions or anything like that. He allowed me the time and the space to process all of this. And he seems to read me as easily as I read you," Kat joked, now turning her head to face Sadie. Sadie could see the watermarks on Kat's face under the sunglasses. They were faint, but they were there. And seeing them made Sadie's throat lump up. She tried to swallow it down as Kat continued.

"Shortly after you came to visit, I realized what I was doing but I didn't know how to fix it. I didn't think there was a fix for the shame and guilt I was feeling. Last week, as Grandpa Jack was leaving for work, he put a hand on my shoulder, flashed that tender smile and handed me this."

Kat gave Sadie a small sheet of paper, which she slowly unfolded. There, in her grandfather's impeccable cursive, was this:

In him we have redemption through his blood, the forgiveness of our trespasses, according to the riches of his grace, Ephesians 1:7

"I hadn't said a word to him about how I was feeling. He just knew. He knew that I needed to know that God would forgive me, had forgiven me, for what I've done. For all of it; the actions and the thoughts. He had forgiven me, not because of anything that I've done but out of his grace, because of the blood of Jesus. It's something that I've known my entire life, thanks to you and your family, but it finally became real. It was also his way of reminding me that not only has God forgiven me, but people that love me have also forgiven me." The tears were starting to stream now, and Kat's quiet voice had started to shake. She put her head down and wiped her face with her hands. Sadie sat there quietly and let Kat do whatever it was that she needed to do. It's what Kat always did for her. Kat took a deep breath and then continued, her voice still a bit shaky.

"And because of all of that, I needed to forgive myself. I cried all day that day and into the night. When your grandfather got home from work, I didn't even come down to say hi. It took me until the following night to get to the point where I could face him. But when I did, I talked nonstop for over an hour." Kat chuckled through her tears and her voice started to find its strength again. "See, the issues in my life have always been because of someone else's choices. I had no control over that fact that my mom was always running out on me, or that she'd leave without getting groceries or paying the utility bill. Or that the rest of my family was virtually nonexistent and that I never knew my father. It was just the hand that I was dealt, so to speak, and I tried to make the best of it. And that was made a whole lot easier because of you. But this, this I did to myself. This was my choice. I didn't know how to handle that. And I also felt like I let down the only person in my life that never walked away. The one person who cared enough about me to warn me about JJ. Repeatedly, I might add. I was so scared to tell you. I turned around three times that day in December when I came up here. And my car broke down because I was thinking about what to say to you and wasn't paying attention and ran over something that destroyed the axel. And, even though we hadn't seen each other in a year, and the fact I know you had questions and had trouble understanding, you were so gracious and caring toward me. You didn't yell or chastise or anything. You brought me home, shared your family with me, again, and made sure that your grandfather would find the very best care for me."

Sadie stiffened a little. Kat turned her body so that she faced Sadie, lifted her sunglasses and wiped her eyes again. When her face was clean, she left the sunglasses on the top of her head and looked Sadie right in the eyes.

"Yeah, he told me what you did. That you asked him to find the best doctors and gave him the money that you had been saving for grad school to pay for my expenses. The envelope of cash is in my bag, by the way. He wasn't going to let you pay but didn't want to give the money back right away."

Sadie looked away from Kat. Her face was heated and not from the sun. She had specifically asked her grandfather not to say anything to Kat about that. To just get it done because she knew that he could. It was her way of helping and it was really the only way she knew how. And not only had he told Kat, he'd also given the money back. Sadie closed her eyes and tried to calm herself. This was not the time to get angry.

"That's a crap ton of money, Sadie. I can't believe you did that. Actually, yes, I can. Because that's who you are. And that's the person I felt like I let down. The generous, caring, loyal person who has long been the best friend of a really messed-up kid. And your response to everything made me feel worse. But then we got in that fight and when you got angry at me for my choices, it confirmed my greatest fear: that I screwed up so much that even you would leave me. But you didn't. I wanted you to. For some ridiculous reason, I wanted you to prove me right. But you kept showing up, even when I tried to push you away. Even when I blamed you for things that you weren't doing. Sadie, I'm so sorry. So sorry. I know you've forgiven me, even though I haven't asked. But I needed you to know what happened, what I was doing and why. And I needed to apologize."

Sadie turned to face Kat, feeling her own eyes fill with tears. For a multitude of reasons. Her heart hurt for Kat and for the emotional rollercoaster that she had been on. Sadie knew that ride all too well. She was stunned and saddened by the fact that Kat thought she had let her down; something Sadie didn't think Kat would ever be able to do. And Sadie would never even consider leaving her. Ever. For the duration of their friendship, Kat had always been the one waiting on Sadie to deal with the enigma that was her own brain and Kat never thought about leaving, at least not to Sadie's knowledge. So why would she leave Kat? Especially during the one time that Kat actually might need her. The tears finally started to run down her face. Sadie sat there in silence, not knowing what to do or say. Kat had pushed her sunglasses back down over her eyes and had turned to look back out over the pool. It seemed to Sadie that she, too, was at a loss. So, Sadie followed the only thought that entered her head. She moved over to Kat's pool lounger and sat down next to her. She put one arm around Kat's shoulders and said,

"You're stuck with me. Just accept it. I speak truth and there's nothing you can do about it."

Kat broke into a fit of laughter at Sadie's quip. Sadie wiped her tears and laughed along with her. Then Kat laid her head on Sadie's shoulder and said,

"Thanks. For everything."

"You too," Sadie responded.

CHAPTER 34

BECCA

Spring break could not come soon enough. Becca needed a breather. For whatever reason, all her teachers decided that the third quarter of eighth grade was going to be insanely intense and filled with major tests. There was a part of her that was thankful that she didn't have to balance all this work with lacrosse and club volleyball. A very small part, but still. Add the work to the failed conversation with EJ, and every other insane thing that had happened this year, and Becca's mental state was pure exhaustion.

Because of their family's participation in spring sports, spring break had never been a week of travel but a week of rest and recuperation. Usually, Becca was thankful for the physical rest. This year, however, it was mental rest that she so desperately needed. Physically, she needed to go in the opposite direction.

Her dad had taken the week off and they decided to take the boat down the coast about an hour to a beach house that had been in Becca's family for decades. It was old and kind of small, but the front door opened to a small canal with a dock and boat lift, and the back door opened to the sandy beach and the sea. To an agent, it was probably a multi-million-dollar piece of real estate. To Becca, it was a cramped house with out-of-date furniture that thankfully had three bedrooms, so she didn't have to share a space with her brothers. She often wondered why no one bothered to update the place. Her extended family did not have Jones level money, but they were also not poor. But that was neither here nor there.

She needed this week to be a week of calm and this house a place of refuge. After Becca and Cooper had attempted the intervention, EJ had responded with a public shunning of both. She returned to actively avoiding Becca and then added Cooper to the list of unapproved interactions. EJ also began flaunting Weston in front of Becca and purposefully overplaying her friendships with Quinn and the other cheerleaders. It was beyond irritating. But instead of ignoring the situation, like she desperately wanted to, something inside of Becca prompted her to pay more attention to EJ specifically. And when she did, she saw that EJ's face was full of apathy. There was no joy, no spark. She was merely acting, or maybe reacting, but there was no happiness to be found. It made Becca sad, but she had no idea what to do at this point. She'd tried talking to EJ, she'd been praying for EJ and for wisdom about how to handle all of this. In her mind, she was doing all the right things and things were turning out all the wrong ways. It was confusing and, to be quite honest, exhausting. And to top it all off, the extra focus on EJ stirred up an internal war against anger and jealousy, because there was no way to completely avoid her escapades with the Gold siblings. For maybe the first time ever, Becca was grateful that she had neither a phone nor access to social media.

The week began in full relaxation mode. Brendan drew some incredibly vivid pictures of the beach and the sunsets. Bryson complained about not seeing his friends and not having access to his Xbox, but he quieted down when another family with a boy his age rented a house two doors down. They rarely left the beach, going skimboarding, body surfing and even trying a bit of surfing, although neither boy was very good. Nor were the waves. In the evening, Becca's family took the boat out and did a little fishing and/or tubing before finding some hole in the wall restaurant on the water for dinner. Every restaurant looked to have been built in the same century as their house, and it was not this one, but without fail, the food was delicious. This was like the island that time forgot, and Becca kind of hoped that it would have the same effect on her. She wished she could go back to

August and the Grove and a time before the current chaos of her life. And she wished she could stay there. Forever.

Before removing herself from all access to civilization, Becca and Cooper had talked about how to handle EJ and her current snubbing of their presence and overall antagonism. Honestly, Becca was at a loss. She didn't understand why EJ remained so hostile despite Becca's apology and efforts to restore their friendship. Especially given that both she and Cooper knew about the divorce and were more than willing to be there for EJ. If Becca was going through something even half as traumatic as a divorce, she'd want nothing more than to be with her best friend. To cry, to vent, to bring some semblance of normalcy. She struggled to figure out why EJ didn't want the same. The whole thing made her sad, confused and maybe even a bit depressed. She moped around the house like she did right after her injury: moody and frustrated. The silver lining was that this time she could walk without the aid of crutches. Her parents had initially allowed her space to feel what she was feeling but they were now over the moodiness. And they had said as much, to which Becca simply rolled her eyes and told them that they didn't understand.

The one positive note in all of this was that Becca's knee was feeling great. She had just passed the six-month mark from surgery and had been progressing well through her rehab. She'd been doing some sprinting and cutting in therapy, all with her functional brace, and her mom decided that she was strong enough to do a bit of running and working out on the beach. Still with the brace, but it was progress. She'd never really been one to sleep in very much so each morning Becca and her mom would go for a run on the beach. For the first day or two, Becca paid close attention to her knee, hoping that it really was as stable as she thought. Once it proved her right, she focused her attention on the beauty of God's creation. The little slice of barrier island was surrounded by bright blue water that was nearly transparent. The gentle lap of the waves against the powdery white sands created a sense of calm like Becca had never known. Or maybe never realized. The water was much calmer in the mornings than in the afternoon, when the surf broke further from the shore and allowed for a little more adventure. This early though, it was calm enough that Becca could see schools of little fish, of which she knew not their name, swimming just beyond the mark where the ocean met the sand. Occasionally, a dolphin would pop its dorsal fin out of the water in a pristine arc and then plunge back below in search of breakfast. The scenery was incredible, and she wondered why she had never paid attention before. Probably because, as a kid, she just wanted to play. And life was easy. And she wasn't actively searching for peace. And answers.

One morning, she and her mom decided to run to the pier on the opposite side of the island. It was a good two miles away from their house and Becca could definitely tell that she was still a bit out of shape. The huffing coming out of her mouth was pretty loud. They decided to grab a bagel and water from the little coffee stand by the pier and walk the two miles back. Becca then decided that this was as good a time as any to ask a question that had been circulating in her mind for a while.

"Mom, if God is good and he blesses those who believe in him, why do things still go wrong for people who are doing the right things?" she asked.

"Asking the hard questions before the coffee," her mom said jokingly.

"You don't drink coffee," Becca responded blatantly.

"Right," her mom responded, as she took a sip of her water. "Maybe I should start."

Becca watched as her mom looked out over the water, contemplating her response. They walked in silence for a while and Becca was unsure if her mother was going to give an answer. So, she started talking again.

"I get that we are all sinners, but there's got to be more to it. It doesn't really make sense," she said, kicking at the soft sand with her foot.

"That is pretty much the gist of it," her mom said as she kept walking, still looking out over the water. There were times that her mother had a seemingly bad habit of delaying her answers. Or maybe it was a good habit, Becca wasn't quite sure. When she was younger, Becca thought it was because her mom thought that she couldn't handle the answers. And it frustrated her. But recently, she realized it was because her mom wanted to give her the right answer. Or the closest thing to a right answer. And the questions that Becca had been asking were probably much more difficult to answer than two plus two. Her mom turned her face to look at Becca and then said,

"The why questions are always the most difficult for me to both understand and answer, because there's a lot that we will never understand. But I'll do my best. I heard this comparison once and it stuck with me. A little girl sees a sheep eating the green grass and thinks, 'wow, that sheep is really white and clean.' And then it starts to snow. And now that same sheep is in a field of white snow and the little girl thinks, 'Wow, that sheep is really dirty.'"

Becca stared at her mom, waiting for an explanation. Her mom chuckled at whatever expression was on Becca's face and then continued.

"Compared to the world, our sins may seem insignificant, or we may seem really good and really clean. But then, compared to the law of the holy and perfect God, we are absolutely filthy. Every one of us, Romans says. There are no quote-unquote good people in this world. The gospel of Luke says that no one is good except God. We are all affected by the sin in this world, be it ours or someone else's."

"Ok, I get that," Becca responded. "But shouldn't there be some kind of reward or blessing for the people who are doing the right thing, like forgiving others and reading the Bible and praying?"

"Shouldn't there be a punishment for the people who get angry and therefore commit murder in their hearts?" her mom countered.

Becca felt her face heat up and she pursed her lips together.

"Listen, Bec," her mom continued. "I know this stuff with your knee and the stuff with EJ has caused you to question things. And I'm glad you are. Digging in to find the answers will only serve to strengthen your faith. And honestly, I'm glad you are dealing with this now. It's a lot harder to work through those questions as an adult while everything you thought you knew is crashing down around you. The Bible says that God works all things out for good, for His purposes. But God gets to define what 'good' is and we will never fully understand how He goes about fulfilling His plan, reconciling us to Himself. This is where faith and trust come into play. Do you trust God enough to know that He is sovereign and good even when bad things happen? Especially when you didn't directly cause them to happen. Or when good things don't happen, even though you are doing everything 'right'? Do you trust Him enough to believe that no matter what happens to us in this life, He understands because He endured it, and more, as well? Second Corinthians says that 'God made him who had no sin to be sin for us, so that in Him we might become the righteousness of God'. Jesus was the very best to ever walk on earth, the only perfect person, fully God and fully man, and he endured the absolute worst. Not only death on a cross which was meant for the worst of the worst in the Roman empire, but also in taking on the sins of the world. To atone for all of our sins. He did that for you and for me, and for all who would believe in him, because He loves us. The Creator of this entire universe loves you so much that He sacrificed Himself, so that we can be with him, so that this world is not the end for us."

Her mom took a deep breath. Becca continued to walk, staring at the split screen of water and beach in front of her.

She was mentally wading through the heavy surf of her mother's words. As if reading her mind, her mom said,

"I know it's a lot. But this is part of the surrender that He asks of us. To surrender our will and what we think is good and right and trust Him. Even if it seems wrong and bad to us. To surrender our plans and our timing." Her mom stopped walking and turned to face Becca completely. "You are following in obedience to God. You've asked for forgiveness, and you've forgiven EJ. You have refrained from gossip, and you even tried to talk to her in the presence of a friend. With a pure heart and pure motives because you care about her. But just because EJ didn't respond in the way that you thought she would, or should, doesn't mean that God is punishing you or that He isn't good or that you should go do all the stuff you haven't been doing. His timing is hard to wait for sometimes, but it's always perfect. Trust that He is working even when you don't see it. Like David did in First Samuel when he was both running from King Saul and waiting for his own time to be king."

"How do you know all of this stuff? Did you go to Bible school and not tell anyone?" Becca asked, her mind still kind of swirling from her mom's answers.

"I wish," her mom responded, her gaze leaving Becca and fixating on the open expanse of water beside them. "Personal experience. Learning the hard way. Still learning to be honest. But God can handle our questions. He can handle our doubts and concerns. He wants our hearts and He's willing to prove himself faithful again and again to get it. Why? I don't know. Because He's God, I guess. I would have given up on me years ago. But He never did. And I'm so grateful."

"But why is it all so hard?" Becca asked.

"You know what they say about that. 'The hard is. . .'," her mom started before Becca cut her off with a moan and a very big eye roll.

"Not again, please not again," Becca pleaded.

"Ok, but the statement remains true," her mom said as she took another sip of her water.

"Well, nothing about this is great right now," Becca said.

"No, I suppose it's not. Most of the things that are worth it, are usually hard. Remember, it's iron that sharpens iron, not a pillow. Keep trusting God. And honestly, don't just take my word for it; keep reading your Bible. That is where you will find truth. Maybe not always the answers that you're hoping for, but always the truth."

Becca let all her mother's words marinate in her mind. She didn't fully understand everything but at the same time, she understood. Maybe that's what her mom was talking about in terms of faith and trust in God and the Holy Spirit. She had to admit that it wasn't the answer she was looking for but deep inside of her, she knew that it was the answer that she needed. *God, help me to trust you even when I can't see you. Even when things that seem so obvious and so true get lost behind the smoke and fog of everything else in this world. Help me to be patient through the hard times and the loneliness. And please be with EJ. I want our friendship back but more importantly; I don't want anything bad to happen to her while she's making bad choices.*

CHAPTER 35

SADIE

*T*he first threat had come shortly after Sadie's fight with Kat, but since they were temporarily not speaking to each other, Sadie was never informed. It came in the form of a letter, typed and wiped, and placed underneath the wiper of Kat's car. For the most part, it was relatively benign, once again asking Kat to abort the baby, that it would be paid for, and everyone could just go their own way. It was ignored. By the time Kat broke the news to Sadie, during that same spring break visit, there had been at least four more, each more foreboding in nature. They ranged from slashed tires to ominous phone calls threatening her life if she continued with the pregnancy. Sadie had been incensed, threatening JJ in the quiet corners of her brain. She asked Kat for the phone number of the callers, but Kat told her that caller ID had been blocked, which only further enraged Sadie. She even went so far as to call Kat's cell phone provider pretending to be Kat and asked them to look into it because of the nature of the calls. She was met by the scene played out in every *Law & Order* episode; she'd need the police to stop by with a warrant. Kat wanted no part of the police, particularly because she believed that the threats were coming not from JJ himself, but from his family. And his family had contacts in the police department. Sadie felt as though she was living in the aforementioned television show. This entire situation felt as though someone was writing a ridiculous movie script. None of it seemed real. But it very much was. Sadie was still of the mindset that JJ was behind the childish prank calls but Kat, being the recipient of said calls, felt that there was nothing childish about it. She was genuinely scared and starting to waver in her determination to keep her child. That was until last week and a surprise visitor at Grandpa Jack's door.

Sadie had received a tearful voice mail from Kat requesting that she call as soon as she possibly could. The panic that Sadie felt upon listening to the voice message caused her chest to tighten like hands clinging to a rope. She feared the worst and then panicked even more when she saw that Kat's call had come two hours prior. Sadie had been in the middle of practice and had no access to her phone. Kat hadn't even gotten through "hello" before Sadie was asking if she was ok. Kat assured Sadie that she was ok but that someone had stopped by Grandpa Jack's to see her. Sadie immediately launched into a diatribe about how awful JJ was and how he should be grateful that she wasn't around because she would have let him have it. She went on so long that Kat had to interrupt her with,

"It wasn't JJ. It was my mom."

Sadie had immediately fallen silent. Kat hadn't had any contact with her mother in almost two years, so her mother's presence alone was a huge deal. But the real kicker was that not only did her mother know of Kat's situation, but she was also actively pleading with Kat not to ruin her life. Despite Kat's persistent questioning, her mother would not divulge the source of her information, only telling Kat that "moms know everything." Her mother begged Kat to leave with her, stating that she knew people that could take care of all of this, even if it was "stupidly going through the rest of the pregnancy," her mom's words, not Kat's. It was at that point that Kat told her mother to leave and to never contact her again. And that Kat became even more adamant that she was going to keep this child and be every kind of mother to him or her that her mother had never even tried to be. It was also the moment that Sadie realized that this might just be bigger than JJ being an irresponsible spoiled brat.

Sadie answered Kat's call one week later and was greeted with,

"The threats are getting worse."

"I'm not sure they get worse than threatening your life or sending your mother to threaten the life of your child," Sadie responded. "I still have a hard time believing that JJ's parents would do this to their own grandchild. It shouldn't matter that it's out of wedlock. I mean, really, they should have expected something like this with JJ. Eh, sorry Kat, that sounded bad."

"But not wrong," Kat replied.

"So, what did this one say? We'll be at the hospital to take the kid away?"

"This one wasn't to me," Kat said. Sadie could hear the frustration in Kat's voice.

"What do you mean?"

"It was to Grandpa Jack," Kat revealed. "It says, 'If you want to continue practicing medicine in this county, get rid of that whore and her kid. Now'."

Sadie felt her hand tighten around the phone and anger begin to bubble in her soul. No, it wasn't anger. It was pure rage.

"I don't think I was supposed to see it," Kat continued. "At least he didn't mean for me to see it. I was emptying the trash cans and when I dumped the contents from the trash can in his study, a piece of ripped paper with the part that said 'get rid of' fell out onto the floor. Typed, like all the other ones. And I just knew. So, I found all the pieces and put them together."

Sadie found herself full of fury. JJ, or whoever it was, had the audacity to threaten her grandfather's livelihood. And to suggest 'getting rid' of both Kat and the baby. Sadie could feel the heat emanating from her face and her mind swirled with thoughts of mass destruction to JJ. She was so caught up in her ire that it took Kat nearly yelling at her through the phone to bring her back to the present.

"Yeah, I'm here. Just deciding on my method of retaliation," Sadie said through gritted teeth.

"You're not doing anything. They'll come for you too. These people seem to have no end to the lengths they will go. I'm going to leave so that nothing happens to Grandpa Jack."

"Why?" Sadie asked. "Don't let them win!"

"If I'm alive and my child is alive, they're not winning."

They had debated at length as to who "they" might be. The idea of an external source was negated because both Kat and Sadie felt that if someone outside of JJ's family or Sadie's family found out about the situation, they would be focusing their attention on blackmailing Edgewater's 'most upstanding family,' the title bestowed by the local newspaper. Kat landed solidly with JJ's parents, given their prior contempt towards her. Even with the unexpected appearance of Kat's mother, Sadie still felt as though JJ was behind it all, even if he were employing others to do some of the dirty work.

"C'mon Kat, you don't really believe that anything is going to happen, do you? JJ's not man enough to do anything if he's behind this. No offense, but he's only man enough to do one thing and that's procreate."

"None taken."

"And even if you're right and his parents are behind the threats, do you really think that they would be as cruel and unusual as to harm their own blood?" Sadie asked.

"I don't intend to find out. I'm going to talk to your grandfather tonight and come up with some options, but all of them will include leaving Edgewater. That was always the plan anyway," Kat answered.

Sadie sighed. She hated the idea of letting whoever was behind this even think that they were winning. But Kat had a point. She had only intended to stay with Grandpa Jack until she could get back on her feet and feel well enough to get a job. And in the very rare case that these were more than empty threats, Kat and the baby remaining alive was the most important thing.

"You can come here," Sadie offered. "We're in the homestretch of the season so we won't be around much but I'm sure my roommates will be fine with it. I can go find another mattress and I'll sleep on that."

"Thanks Sadie, and I really mean that, but I need to get back to being independent and taking care of myself. I'm fine, I promise. I'm going to try to get my old job back and see if I can find an apartment or room back there."

"But JJ," Sadie started, but Kat cut her off.

"He's in Edgewater. Another reason for me to get out. He's interning with one of his dad's companies, so he's out and about a lot. I'd prefer to avoid awkward, unplanned run ins."

Sadie more than understood that. Although if she had an unplanned run in with JJ, it'd probably be awkward and very uncomfortable for him. Physically.

"Ok, but if you need anything. . ."

"I know, I know," Kat interrupted again. "I promise that I will call or come to you. Promise. I speak truth remember?"

Sadie could hear the confidence in Kat's voice and truly felt that everything was going to be ok. She could also hear the humor in that last statement and was so grateful to have Kat back. Not just in her life but the real, crazy, funny, full of life Kat back.

"I'm holding you to that," Sadie said.

"Oh, I know. That brain of yours forgets nothing. Talk later, sister."

Sadie shook her head at Kat's sign off and hung up her phone. Gosh, it felt good to have Kat back. Like normal. Like home.

CHAPTER 36

BECCA

"**I** don't know what else to do," Becca admitted to Cooper one afternoon after school. "I've apologized, I've tried talking to her, I've given her space. I've even talked to my mom about what to do!"

"You make it seem like talking to your mom is a completely foreign thing for you to do," Cooper said as he tossed the basketball into the hoop that adorned Becca's driveway. "And we both know that it's not."

"Ok, well, you're not wrong," Becca admitted with an eye roll as she retrieved the basketball and passed it back to Cooper. "But that's not the point. The point is that I've exhausted all options with EJ, and she clearly wants nothing to do with me. Over what? Will? There's nothing going on there. I can't help it if he likes me and not her. But I'm not doing anything about it. Clearly."

Cooper's next shot clanged off the front of the rim. Becca grabbed the rebound and dribbled the ball over to her favorite spot to shoot from: the equivalent of the right elbow of the key. She drained her first shot and Cooper ambled over to grab the ball and pass it back to her.

"What did your mom say about it? Oh, shoot, I hope no one heard that," Cooper joked as he looked around, pretending that Becca speaking to her mom was some sort of secret.

"Ha, ha, very funny." She lined up her next shot and drained that one too. "She gave me a long speech that basically summed up to, 'keep waiting. God's timing is perfect.'" Becca caught Cooper's pass and in one fluid move drained her third shot in a row.

"Our parents must have gone to the same motivational speaking school," Cooper quipped as he once again gathered

Becca's made shot and passed it back to her. "But if anyone knows anything about waiting, it's me. And I know that it's not an easy thing to do."

Becca bounced the ball a few times, mulling over his words. He was certainly right about that. He endured almost four long years of waiting for the 'cancer-free' words and even longer for a return to normalcy. She took two steps back and tossed up another shot. Another swish.

"Can I ask you a serious question?" Cooper said, letting the ball bounce into the grass beside the driveway. Becca stared at him. "Why don't you play basketball again?"

"Because I play soccer," she answered, looking at Cooper but pointing to the basketball laying in the grass. Her features changed as a realization swept over her. "Oh gosh. If all this keeps up, I may have to switch sports. Hurry up and toss me that ball."

Cooper obliged and Becca tossed up another shot that ricocheted off the back of the rim, hit the backboard and fell harmlessly to the ground. Becca grunted in frustration and grumbled about how terrible she would be on the basketball court.

"Only four of five? Please stick with soccer," Cooper said sarcastically as he grabbed the rebound and dribbled out to the opposite side of the driveway.

Becca glared at him and rolled her eyes. "Back to the topic at hand," she said, eager to return the focus from her basketball prowess to her issues with EJ. "What's the play?"

"You're naturally athletic so you're going to succeed at either one," Cooper said as he launched the ball from the far end of the drive. It landed hard against the front of the rim and bounced back toward him. "But I'll stick to hockey, thank you very much."

"Cooper!" Becca yelled, becoming annoyed by his avoidance of the problem.

He sighed as he corralled the ball and took a few dribbles before passing it over to Becca. She caught it easily and tucked it under her left arm, impatiently awaiting Cooper's response.

"I have no idea. She won't speak to me either. And I'm me," Cooper said, half in jest but also in truth, because everyone talked to Cooper. Mr. Personality had no enemies. Until now. And it was kind of Becca's fault. But was it really? Cooper was just as big a part of the 'intervention' as she was. But there wouldn't have been the need for an intervention if. . . if what? What could she have done differently? She apologized for the way she reacted to Weston, and she hadn't done anything regarding Will, despite both her growing feelings for him and EJ's betrayal. She'd tried on multiple occasions to talk it out, with zero success. In her mind, she'd done everything right. Really right. And it was still going wrong. Her mom's words rang in her ears: trust that God is working even when you don't see it. His timing is perfect. Maybe so, but it sure didn't feel like it.

"Ugh, why is this so hard?" Becca complained.

"To quote the great Tom Hanks, aka Jimmy Duggan," Cooper began.

Becca threw the basketball at him and commanded him to stop. "You sound like my mother. Exactly like my mother, in fact. And it's pronounced, Doo-gan, not Duggan."

Cooper laughed as he caught Becca's throw and then said, "Well, great minds think alike." He dribbled twice and tossed up another shot that once again hit only the rim. "Yep, hockey it is. But seriously Becca, I think the only thing we can do is wait her out. She knows how we feel about her, and we can't make her change her mind about talking to us. Or allowing us to be her friends again. But even though she's acting like someone we don't know, we do know her and she's EJ. She'll come around."

"I hope you're right," Becca mumbled.

"When have I ever been wrong?" Cooper remarked.

"Aside from calling him Jimmy Duggan, you mean?" Becca retorted with a sly smile.

"Ok, ok, maybe you shouldn't answer that question."

Becca shot him a look that said, 'exactly' and jogged to get the basketball. She offered it to Cooper, but he declined and told her to shoot until she missed. She went ten for ten. On the eleventh shot, Cooper made the projection that if this went in, they would be back at the Grove with EJ before the summer. That, too, went in. But teenage prophesies are often wrong.

CHAPTER 37

SADIE

Kat's first call after her decision to leave Edgewater was to her first roommate, Emma Grace. Kat had moved from that apartment after a year but the two had kept in touch and when Kat explained her situation, Emma Grace practically begged her to move in. Em had said that her previous roommate had moved out at the end of the last semester, and she hadn't been able to fill the room. Now she knew why. "God knew we were going to be roomies again," Emma Grace had said. Grandpa Jack had apparently handled Kat's rent for a couple of months and as grateful as she was for all his help, Kat was bound and determined to find a job and not only pay him back but support herself and her child. Emma Grace helped with that as well. It turned out that her father had just expanded his business into the area, and they were looking for an office manager. Despite all the craziness that surrounded her life, Kat's organizational skills were impeccable. It was the perfect job: good pay, low stress, time off, and most importantly, away from any prying eyes and loose lips that may divulge Kat's whereabouts to JJ.

Kat had told Sadie that the threats seemed to have stopped. She hadn't gotten anything since she moved. Whether that was because they were satisfied with her actions or that they couldn't find her, neither Kat nor Sadie knew for sure. But Sadie suspected the latter. She didn't have any physical evidence to support her theory but when she had recently asked her grandfather about it, his answer was a vague, "That's not something to concern yourself with." Sadie knew him well enough to know that if they had ended, he would have said so. But she wasn't about to say something to Kat and send her into any sort of fear spiral that caused another move. Four hours away was far enough. And she still seriously doubted JJ's ability to do anything other than make empty threats.

All in all, Kat seemed very happy. And that made Sadie very happy. It seemed that the events of the past few months as well as the distance of the past few years had disappeared. Their friendship was nearing the closeness that had defined it for the duration of their childhood. To Sadie, everything was finally as it should have been all along.

Sadie headed down to see Kat as soon as her season ended. She was going to have to spend most of the summer at school but had a week to burn before classes started. And to be honest, she needed to get away for a little while. Softball continued to be a struggle, both physically and mentally. Her shoulder was getting worse, and it was affecting her play on the field. The stress of trying to be perfect and not losing what little playing time she had, as well as secretly dealing with her deteriorating shoulder, left her both physically and mentally exhausted. And in a dour mood most of the time. That, coupled with sixteen credit hours of medical classes, left little time, focus or energy for anything else, including Christian. He understood to a point, as he had his own athletic and academic career to focus on, but he was not necessarily happy with the lack of time together. They probably should have been spending this week off with one another, but he had already committed to a camping trip with some of the guys from FCA. Sadie was not the least bit upset; she was going to see Kat whether he was in town or not. It had been a very long two months since Kat had come to visit and Sadie needed a week of friendship and fun. She'd figure things out with Christian when she got back.

The apartment Kat shared with Emma Grace was in the same complex as the first apartment that they shared, although this one was on the newer side of the complex and was on the second floor as opposed to the third. If Sadie was grateful for one less flight of stairs, she could only imagine how thankful Kat was. As she climbed the steps, the door to the right of the staircase opened. Kat was standing in the doorway, signature messy bun on top of her head. The sickly look that she had in January and February had completely disappeared and she looked healthy and radiant.

"Still driving too fast, I see," Kat said, in a tone of mock disapproval. Sadie had called when she left her place. A normal drive should have taken anywhere from three and a half to four hours. Sadie Andretti made it in three fifteen.

"Why drive slow when you can drive fast?" Sadie questioned as she ascended the last few steps. "Traffic was light and I. . ." She stumbled over the last step as well as those last words because she caught a glimpse of Kat in profile.

Kat noticed the look on Sadie's face and started to laugh.

"Yeah, can't hide it anymore, can I?" she said.

Sure enough, there it was. Sadie wasn't sure what she was expecting but she was still caught off-guard by the bump in Kat's belly. From the front, she looked like the same old Kat but from the side, well, there was no denying it anymore. Sadie regained her balance and stood there statuesque in front of Kat, not exactly sure what to do next. When Kat reached out for a hug, Sadie remained motionless.

"Is it ok to give you a hug?" she asked, as she had literally zero experience with pregnant women. "I'm not going to hurt the baby, am I?"

"I'm not made of porcelain, ding dong. No, you're not going to hurt the baby." Kat hugged Sadie tight to prove her point. "See. Just fine. You know, Sade, for a pre-med student, you don't know a whole lot about pregnancy."

"Bones and ligaments, not babies and, well whatever else goes with them."

"Told you," Kat said over her shoulder. Sadie could hear laughter coming from inside the apartment.

"Hey Em," Sadie hollered through the still open door.

"Hey Sadie! Come on in!" 'In' had two syllables in Emma Grace's vernacular and the 'a' in Sadie's name was still just as long, despite being out of Charleston for the better part of three years. Sadie found Emma Grace's lack of change very comforting. She grabbed her bags and walked past Kat, careful not to accidentally hit her stomach. Kat rolled her eyes and she and Emma Grace burst into a fit of laughter yet again.

"Seems like this is going to be a week full of laughter," Sadie said. "Mostly at my expense." And she was right. That may have been one of the best weeks ever. It genuinely felt like old times, even with Emma Grace joining them. They stayed up late chatting about school and boys and life in general, and then, because Em's dad was kind enough to give Kat the week off, they spent most of the daylight hours lounging at the pool. Thanks to Grandpa Jack's generous end-of-the-school-year gift to Sadie, they ate out every night, went to the movies three times (twice watching the same movie) and found themselves at an arcade in which Kat dominated both Sadie and Emma Grace in nearly every arcade game known to man. If Sadie thought that a baby bump would alter Kat's ability to shoot hoops, she was sorely mistaken as Kat won five games in a row of pop-a-shot before Sadie had enough. On Sadie's last day in town, Emma Grace treated them all to mani-pedis and massages at a swanky spa. It was glorious. They then took Kat on a trip to the local baby store to pick out items for the upcoming, still unscheduled, baby shower that neither Emma Grace nor Sadie would let Kat go without. It was as enjoyable and relaxing a week as Sadie could have imagined, full of love, laughter and friendship. and she was so disappointed when she had to return to school. But real life beckoned them all. At least they had the week as well as the memories. As she drove back to her college campus, she thanked God for his graciousness in restoring the best friendship of her young life.

CHAPTER 38

BECCA

Eighth grade ended on a decent note. At least academically. And maybe even athletically. Becca made dean's list with her 4.0 GPA, thanks not in small part to Maddie's cliff notes in English. There was no valedictorian for middle school, just recognition of those on the dean's list and principal's list, 4.0 GPA and over 3.5, respectively, but everyone knew that Maddie was the queen when it came to academics. Becca was grateful for her, and not just because of the schoolwork. Maddie, like Lindy, had become a significant source of comfort and friendship, both trying to fill the void that EJ left. Or maybe it was Becca herself trying to fit them into an EJ shaped hole. Either way, they had both been of immeasurable support for her this year. And with Maddie's knowledge of the history of Becca's friendship with EJ, she was able to bring an extra bit of understanding to the situation that Lindy could not. That reality did not go unnoticed or unappreciated.

Becca was cleared to return to sports at the beginning of June, nine months after her injury. She was equal parts thrilled and nervous. Even with the brace and the constant reassurance from her mother that her knee was stronger than it was before, Becca couldn't completely shake the ravenous pterodactyls residing in her stomach. Maybe it was out of fear of reinjury or maybe it was a nervousness about jumping back into competition after nearly a year away. Becca wasn't completely sure but regardless, there was an unsettled feeling that was proving difficult to remove. Her mom made her start slow, monitoring practices and interspersing extra strengthening sessions to help maintain strength and reassure Becca that her leg was good. Both Becca's stomach and brain were grateful for the extra steps her mom was taking, even though her mouth complained incessantly.

June dragged into July, the way that summers do when time is relative, and everyone is out of town. Lindy was gone for almost two weeks visiting family and it just so happened to coincide with Maddie and Sebastian's vacation. Cooper was home but with his strength back to one hundred percent, he dove headfirst into sports. Literally. He joined a swimming club to cross train for hockey and found that he loved swimming. Becca was certain that he spent most of the month in the pool and Becca found it difficult to have conversations with someone who was underwater more than they were not. After nine months of isolation (as defined by a normally gregarious teenager), Becca was desperate for social activity but, with everyone either gone, busy, or not on speaking terms, she found herself once again relegated to the chaotic solitude of her own mind, a place she'd been trying to evict herself from for a while. She needed a distraction. And she was about to get one. A very big one.

The school held a volleyball camp during the first week in July and, for Becca, the timing couldn't have been more perfect. Her first competitive tournament of the summer was ten days away and camp would be the perfect place to work out those nerves. Lindy had returned from Tennessee a few days ago, stating that she would have cut her vacation short if she had to; she was not missing camp. The girl lived and breathed volleyball. But there was a significant and noticeable absentee: EJ, their primary setter. Becca couldn't really say that she was surprised. Cooper's driveway basketball prediction proved very wrong, and EJ was continuing to play keep away with her presence. She'd heard through her mom, who continued to maintain her close friendship with Ms. Elisabeth despite the inability of their daughters to do so, that EJ had made the U15 junior national soccer team and that her time was tied up with that this summer. She was genuinely happy for EJ yet still fought the feelings of betrayal and sadness when hearing about things secondhand that she should have been celebrating with EJ herself.

The first four days of camp went flawlessly and with each new day, Becca's butterflies quieted, and her confidence grew. But when she awoke Friday morning, the butterflies made an unwelcome and somewhat unexpected return. Perhaps it was because today was a shortened day of camp that was filled solely with scrimmage games, her first real action since September. Or maybe it was because today was the Fourth of July.

July Fourth had long been Becca's favorite holiday but the reason for that had nothing to do with why that date was celebrated. It was Becca's favorite holiday because both her family and EJ's family always came together for a full day of activities on the Jones' "big boat," a forty-two-foot Sea Ray cabin cruiser that easily held both families, with extra room for all the inflatables, skis and fishing poles. They'd spend the entire day on the water, both in the river and traversing the coastline, engaging in all manners of water-related fun and ended the day watching the huge fireworks show that the marina put on. But with the divorce finalized and EJ's dad still in Europe, the big boat wasn't an option, even if the girls were on speaking terms. That thought, and the uncertainty of the entire day, weighed heavy on her shoulders as she methodically descended the stairs.

She was surprised to hear Bryson's voice coming from the kitchen. He'd always been somewhat of an early riser but lately, be it a growth spurt or staying up too late playing Xbox, he'd been sleeping in a decent amount. As she grabbed a protein bar from the pantry, she heard him negotiating with her parents.

"Come on, please. We are always on the water for the Fourth. And it's just two more people, you know EJ's not going to come. Please. I'll even read today," he was saying.

Bryson's statement about EJ caused Becca to close the pantry door a little too hard, drawing a look from both of her parents.

"Good morning, Bex," her dad said cheerfully as he gave her a sweet smile. *A little too sweet,* Becca thought to herself.

"How are you feeling? Little nervous about the scrimmages today?" her mom inquired, giving Becca a knowing glance before turning back to the eggs and bacon she was cooking on the stove.

"I'm fine," Becca quickly responded. Not wanting to engage in either part of the conversation any more than she already had, Becca turned back towards the stairs, content to eat the bar in the quiet of her room.

"Nope," her mom said calmly, without so much as turning away from the stove. "You can eat down here. If you don't want bacon and eggs, that's fine, but no going upstairs."

Becca huffed loudly at her mother's demand. This was the very last thing that she wanted to do right now. She plopped down noisily into the chair next to her father and started unwrapping the protein bar. Bryson, from the opposite side of the table and apparently still eager for an answer, continued his petition.

"The boat holds eight easily so there's plenty of room. Me, Xan, Brendan, you and you," he said pointing to each parent, "And Ms. Elisabeth. That's six. And Becca, if she has to come. But EJ definitely won't come because she hates Becca."

"Bryson!" Both of her parents yelled in unison, her mom turning once again from the stove, spatula still in hand.

Becca threw her half-eaten protein bar at him and hit him square in the face. She then shoved back her chair and started to leave the table once again.

"Wait, Becca," her mother called out. "Just wait a second."

Becca paused at the foot of the stairs, her body nearly completely out of the kitchen area, but she did not turn around.

"Bryson, that was completely uncalled for," her mother started and then pointed the spatula straight at Bryson when he tried to interrupt. "Ah, don't try it. You will apologize to your sister, and I have half a mind to ground you today and make you do nothing but read."

Bryson dramatically dropped his forehead to the table as if his mother's words just shattered his entire existence. Becca chuckled and turned back around to watch her brother's agony. It brought her a small bit of pleasure on a thus far unpleasant day.

"Becca," her mom said, pausing for dramatic effect. "I'm so glad you find pleasure in your brother's pain," she said sarcastically. "Please pick up the protein bar and sit back down for breakfast.

"But I don't want eggs or. . .,"

"Have a seat," her mother interrupted.

Becca moped back to the table. As she sat back down, her mom continued. "Mrs. Montgomery called last night to see if you wanted to go out in their boat today after camp with Maddie and Lindy. I said it was fine with me, if that is something that you want to do."

"YES!" Becca shouted, a smile breaking the somber look that had covered her face since she had awakened this morning.

"I thought you might," her mom said. "I'll pick you and Lindy up from camp and then drop you off at Maddie's. And Bry, yes, Xan can come with us on the boat."

"Sweet!" Bryson replied, his head bouncing up from the table like a rubber ball. "I'll go call him!"

"Eat," her dad said, putting his hand on Bryson's shoulder and gently pushing him back down into his seat. Becca's mom placed a plate in front of both Bryson and her dad and then grabbed two more plates of food and hollered for Brendan to join them. As she placed the plate in front of Becca, she leaned down and whispered,

"Trust the preparation. With everything. You've got this."

Whether it was the smell of the food, the thought of exciting plans for the day or her mother's encouragement, she did not know, but suddenly, Becca found her appetite. Maybe those butterflies were going to calm down after all. She hoped the bacon and eggs would appease them for the remainder of the morning.

CHAPTER 39

*T*he food did its job for about one hour, right about the time the whistle blew to signify the start of the first scrimmage. Of course, fate, or God, would have it that Becca start at the outside hitter position on the same side of the court that she destroyed her knee. The butterflies were flying around so hard and so fast, it felt as though they were going to fly right through her chest. Or maybe that was her heart. At this point, she couldn't really tell. But she was having some trouble catching her breath and the red, white and blue walls of the gymnasium felt as though they were starting to collapse in on her. Fortunately, they were on serve possession and the opposing team shanked the first two serves, meaning she didn't even have to move from the net. Lindy looked at her from her middle hitter position and said something that Becca could not quite make out over the sound of her own pounding heart. She just smiled and nodded. That, apparently, was the wrong response because Lindy eyed her and then slid over closer while the other team was busy retrieving the ball.

"You've got this," Lindy whispered, her voice holding enough optimism for the both of them.

Becca's head nodded in agreement but the rest of her was having trouble believing that statement.

Lindy took a deep breath, and then, as serious as Becca had ever heard her voice, she said,

"I can't guarantee that you'll never blow your knee out again."

Becca felt her face contort into a confused look. Lindy continued.

"But I've watched you hit for four straight days, and I can say with certainty that you are stronger than I've ever seen you. You've done the work. Now trust it and just do it. You're getting the first ball."

She slapped her hand down on Becca's, effectively giving her a five, and then walked over to the setter and, with a huge smile on her face, pointed at Becca. Becca felt momentarily paralyzed, brought back only by the service whistle. The ball flew over the net and this time it was returned as a free ball to the back row. Becca's mind was blank, or maybe it was full of so much chaos that it seemed blank, but her legs were moving, and she didn't think that her brain told them to. She was back by the ten-foot line, setting up her approach. The setter pushed the ball in her direction. It was a little farther out than she anticipated, again. But her body effortlessly and completely subconsciously made the necessary adjustment. She felt herself go airborne, struck the ball at the highest point and watched it sail out of bounds. And she landed. Perfectly. No wobble, no pain, no tear. And then she felt herself exhale. Hard. Despite it being a point for the other team, Lindy looked at her and smiled her mega-watt smile, sending the perfect message. *I do have this. Let's go!*

It was all Becca needed. Those butterflies went completely dormant after that, allowing her to find her rhythm and have one of the best practices she'd ever had. She and Lindy were talking over each other as they got into her mom's car. Her mom never had the opportunity to ask how practice was, not that she needed to; the girls recapped the entire morning on the ride to Maddie's, full of excitement, laughter and teenage silliness. Lindy nearly jumped out of the SUV as soon as Becca's mom put it in park in the Montgomery's driveway. Becca laughed and finished unstrapping her knee brace. As she grabbed her bag from the floor and climbed out of the car, she heard her mom call her name.

"Becca."

Becca looked back towards her mom and saw her smile in delight.

"I'm proud of you."

Becca climbed back into the car and slid across the middle seat until she was close enough to wrap her mom in a hug.

"Thanks Mom. For everything."

"Becca, let's go. We're wasting precious daylight!" Lindy hollered from the front door of Maddie's house.

Becca and her mom both laughed, and Becca climbed back out of the car and jogged up to the house. Once inside, she found Sebastian and Will gathering a bunch of fishing gear and hauling it to Cooper's boat that was tied up to the dock. Before the boys left on their excursion, the teenagers made a plan to meet up by the old bridge later in the day. As the boys boarded Cooper's skiff, the girls grabbed some water bottles and decided to do a little tanning by the pool until Maddie's parents were ready to leave. The midday July sun was blistering and the girls quickly found themselves in the water, trying to cool down. The afternoon was going to be a scorcher.

After a couple of hours of traversing the river and chatting with other boaters, the girls and Maddie's parents made their way to the old bridge. The boys were waiting and, after Cooper anchored down just off the shoreline, they swam over to the bigger boat to try their turn at wakeboarding. All except Becca. She didn't dare ruin the good fortune that her knee brought her this morning. And her mom would have killed her if she found out she hopped on a wakeboard. Maybe in a few months, but not now. Volleyball was far more important.

Tubing was a different story though. She was more than happy to participate in that, especially when she was paired up with Will. Becca had done her best to temper her feelings for him but her best turned out to be not very good. He still made her butterflies jump when he smiled at her. And she wasn't great at hiding her reactions either as her face would turn pink and her mouth would twist into a perma-smile, as was the case right now. Maddie made a swooning sound as Becca donned her life vest, which caused Becca to both roll her eyes and turn a deeper shade of pink. Once buckled, Lindy gave Becca a wink and promptly shoved her into the water after Will.

Despite her physical reactions to him, there was never any awkwardness in conversing with Will. They chatted as they swam out to the tube. Becca knew that he still liked her; he had said as much on the last day of school. And since EJ seemed to no longer be in the picture, Becca had returned the sentiment but also stated that under no circumstance was she allowed to date until she was sixteen. And that she preferred to just be friends right now. He agreed and continued to treat her just as he did any of their other friends. It only served to strengthen her feelings for him. But that was as far as she was willing to let it go. Out of respect for her parents, for Lindy and even a little bit for EJ.

Becca's morning had started with a nervous concern that the day would be filled solely with sadness at a lost tradition. But the joy and laughter she shared with this wonderful group of people was causing her to forget the recent past. Almost.

CHAPTER 40

After a raucous afternoon of watching teenagers both succeed and fail at various watersports, Becca and crew headed back toward the marina for the rest of the Fourth of July festivities. Their path to the marina would take them right past the Banks. A summer holiday on the weekend meant that the area was prime for teenagers and twenty-somethings, all with their daddy's boats and an endless supply of swiped party favors. Nothing good would come of the mix. Both vessels had to slow their speed as they passed by, given the number of boats parked around the sandbar. As they eased through the traffic, Becca found herself looking for EJ and at the same time hoping that she would be nowhere near this place. The late afternoon sun was setting in their eyes but was not in position to impede their vision. What Becca saw made her wish that it would have been.

Her eyes spotted Weston wading through the water towards a parked boat, alcoholic beverage in hand. She hated to admit it, but between all the rumors, and what she was seeing with her own eyes, it seemed as though her mom was right about him being bad news. She chastised herself for ever having any interest in him. Becca watched him as he continued toward the vessel. She saw Quinn sitting on the captain's chair, loudly talking to anyone who would listen. And next to Quinn, leaning against the gunwale of the boat, was the person she was hoping not to see. EJ looked tanked, even from this distance. The gunwale seemed to be the only thing keeping her in an upright position. Someone hollered in their general direction, but Becca's focus was fixated on EJ, and she heard nothing. Lindy and Maddie both followed her gaze and just about the time that they were even with the stationary boat, EJ turned her back to them and vomited into the water. Becca turned around and could see Cooper watching the same scene. He looked at her and she could tell that they were thinking the same thing. Cooper slowed his boat to a stop as Becca, as politely as she could, asked Maddie's dad to stop his. He complied, as he too had noticed the scene beside him.

As soon as Maddie's dad cut the engine, Becca hopped out of the boat. The water was nearly chest high, so she swam after Cooper, whose swim team participation made him significantly faster than her, and he made it to EJ just as she started to fall over the edge of the boat. Cooper had already pulled EJ up out of the water and was holding her upright, one arm around her waist, when Becca caught up. Together they swam her to Cooper's boat. Seb and Will assisted in lifting EJ in and then eased Cooper's boat up next to the other one. Becca grabbed her things and told Lindy and Maddie that she was going to go with Cooper to take care of EJ.

"I'll go with you," both Lindy and Will said in sync. There was something about those twin genes that made them so very much alike.

"Thanks, both of you," Becca replied. "But it's probably better for just me and Cooper to take her home."

By this time, the divorce of EJ's parents was public knowledge but given the standing of the Jones family in general, very few people made any public comment about it. Privately, however, rumors were running rampant. Becca had heard a few things in passing that made her both sad and angry. Maybe it was her protective nature kicking in, but Becca wanted to shield EJ from any more humiliation. Even if this was self-inflicted.

"Are you sure?" Will asked. "I can help with the boat or whatever you need."

"Thanks, bro. But we got this. You go enjoy the fireworks. This is going to be a mess that you don't want to deal with," Cooper said.

"He's right," Becca concurred. She turned to Lindy and Maddie. "Seriously. I appreciate it. But you guys go enjoy the show. I'll have Cooper text Seb as soon as we get her home."

Will relented and followed Seb into the other boat. Becca thanked Mr. and Mrs. Montgomery for taking her out and for allowing her to tend to EJ. She had no doubt that they had already contacted EJ's mom and informed her of EJ's antics. Which also meant that her parents would know, since Ms. Elisabeth was on the boat with Xan and the rest of her family. Part of her hoped that no one would answer the phone so that she could have some time to talk with EJ but the bigger part of her hoped that they would beat them to EJ's house, since Becca had no earthly clue how to handle a drunk person.

As she and Cooper navigated his boat toward the Joneses' house, EJ started to moan. She hadn't fully passed out at any point thus far, but she also wasn't very aware of what was going on. She mumbled something unintelligible and then pulled herself up to the side of the skiff and puked once more. After spewing the contents of her stomach and wiping her mouth with the back of her hand, she sat back against the side of the boat. She cast her gaze from Cooper, at the helm, to Becca, who was sitting on the seat next to her, and back.

"What are you two doing out here together?" she asked. "K-i-sh-sh-shg?" EJ was slurring her sounds so badly it sounded as though she was hushing a baby to sleep instead of spelling a word.

"I could ask you the same thing," Becca said. "In fact, I will. What are you thinking? Why in the world would you go to the Banks?"

"To drink," EJ stated in a matter-of-fact tone.

"And why would you do that?" Becca admonished.

EJ merely shrugged. The sun had now slipped below the horizon, the orange and pink of the western sky fading quickly into the purple haze of dusk. Some lowkey fireworks were already lighting up the sky, but the main event at the marina was still a good twenty to thirty minutes away. Becca knew that she had no chance of watching them tonight, as it would take them at least that long to get EJ out of the boat and into the house. But then EJ's next words set off a different set of fireworks.

"You know why Coop didn't want Will's help, right?" EJ asked, staring directly at Becca. Without waiting for an answer, EJ continued. "Because he's jealous. Cooper wants you all to himself. Always has. Isn't that right, Coop?

Becca eyes widened at this revelation, and she turned her head to stare at Cooper. She could only see his profile and in the twilit sky, couldn't see it well.

"Shut up, EJ," he said sternly. "Don't listen to her Becca. She's drunk and doesn't know what she's talking about."

Becca wanted to believe his words but as a firework lit the sky overhead, Cooper's face was as pink as the summer sunset.

"It's true," EJ tried to whisper to Becca, although her inebriated state precluded her from lowering her voice. "You can't be that naïve."

Then EJ's eyes and mouth both closed, leaving Becca and Cooper to endure the remainder of the ride in complete silence.

CHAPTER 41

*G*etting EJ out of the boat turned out to be more difficult than either Becca or Cooper had imagined. EJ was still conscious but was proving to be no help whatsoever. Whether that was because she was unable, or just unwilling, was a source of debate. Either way, she was nearly dead weight, and they were having to drag her up onto the dock. Becca was now wishing she had not been so hasty in declining Will's offer to help. Although his presence may have made an already uncomfortable situation intolerable. Becca was grateful that no more words were spoken for the duration of the boat ride and that Cooper's only comments were on ways to successfully remove EJ without anyone getting hurt. She was not ready for anything else.

Becca was on the dock, holding onto EJ's torso, when a voice behind her beckoned her to move. The voice startled her, but then she willingly stepped to the side. Gavin wrapped one muscled arm around EJ's upper body, the other under her knees and then carried his younger sister into the house. Becca stared at him, unmoving, as Cooper hopped out of the boat, brushed past her, and followed Gavin inside. Her legs carried her slowly behind them, although, once again, she wasn't sure that her brain had told them to move. It seemed to be a theme today. Becca watched Gavin as he maneuvered EJ into the guest bathroom downstairs, placed her in the shower and turned the water on cold. EJ jumped, yelped and tried to escape but Gavin pushed her back down into seated position and told her not to move. And then the grilling began.

Cooper did most of the talking, as Becca was still stunned by Gavin's presence. She heard that Gavin had bolted right after his graduation and was spending the summer in Europe. Although the source of said information was a ten-year-old boy, so the reliability was questionable at best. He looked strong and healthy. And sober. Not at all like the guy that nearly ran them off the driveway ten months ago. Somewhere in the recesses of Becca's mind, she recalled hearing a rumor that Gavin had ceased with the alcohol and partying, but she thought it was just that: a rumor. Apparently not. Unfortunately, it seemed like EJ had picked up where her brother had left off.

Gavin left with instructions to keep EJ in the shower until Ms. Elisabeth returned. Becca assumed that he was making his way to the Banks with every intention of crushing Weston Gold. Mainly because he said he was headed to the Banks to crush Weston Gold. Becca glanced up at Cooper, who quickly looked away and said he would wait by the door for EJ's mom. He looked as uncomfortable as she felt. Becca turned her attention to her oldest friend and wondered how things got to this point, between them, and between her and Cooper. Nothing was the same anymore. And she didn't think they could ever go back, any of them. The thought made her spirits sink deeper than the Titanic in the Atlantic.

Becca was still lost in the misery of her thoughts when Ms. Elisabeth rushed into the bathroom and turned the shower off. She was followed closely by Becca's mom, who calmly placed an arm around Becca's shoulders and pulled her close. Ms. Elisabeth turned to thank Becca for bringing EJ home before peppering EJ with questions. A soaking wet EJ remained seated on the tile floor of the shower, gently rocking back and forth, mumbling more incoherent words. Becca's mom directed Becca out of the bathroom, made a quick remark to EJ's mom about coming back to help, and walked her to the dock where their boat was waiting. She didn't think the night could get any worse, but then her dad told Cooper to leave his boat at the Joneses and they would take him home. To his credit, Cooper tried to protest, but her dad would have none of it. Becca despairingly climbed into the waiting boat, as did a very uncomfortable looking Cooper, and they once again traveled the river in awkward silence.

The following week was as dark as winter in Alaska, at least in Becca's soul. The weather itself was sunny, hot and humid, like every other July day in the history of Edgewater. But the external sunshine did nothing to lift Becca's spirits. Her mind was a jumbled mess of incomplete thoughts and intense emotions, and she had no blueprint as to how to handle everything that the last week, or really, the last year had thrown at her. Ms. Elisabeth had called and told her that EJ was ok and had once again thanked her profusely for being there and bringing EJ home. She apologized for EJ's behavior and for the tension in their friendship. That was all well and good, but it meant very little to Becca since it didn't come from EJ herself. She wasn't sure what she expected after basically saving EJ's life, but apparently it was not a phone call from EJ's mother. Was it too much to ask for EJ to call her herself? And then there was the whole mess with Cooper. Becca had avoided him like the plague at church last Sunday. So much so that Lindy made a comment about it after the service. Becca brushed it off and told Lindy that she was just tired and didn't feel like talking to anyone. Which was not a lie. But it also wasn't the entire truth. Part of her wanted to tell Lindy about the incident on the boat, to have someone to help her untangle the web in her brain, or at the very least, someone with whom to commiserate. But she was fairly certain that Lindy had a thing for Cooper. Becca already had one love triangle destroying her life. She had no intention of creating another one. So, she left it all in knot; both in her brain and in her soul.

After a week of ghosting him, Cooper stopped by to try to talk with her, but Becca left him standing outside in the heat, shooting hoops. After about ten minutes, Becca could no longer hear the bounding of the basketball on the pavement. She hoped that Cooper had gotten the hint and that he would stop his fruitless attempts to chat. She had no interest in talking to him right now, even if she had something to say, which she didn't. Her mom could sense the tension surrounding Becca and, after only asking once if she wanted to talk about it, had been doing a decent job of giving Becca space. But a week of solemn-faced sulking in her room was apparently more than her mother could handle, and she forced Becca to go outside and do something. Anything. Becca reluctantly acquiesced, stuck her knock off air pods in her ears, grabbed the phone that her parents finally allowed her to have, and went for a run towards the Broken, in more ways than one.

CHAPTER 42

SADIE

By all outward appearances, life was going great for Sadie. And finally, the inward thoughts matched those outward signs. For the first time in her life, or at least the first time in a very long time, her mental state was solid. Summer semester was a breeze, by the previous semester's standards, and, although she was missing the warm currents of the river and the fish beneath, she was thoroughly enjoying the time spent at the pool with friends. She and Kat were talking every day and Kat was excited and happy. They laughed and joked and, with Emma Grace, planned a wonderful baby shower. At times, Sadie could tell that Kat was nervous about being a mom, but they both figured that every new mom felt that way, regardless of age or marital status. Overall, Kat very much seemed like the Kat of their youth.

Sadie's relationship with Christian was stronger than ever. The week away at the beginning of the summer had proven to be the best possible thing for them both. For her, it created the space she needed to realize how significant Christian had been, and continued to be, in this crazy journey that she was on. He seemed to agree and said that his time away had allowed him to see that sometimes people need space and it's not always a bad thing. The decision was made to prioritize their relationship this summer. They spent most nights together either bowling or playing cards with their FCA friends and enjoyed a date night at least once a week, usually at the movies. By the end of the summer, Sadie was seriously considering whether Christian was 'the one.'

Sadie would also say that her relationship with God was better than it had ever been, and it probably was, but it was far less focused on relationship and more on religion. She'd been diligent in reading her Bible and in writing in her prayer journal, had invited a few of her teammates to FCA events and even found time to volunteer with the kids' ministry at her church. She was doing all of the right things, as she had tried to do for the entirety of her young life, and it seemed as though it was finally paying off. Life, at long last, was going according to every plan that Sadie could have conjured up in her head. Everything was coming up aces, as the saying goes, and she thought that this was God's path that would carry her into her own version of happily ever after. She was about to experience firsthand how wrong that mindset was.

Summer session ended on a high note, straight A's across the board, and Sadie was eager to enjoy a couple of stress free weeks fishing the river Broken before her senior year officially started. She delayed her return home a couple of days, wanting to spend some extra time with Christian. Soccer training was in full swing, and he was required to remain on campus. Or at least close to it. Her reasoning to stay through the weekend was also influenced by not wanting to miss church on Sunday. Someone was scheduled to speak about a recent mission trip that her church had taken to Poland to facilitate a sports camp. The idea of sports missions thrilled her, and she was eager to hear more.

Her phone rang at 11:02p.m. on Saturday night. She and Christian had just returned from a movie, and Sadie was in the middle of packing. All that meant was that there were clothes scattered across her bed and a large duffel pulled out of the closet. College had only served to worsen her procrastination.

The Caller ID told her it was her father calling. Odd that he would call so late but not necessarily abnormal. Her dad was an avid LA Dodgers fan, much to his father-in-law's dismay, and could frequently be found on the couch watching West Coast games into the wee hours of the morning.

"Hey Dad, I don't have the game on tonight. How's it going?"

"Sadie, there's been an accident." His baritone voice sounded lower than normal, deeper and almost somber.

Sadie felt certain that she heard him wrong. "What?", she asked.

"It's Kat," he continued.

Sadie felt her heart plummet into her stomach and her knees start to buckle. She almost dropped her phone. *Please God, no.* She tried to string together a coherent thought as she sat down on her bed. Her mind tumbled between what, how and where, as she tried to process what to do next. She had talked to Kat earlier that day. She said she was driving to Edgewater to talk to JJ, that he had something important to tell her. *Freaking JJ, I'll kill him.*

"Sadie. Sadie. SADIE," her dad yelled through the phone, his voice stirring Sadie back to the present.

"Yeah, I'm here."

"Sadie, you need to come home. Now."

CHAPTER 43

BECCA

*I*t took over a month before Becca got the phone call that she'd been waiting for. A long, unpleasant month riddled with avoidance and confusion. She'd not settled anything with Cooper and found a hint of peace by simply avoiding him all summer. Becca was certain that it created zero peace for him and the rest of their friend group, but it was the only thing she could think to do. The avoidance hadn't done much for her overall mood, as she still tended to spend most of her time in the dark dungeon that was her room. And her mind. Deep in her subconscious, Becca knew that she needed to settle things with EJ, or at least talk about what happened at the Banks, before she could move on to Cooper, but she had no way to put that into a coherent thought. Until now. EJ had finally called. Maybe this was the turning point. Maybe all would be forgiven, and maybe, just maybe, they could go back to the way things were. It was the one ray of hope peeking through a grey sky. Which was quickly consumed by an all-encompassing thunderstorm.

Becca never even had the chance to ask how EJ was. EJ was hot from the jump. Her mom had grounded her, forbid her to leave the house, with soccer as the only exception, and had taken all electronics from her grasp. She had no access to her new friends or to social media, and everyone was moving on without her. They weren't even talking about her anymore. And EJ blamed it all on Becca. She told Becca that she should have minded her own business, and that there was no reason to have brought her home. She could handle her own life and her own choices and certainly didn't need Becca to babysit her. She said that her reputation was teetering on the edge because the 'basics' had to bring her home. EJ even went so far as to tell Becca that she hoped she never saw her again. And then the phone went dead.

Becca sobbed that afternoon. And into the evening. She only came down for dinner because her parents refused to take no for an answer. But then she immediately returned to crying in her room. It had been a rough month of moodiness but tonight had hit a new level. It was a level that her parents apparently could not ignore because later that night, her mother knocked on her door. It was a knock announcing her presence, not asking for permission to enter.

"Becca, I understand that things have been difficult and that you are sad and upset, but it's time to talk about it and move on. You cannot continue to live in these feelings."

"Why not? And don't give me some crap about feelings changing or they can't be trusted or whatever. You don't know what I'm going through. You don't know anything!" Becca yelled, plopping face down on her bed and refusing to look at her mom.

Becca's mom walked out of her room with a loud huff, and Becca thought she might have finally won a battle with her. It took all of thirty seconds for her mom to prove her wrong. Becca heard her walk back in, taking a deep breath as she sat down on the bed next to her.

"I want you to know that I am not trying to be insensitive to the hurt that you are experiencing. But I also cannot allow you to wallow in it. I want to be able to help you through it, but I can't do anything if you do not tell me what is going on," her mom said. Becca could hear the restraint in her mother's voice but could also tell that, despite her irritation, she really did want to know and find a way to be helpful. Or maybe she just wanted the moodiness to stop. Either way, Becca's mom sat there and waited patiently for an answer. And waited. And waited some more. Becca just continued to cry into her pillow.

She was unsure how much time had passed but Becca was certain that her mom had better things to do than to sit here with her in silence. But her mom didn't move. She didn't sigh, she didn't nag, she just sat there. Becca also didn't know if she really wanted to talk to her mom or if she was giving in out of spite, but she began to feel the desire to be heard overtake the desire to remain angry. She sat up and wiped the remaining wetness from her face. And then the words started tumbling out of her mouth like they had accidentally sailed their boat over a waterfall. She told her mom about what she saw at the Banks on the Fourth of July, about the boat ride home and EJ's revelation about Cooper's feelings for her and about how she still had feelings for Will. Her eyes started to well up again when she told her mom about EJ's phone call earlier that afternoon.

"Mom, I don't know what to do," she said as the salty tears ran slowly down her face. "I've been waiting on God to restore my friendship with EJ. I've been doing everything that you've suggested and have tried to be patient, but not only is it not happening, it's like everything is running in the opposite direction. Fast. And now I'm stuck between Cooper and Lindy, and it seems like every friendship I have is blowing up in my face somehow or another. I don't know how to do this. And it hurts. It all hurts so bad. I feel so confused and so broken. I just want it all to stop."

Her mom was silent through Becca's entire monologue. She remained silent for a few moments after Becca had ceased talking, like she so often did, processing. Maybe even praying. Becca was still a little unsure as to her mother's reasons.

"I'm sorry, Bec. I'm sorry that you are having to go through this." Her mom paused for a second. "Maybe sorry is not the right word. I don't like that you are having to go through these trials and this confusion and this pain, but I'm not sorry that you are going through it."

Becca scoffed at her mom's words. This was definitely not the sympathetic talk that she thought it was going to be.

"Hear me out," her mom continued. "I read a verse in the Psalms this morning that may be one of my least favorites in the entire Bible. 'Wait for the Lord; be strong, and let your heart take courage; wait for the Lord.' Sometimes I think that waiting is the hardest thing that God asks us to do. Because we want to control things. We want answers to our questions now and we want them to be the answers that we want to hear. We want to fix things and fix them now. And honestly, there is a part of me that wishes we had the ability to get those answers and be able to fix the things that I think need fixing. There are so many things in my life and in this world that I would want to fix or restore or reconcile. But I can't. And I am really glad I can't. Because even though it hurts like heck, the pain makes me realize my need for God. My dependence on. . ."

A knock on the door interrupted her. It was Becca's dad, and he looked nervous. He glanced at Becca and then stared hard at Becca's mom.

"There's been an accident," he said. "Over by the old bridge. It's Gavin and EJ."

CHAPTER 44

SADIE

Sadie made the two-hour drive in less than ninety minutes. Thank the good Lord for minimal traffic and no cops. She had bolted down the stairs, leaving a worried Christian standing at the top, and hollered a promise to call later as she ran across the parking lot to her car. Her right foot never let off the gas. The drive was filled with a lot of praying, a lot of begging, and a lot of yelling. The yelling was her only way of staving off the tears that she could feel filling up in her eyes. God wouldn't take Kat away right when she got her back, would He? As she drove into town, she could see a strange burgundy glow on the river by the Banks, the result of an amalgamation of police and tow truck lights. The only information that she received from her father was that Kat had been in an accident at the old bridge, near the Banks. Even though she didn't know all the details, she knew enough to hate JJ and the Banks more than ever.

She swung her old SUV into a parking spot outside the emergency room. Jumping out of the car, she slammed the door behind her and tried to run toward the hospital, only to be yanked backwards. A strap from her purse had decided that it did not want to leave the car and had wrapped itself around a knob in the inside frame of the door. Sadie mumbled a few choice words that would have prompted her mother to wash her mouth out with soap had she been around to hear them. As she opened the door to extract the strap, she realized that she had left the car running. Sadie slammed her fist against the door frame in frustration, feeling a pop on the side of her hand as she did.

Sadie yelled out in both pain and anger, the combination of the two causing a few rogue tears to escape from their self-imposed prison. She turned the car off and, making sure all objects were free and clear, shut and locked the door, and then took off at a dead sprint toward the hospital doors. Her dad's timing was impeccable because he stepped out of the automatic doors just as she was sprinting in.

"Dad! Is she ok? What happened? How bad is it?" The questions were coming faster than Sadie had been driving.

"Don't know much," her dad answered, wrapping her in a hug. As Sadie melted into his arms, she realized her entire body had been shaking. "Grandpa Jack has her right now, so you know she's in the most capable hands around." That gave Sadie comfort on so many levels not only because of the connection between her grandfather and Kat but also because he truly was the best surgeon in the area.

"The baby?" Sadie asked, tensing up again in anticipation of bad news.

"Don't know that either. Let's go inside. Mom and Sam are in there."

"Sammy's here?" she asked. She was not sure why her brother being here surprised her, but it did, nonetheless.

"Ah, yeah. And, um, Sade, he sort of saw it," her dad said as they walked down the hall, his arm around her shoulders.

"What do you mean, 'sort of saw it'?" She stopped immediately and turned to her dad, shock covering her face. "You mean he saw the accident?" Sadie could feel her eyes widening, her thought process bouncing around like a pinball machine.

"Did he cause the accident?" she said, louder and angrier than she should have.

"No and no. But I'm going to let him tell you the rest," her dad replied, his voice not giving anything away.

They walked in silence the rest of the way to the waiting area, although Sadie's mind was not quiet at all. She had no idea what her brother might say but was imagining possible scenarios and their subsequent outcome. *She was supposed to be talking to JJ tonight. They obviously would not have met anywhere close to his house, since no one was supposed to know the kid was his. He wouldn't have risked a meeting at the Banks tonight either since it was still summer and other people would be there. But then why was she near the Banks? She would have come into town from the opposite direction. And what did Sammy see? I assume he was at the Banks with his buddies for one more hurrah before heading back to school.*

She was so focused on the thoughts in her head that she didn't realize they had entered the waiting room until her mom came over to give her a hug. She started to return the hug but then her eyes caught sight of her brother sitting near the far end of the room. At this moment, his information was far more important than a hug from her mother. She broke through and headed straight for him, her features contorting from a look of deep concern to one of fury. Sadie's default had always been anger. She didn't know why, but it was always the first emotion to unveil itself in situations over which she had no control. Maybe that's why. Regardless, Sam saw the look on her face, one he knew all too well, popped out of his chair and started talking before she had a chance to attack.

"I didn't know it was Kat, Sadie. I promise. I would have stayed; I would have tried to help. But I didn't even know she was in town. I'm so sorry."

She slowed down trying to process what he was saying. She still didn't know what had happened and therefore had no context for his words. But the pain and anguish on his face, and in his body, caused Sadie to pause. She had to remember that no matter what had happened, Kat was basically his sister too and this looked as though it was tormenting him. She stopped a couple of feet from him.

"I don't understand. What happened? Did you see the accident or not?" Sadie asked, the confusion evident in her voice.

"Dad didn't tell you anything?" Sammy asked.

"He just told me that you were there."

"Well, not really. Mikey and I were taking out the skiff to do a little night fishing." Mikey was their cousin. He and Sam were close, and they frequently fished the river at night. Or at least that was what they told their parents. It was only a partial truth.

Sam lowered his voice and turned away from his parents, as if the next bit of information was not something he wanted them to hear. "We stopped by the Banks to see if anyone was there yet, but it was empty. When we got up near the old bridge, we saw a car flipped over in the water. It was smashed up pretty good, so it obviously hit something, or a lot of somethings, before it stopped. We had no idea how long it had been there but there were a couple of small fires in the brush so it couldn't have been there too long. I couldn't get the boat close because of how shallow it is right there, but I did hop in and wade over to it. Mikey and I both kept calling out to see if anyone was there, but no one answered. I got as close to the car as I could; it was on fire too, but just a little, but didn't see anyone. I just figured a drunk had driven their car off the road and then walked away. I called it in, told cranky Pete at the dispatch, and headed off. I didn't know she had been thrown from the car and was near the bridge. We looked in the water, I swear we did, but we didn't see anyone or anything. I promise. When Dad called me and told me that Kat was in an accident, we high tailed it back, but the police were already there and had it all blocked off. So, we took the boat back and I came here. I'm really sorry Sadie. I didn't know."

Sam's eyes had filled with tears as he relayed his story. Upon hearing that Kat had been thrown from the car, Sadie's did too. And she felt as though someone had punched her in the gut. Hard. Her heart hurt for Sam, because she knew that he would hold himself responsible for not doing more. Her heart hurt for her best friend and at the thought of losing her again. But before she could give in to those feelings, there were questions that needed answers. The memories of threats against Kat bubbled to the forefront and Sadie's anger burned against JJ.

"Was there another car?" she probed.

"Uh, I don't know, I couldn't see the road from the boat. I guess there could have been one up there, but hers was the only car in water," he replied. "The car was smashed up pretty good, so it definitely hit something, but I don't know if it was another car." Sam paused for a moment, eyes darting towards the ceiling as he thought back on the night. "When Mikey and I were bringing the boat back, I could hear Cranky Pete on the cops' radio. I think he said something about a Jeep. I don't know if it is related at all. And I could have heard wrong." Sam gave a little shrug.

Sadie bit her lip, digesting the words. She didn't know every car that JJ's family owned but she didn't think that they had a Jeep of any sort. Maybe no one else was involved. The road was a little windy down by the old bridge, but Kat had never been one for reckless driving. Or even driving over the speed limit. Being almost nine months pregnant would have been cause for even more caution. *What happened, Kat? Why were you over there?*

She used Sammy's words to recreate the accident scene in her mind, and when she did, her brain caught on something. *It was the end of summer, and a Saturday night at that, and yet he said the Banks was empty?* That made no sense. Yes, she'd basically been gone for the last three years and was never in the 'party' crowd but there's no way that things had changed so much around here that there would not be a Saturday night party at the Banks.

"Wait, did you say the Banks was empty?" Sadie asked.

"Can you keep your voice down?" Sam responded, eyes darting toward their parents who had taken up seats closer to the entrance, kindly giving the siblings space to talk.

Sadie rolled her eyes. "Everyone already knows you party there, Sammy. It's not a secret. Why do you think Mom and Dad are way over there? They want you to tell me what you really know instead of omitting things so you don't get in trouble."

Sam thought about that for a second and nodded his head, realizing that it was probably true.

"Yeah, no one was at the Banks yet. It was a little after ten and most people were probably still at the yacht club for JJ's going away party."

"Going away party?" Sadie inquired. "And where might JJ be going?"

"You don't know? His parents are sending him to Europe to negotiate some contract with some Swiss company. He leaves Monday. I figured that's why Kat was in town."

"Of course they freaking are," Sadie said in frustration. "Send JJ as far away from his mistakes as possible so that he never feels responsible for them. Let alone takes responsibility for them." She paused. "Did you go to the party?"

Sammy looked at her as if she had three heads. "Seriously? I hate that dip-sh..." He caught their mom giving him a look of admonition. "I hate that guy as much as you do. I was Mikey's excuse not to have to attend."

"Does Mikey know? Or Maggie? That would be disastrous." She thought about that for a second. Her cousin Maggie was the conductor of the gossip train. She was also deeply embedded in the wealthy and popular crowd. If Maggie knew, everyone who was anyone would know. And maybe that wasn't such a bad thing after all.

"I don't think so. I haven't said anything, Mom and Dad wouldn't tell, and you know for a fact that nothing is coming from JJ's side of things. Kat hasn't really been around for anyone to ask about her. And no, I haven't heard anything either. And you know what happens to information once Maggie knows about it." Sam gave Sadie a knowing look and then let his eyes gaze down at the floor. His voice turned somber as he said, "I keep wondering what is going to happen to the baby if Kat's not ok."

Sadie's eyes filled instantly with tears. That was the one scenario that frightened her the most. Sam looked up from the floor, stopping his eyes to meet Sadie's. She could see that his eyes were brimming with the tears he was trying to hold back. Sammy may have been a good six inches taller than Sadie, but he was still her little brother. She wrapped her arms tightly around him, allowing her head to fit just underneath his chin. He enveloped her in his arms. They were much bigger than she remembered. And stronger. He was no longer the lanky teenager that Sadie left three years ago. So much had changed. And change wasn't finished with them yet.

CHAPTER 45

BECCA

*B*ecca and her mom hopped in the car and headed for the hospital. She had watched her mom's features transform when her dad told them that Gavin and EJ had been in an accident over by the bridge. Her mom had pulled herself together quickly but not before Becca saw the intense fear in her eyes. She knew that her mom was putting on a brave face so that Becca wouldn't freak out, but she didn't think it mattered. All those prior feelings of confusion and anger were instantly replaced with fear and worry. The nervous butterflies hit full escape mode and Becca thought at any moment she was going to throw them all up. Until this point in her fourteen years, the only death, or even death scare, that she'd encountered was that of her great-grandfather. She was only seven when he died, so it didn't really register. Plus, he was old. She did not have any concept of how to handle unspeakable tragedy. Shoot, she was having a hard enough time dealing with teenage drama! It was too much to think about. All she knew to do was pray, so that's what she did.

Her mom had called Ms. Elisabeth as they were leaving the house, finding out nothing except that she was already at the hospital. The rest of the ten-minute ride was silent. They pulled into the parking lot and found a space out in front of the emergency room. Her mom hesitated before putting the car in park, as if deciding whether she really wanted to be here or not. *Wow, she really is scared*, Becca thought.

"Mom," Becca said, interrupting the silence. But her mom just stared straight ahead, not hearing her at all. "Mom," Becca repeated, a little more forceful this time.

"I'm sorry, Becca, what did you say?" her mom answered, turning her head toward Becca in acknowledgement.

"Are you going to put the car in park?" Becca asked, as the car was slowly easing forward in the space.

"Oh gosh, yes. Sorry." Her mom slammed her foot down on the brake, causing her purse to tip forward and the contents to spill out. Becca's mom shoved the shifter into park, righted her purse and threw her keys and cell phone back into it.

"I thought you'd be better at putting on a brave face for me," Becca said, trying to add a little humor to a situation that she had no experience handling. Her mom laughed a little and replied,

"Yeah, me too. I guess I'm just a little worried."

"Do you think they're going to be ok?" Becca asked, trying to sound strong but realizing that even a child could have heard the fear in her voice.

Her mom took a deep breath, letting it out slowly before answering, "I hope so." She paused and then mumbled something under her breath that sounded like 'can leather oaken windgin.' Becca looked at her mom questioningly to which her mom shook her head and repeated, "I hope so, kiddo." Then she added "Are you ok?"

"I'm just really scared. What if it's so bad that EJ can't play soccer anymore? Or worse, what if she's, uh, what if we don't get the chance to fix us?" Becca's butterflies were traveling up her chest and it took everything she had to push them back down and not puke all over her mom's car. She could do nothing about the tears streaming down her face though. Her mom gently wiped at them with the back of her hand and then wrapped her arms around Becca. She always felt so secure in her mother's arms, and that hadn't changed, but Becca could also feel some unexpected tension in her embrace. She felt her mom kiss the top of her head and tighten her hug. When she let go, Becca could see that the corners of her mom's eyes were a little wet. Her mom was not an easy crier. In fact, the only other time she remembered seeing her mom cry was seven years ago when her great grandfather died. And even then, it wasn't much. That realization did nothing to calm Becca's butterflies.

"Keep praying for that chance," her mom said, as she gave Becca's hand a tight squeeze.

Becca watched as her mother turned to open the door and diffidently got out of the car. *I've never seen my mom like this before*, Becca thought to herself as she opened her own door and hopped out of the SUV. She knew that her mother had a fondness for Gavin, and for EJ for that matter, but this seemed like something else. Something more. Becca took a deep breath and silently sent up a prayer for not only Gavin and EJ but also for herself and her mother as they encountered the unknown. The unsettled butterflies in her stomach gave her the sense that this would be a long and eventful night. She joined her mom on the other side of the car and together they walked toward the emergency room doors, her mom's arm wrapped tightly around Becca's shoulders. The tension that Becca previously felt in her mom's touch had, in a matter of a few seconds, been replaced by the motherly comfort and confidence that she was so accustomed to. She had never been more thankful for that strong yet tender touch.

CHAPTER 46

SADIE

Sadie sat curled up in her seat, Sam to her left and her parents across the aisle. They were all a bit restless as the uncertainty and impatience were starting to take their toll on them all. Her mom had informed her that Grandpa Jack had taken Kat immediately back for surgery and had called in the obstetrician to assist with the baby but had otherwise given no indication of how bad she was. That was four hours ago. They'd heard nothing since. Sadie was faintly aware of the other people in the waiting room, but as she was not one for people watching, she paid very little attention to what they were doing or who they were. Except the mom in the far corner of the waiting area with her son who looked to be about ten. She briefly wondered who they were waiting for. The mom looked like she was putting on a calm face for her son, but Sadie noticed that her leg never stopped bouncing up and down. *This place will do that to you,* she said to herself. But even they couldn't hold Sadie's attention for very long. For a while, she'd glance up whenever anyone entered the room, hoping that it was her grandfather with good news, but after hours of disappointment, she relegated herself to interspersing prayers in between counting ceiling tiles. There were exactly six hundred of them: ceiling tiles, not prayers. Thirty lengthwise, twenty widthwise. Easy math gave her six hundred, but she also had enough time to count them all individually. Twice. She needed something else to keep her distracted.

Sadie rubbed the area on her hand where she felt the pop after she punched her car door. It was tender and already starting to bruise. She hoped that in her anger she hadn't done anything stupid. Like break her hand. She glanced back over to the mom and her son but that only made her think of Kat and the baby. Her eyes continued to wander around the rectangular room. She had once read that hospitals liked to use soothing colors like soft greens or light blues to exude a calming sensation for patients. Clearly River County Medical Center failed to get the memo as every wall of the waiting area had been painted some shade of off-white, although the layers of dirt made them look more greyish in tint. They were in desperate need of a paint job. A smattering of artwork adorned the dirty walls. On the shorter wall, adjacent to the entrance, sat a pair of flower paintings, the type of flora Sadie could not have named if she wanted to. They were purple and yellow and blue and gave a little bit of hope to an otherwise dismal area. The wall across from where Sadie had taken up temporary residence housed a years old television, placed imperfectly between sketches of tarpon, yellow jack, reds and a snook. Guy Harvey would have felt right at home. The TV was currently showing reruns of *The Andy Griffith Show* on mute. Part of her wanted to walk over and turn the sound on. She couldn't have cared less what Andy or Barney Fife was saying, she just wanted the distraction of the noise. She let her eyes continue to wander around the room. The wall to her left held a magazine rack and a couple of black and whites of various county landmarks. But one particular picture garnered some interest in Sadie's already overwhelmed brain: an old surveyor rendering of the county from 1882. Sadie pried herself out of her seat to take a closer look at the picture.

River County was an expansive county, bifurcated by the Broken River. The bifurcation, however, was as imperfect as the position of the television, with nearly three quarters of the county located on the north side of the river. The county's largest town, at least as far as population was concerned, was Edgewater, which happened to be located on the south bank of the river. As far as Sadie knew, Edgewater was the first settlement in the area and had always been a part of River County. This surveyor's map told a different story. According to this, in 1882, the southern border of the county was the northern bank of the river. Edgewater sat alone, with no county delineation. The old piece of framed parchment paper served as the perfect distraction from her current circumstances, as Sadie found herself racking her brain in vain attempt to remember anything about the acquisition of Edgewater into River Country. Nothing registered. She'd have to ask her grandfather the next time she saw him.

"Sadie."

Her grandfather! She wheeled around so quickly that her knee hit the side of the magazine rack, and she nearly lost her balance. She knew that it was going to leave a nasty bruise but the anticipation of news about Kat blocked out any current pain. Sadie saw Sam and her parents stand up when Grandpa Jack entered the room, but her focus was on his face, which seemed to show nothing but sheer exhaustion. He sat down in the chair that Sadie had previously occupied. Everyone else also sat; Sadie taking a chair opposite her grandfather and next to her mother. She felt her mom reach down and grab her hand, as if already knowing that Sadie needed comforting.

"It's a baby boy, and he seems to be healthy," her grandfather said, and an audible sigh of relief escaped from Sam and her parents. "He will continue to be monitored for the next few days to ensure that there are no lingering issues." Grandpa Jack paused, looked down at the floor and inhaled a deep breath. It was at that moment Sadie realized that not only had she been holding hers, but that the news about Kat was not good. Grandpa Jack raised his head and looked directly at Sadie; his bright blue eyes filled with water. He merely shook his head. Sadie felt her heart plummet to the depths of her stomach.

"Please no," she whispered, her own eyes filling with tears.

"I'm so sorry," she heard her grandfather say. Her grandfather ran one hand through his silver hair. Sam's head collapsed into his hands. Sadie could see none of it as her field of vision had turned opaque. She felt her mother's hand tighten around her own, but she could not return the sentiment. Instead, Sadie ripped her hand from her mother's grip, stood up on wobbly legs and said something she'd probably regret for the rest of her life.

"You were supposed to save her! This is all your fault!" The words came out louder and angrier than intended. Logically, she knew that her grandfather bore no fault at all, but pain overtook logic in moments such as this. She tried to run out of the waiting room, but her legs would not hold her weight. She collapsed in a heap on the gray spackled linoleum floor.

CHAPTER 47

Somehow Sadie managed to get herself up from the floor and found herself running out of the automatic double doors of the hospital. She stopped a few feet into the parking lot, put her hands on her knees and tried to take a breath, but the night air was still full of humidity, and all she got was a coughing fit. Standing up tall, she tried inhaling again, getting only enough air to turn the coughs into wheezes. The tears were coming down so hard that she was surprised to actually see what entered her field of view. And suddenly, the faucet of tears turned off; her sadness and heartache turning into absolute rage.

"You bastard," she yelled as she walked toward the far end of the parking lot. JJ was leaning on the hood of his new Chevy truck, looking uncertain as to what to do. "You did this to her!"

Sadie saw JJ push off his truck and start to walk towards her. In her mind, it would be the last thing he would ever do.

"Sadie, what's going on? No one will tell me anything," JJ said, his voice sounding scared and concerned. Sadie wasn't buying it. She walked straight up to JJ and swung as hard as she could. Her fist connected with his jaw, hard. If her hand wasn't broken before, she was pretty sure that his face finished the job. But the adrenaline kept her from really noticing. JJ yelled out in pain and said, "Jesus Chr, what the heck was that for?" He spat blood and rubbed his jaw. Sadie hoped like heck that it suffered the same fate as her hand.

"YOU KILLED HER!" she screamed in his face. She pushed him away and yelled at him again. "You killed her." The tears started to fall again.

JJ's face looked confused and then the reality of Sadie's words hit. "Kat's dead?" he asked. Sadie could only answer in sobs. JJ's eyes started to well up. "And the baby?"

Sadie nodded and then shook her head. JJ stared blankly at her. She sucked in some more of the thick, moist air and said, "He's ok. Not that you care."

"It's a boy?" JJ asked and then, as if not hearing her before, once again asked if Kat was dead. Tears started running down his face and Sadie was beginning to think that maybe JJ did, in some way, actually care about Kat. Maybe he didn't have anything to do with the accident. And then Sadie saw the front bumper of JJ's truck. The dent looked fresh. Her face filled with anger once again. JJ saw the change and followed her gaze towards his truck. His arms went up and his mouth spilled out words just as Sadie swung at him again.

"That's not from this! I hit a post leaving the Banks Friday night. I swear! I was drunk and wasn't paying attention. I SWEAR!"

Sadie knew that his answer was not out of the realm of possibility, but she still wasn't sure if she believed him. Her disbelief must have been written on her face because he continued,

"I was at the yacht club tonight. I didn't leave until almost midnight. I swear," He thought for a second. "Call my sister. Or call Maggie. She was there the entire time. Sadie, I swear."

"Kat called me this afternoon," Sadie said, her voice trembling with a mix of anger and overwhelming sadness. "Said she was supposed to meet you tonight."

"That's true. I was going to give her this." He pulled out a piece of paper from his pocket. It had a bunch of numbers on it. "It's a bank account and routing number that I set up for her and the baby. I was going to put some money in every month, as long as she kept her promise to keep my name out of all of it. But she never called to tell me she was here." He dropped his head. "I guess I know why."

"How very noble of you, JJ," Sadie said sarcastically, rolling her eyes and shaking her head.

"Sadie, I swear I had nothing to do with the accident. I. . .,"

"What about the threats, JJ?" Sadie interrupted, the anger momentarily overtaking the sadness. "I supposed you didn't have anything to do with those either. BS."

JJ looked at her with seemingly genuine confusion. "Threats? What threats? To Kat?"

"Stop acting like you don't know what I'm talking about. I'm not stupid. Yes, to Kat and to the baby. And to my grandfather as well!" Sadie was yelling again, causing the one other person in the parking lot to glance their way and then walk hastily to his car.

"What? Your grandfather? I'm so confused. Like death threats? On my own kid?"

"You're not a very good liar," Sadie said, although JJ still looked as though he had absolutely no idea what she was talking about. Either he was a great liar, or he truly knew nothing. She was about to find out.

"I already know you told her to get an abortion at the beginning. Which, honestly, was bad enough. But then to threaten Kat's life because she didn't! Even I didn't think you'd stoop to something that low. And now she's dead! Because of you!" Sadie balled up her fists to swing at him again, causing JJ to take a step back as he started talking.

"Sadie, I know you hate me and that you always have. But I swear on everything I have and everyone I know that I don't know anything about any death threats. I would never. Yes, I did tell Kat to have an abortion. Maybe that was wrong. I was scared. So was she. And when she told me that she was keeping the baby, yeah, I was a little angry. But she told me that she wouldn't say anything to anyone and that she wasn't going to hold me responsible for anything that I didn't want to be responsible for. That was months ago, and I haven't talked to her, or even tried to contact her, at all since then. Honestly, I was trying to forget about the whole thing. But I've grown up a little bit since I last talked with Kat, and I decided that it would be a good thing to support her and the baby financially. My parents are sending me to Europe to work for one of the companies that my dad is buying. I'm supposed to leave on Monday. So, I called Kat yesterday, well, two days ago now, to ask her to meet me so that I could give her the information. And tell her that's all I can do right now. First off, my parents would kill me and secondly, I'm not ready. I can't be a dad right now. Sadie, I swear. You have to believe me. I would never do anything to hurt Kat. Or my. . .son."

Sadie's skepticism was still apparent on her face but was waning significantly. JJ's story made sense, to a certain degree. And maybe he didn't have anything to do with the accident. But he was the reason she was pregnant, and he was the reason why she was in Edgewater tonight. Which made him the reason that she was dead.

"What's going to happen to the baby now?" JJ asked, running his hand through his hair, looking even more confused than before.

Sadie narrowed her eyes at the idiot standing in front of her. Maybe he wasn't directly responsible for Kat's death, but he was directly responsible for the child that was still alive and sleeping in the hospital nursery.

"You." Her answer apparently surprised JJ because he stared at her as if she had just spoken a foreign language. Sadie rolled her eyes again and took a deep breath. What she was about to say was out of pure anger, but she didn't care.

"You, you idiot. You are what's going to happen to the baby. He's your son and you are going to be responsible for him, like you should have been from the start. You are going to take him with you to Europe."

JJ tried to interrupt but Sadie merely held up her hand and continued. "I don't care what your parents have to say. Your mom can be your nanny, or if she's mad at you, hire one with the ridiculous amount of money you have. I hear there are great au pairs over there. But you are now a single parent to a baby boy. The baby boy of my best freaking friend. You're going to take him and be his father. You're going to give him the very best life, because you can. And if anything happens to him, I swear to God, JJ, everyone will know your little secret and I will make your fancy little, irresponsible life a living hell." She gave him one final shove and turned around to walk back into the hospital. As she walked away, she hollered back at him,

"I will make this kid my life's mission. He's all I have left of her. So don't you dare try me."

CHAPTER 48

BECCA

A young woman came running out of the automatic doors just as Becca and her mom walked up. Her mom stopped and stared at the woman, a look of recognition and concern covering her face. Becca looked back at the woman but did not recognize her herself. She started walking again, but realized her mom was still staring.

"Do you know her?" Becca asked her mom.

Becca's mom shook her head and turned her gaze towards the doors. "I hope not," she said, as she rejoined Becca inside the doors.

My mom is losing it. Any thoughts about her mom's mental status quickly disappeared as Becca's focus shifted to the significant change in temperature. The languid humidity of the outdoors was immediately transformed into a rabid circulation of dry, frigid air. Becca now understood why her mother had grabbed a jacket upon leaving the house. She wished she had as well.

Her mother was no stranger to this hospital, not only from having lived in this town for most of her life but also from years spent working in the rehabilitation center. Since Becca's only experience with the facility was the rehab area, she deferred to her mom's lead. Becca watched her walk with a confident familiarity through the doors, deftly navigating the maze of hallways to the waiting room without need for directions. Becca's eyes wandered as they walked, taking in the greyish walls in the hallways, pictures of medical advice intermixed with drawings of beach scenes and palm trees. Geometric shapes adorned the flooring in various patterns and colors. The signs designating locations of all the different areas were cracked and yellowing. The hospital had been built sometime in the 1960s or 1970s and

Becca thought that it showed. The rehab area gave Ritz vibes compared to this place, and that's saying something because the equipment there was at least ten years old.

She saw a sign indicating the waiting area with a green arrow pointing to the right just ahead of them. There was no connecting hallway up ahead, just an open doorway without a door on their right.

Here we go. She took a deep breath and prepared to enter the presence of Ms. Elisabeth and whatever information she held about her best friend, or former best friend. That thought made Becca's heart hurt. She had no idea what the future held for her and EJ. Especially now. That also scared her, a lot. Apparently, her mother had the same sentiment, as she had come to a dead stop about ten feet from the opening. Becca looked at her mom quizzically for at least the third time tonight, wondering where this strange behavior was coming from.

Sensing Becca's concern, her mom said, "I just need a minute. You can go ahead if you'd like." She then inhaled deeply and tucked her bottom lip below her top one as if chewing on it. It was something that Becca had seen her mom do when she was concentrating. Maybe she was thinking about what to say to Ms. Elisabeth. But with the weird behavior that her mother was displaying tonight, Becca had to admit that she had no idea what her mom was doing. Or thinking.

Maybe it was because her mom had always been there for her and she wanted to return the favor, or maybe because Becca wasn't sure she could walk in there on her own, but she decided to wait for her mom. In the silence that followed, Becca's subconscious produced a thought that, had her brain had time to filter before her mouth blurted it out, she's not sure she would have said it. Because she wouldn't have been sure that she believed it.

"Mom, it's going to be ok. No matter what happens in there, it's all going to be ok. You've taught me to believe that God's always in control, no matter our circumstances and I truly believe that. I may be sad, and it may hurt really bad, but I still believe that."

Now that it had been said aloud, she realized that, despite the fear and the doubts that she was feeling, she really did believe those words.

Her mom turned to look at her with tears in her eyes but a smile on her face. Becca had now grown tall enough that her mom no longer had to look down at her; they were nearly eye to eye. Her mom wrapped Becca in a quick hug.

"I love you, Becca girl. Let's go." Hand in hand they traversed the last ten feet of blue semi-circle tile to the waiting area. Ms. Elisabeth saw them as soon as they entered and wrapped them both in a huge hug.

"I think I'm the one who's supposed to be hugging you," Becca heard her mom say as she broke hands with Becca and put that arm around her and the other around Ms. Elisabeth.

"You know that I am a hugger by nature," Ms. Elisabeth replied. "I'm so very glad that you both are here." She released her grip and Becca noticed that EJ's mom's face was relatively clean. There was a small smudge of mascara under her right eye but otherwise, Becca saw no signs of heavy tears. Maybe that signified good news.

"Is EJ ok?" Becca asked, her curiosity overriding her manners.

Ms. Elisabeth smiled at her, but the smile did not reach her eyes. "She's in surgery. The doctor said that she suffered a bad break of her left leg and that he was checking for internal injuries. Luckily, she had her safety belt on."

Becca took a deep breath. That report made it seem that, overall, EJ was ok. And for that, Becca was so grateful. But she knew that EJ was naturally left-footed and that the power behind her left foot was one of the major reasons she made the junior national team. Coming off her own leg injury, Becca knew that EJ had a long road ahead of her, both physically and mentally. But at least she was alive.

Ms. Elisabeth continued, "But it does not seem that anything is life threatening. With her."

Becca and her mom both caught the break in the sentences.

"And Gavin?" Becca's mom asked, in a voice that seemed to already know the answer.

Ms. Elisabeth turned to peak behind her. Becca followed her gaze and saw Xan sitting in a chair, knees up to his chin, his gaming system in hand and massive headphones adorning his ears. He seemed completely oblivious to his surroundings. She lowered her voice anyway and said,

"We don't yet know the extent of his injuries. It seems that EJ and Gavin were having some sort of argument, and that EJ grabbed the keys to Gavin's jeep, or perhaps he left them in the ignition, I'm unsure of which, and started to leave in it."

"EJ was driving?" Becca interrupted, speaking louder than intended.

"According to the police, yes, she was in the driver's seat with the safety belt on. Gavin was said to be in the passenger's seat, so I am assuming that he was able to jump in before she left completely. He apparently did not have his belt connected. He was not ejected from the vehicle, thank heavens, but ended up on top of EJ. Part of the frame of the jeep impaled him. As I said, the extent of the damage is unknown at this time, but he was breathing and had a pulse when they brought him in. As per the doctor on call."

Her eyes filled with tears, but she was somehow able to keep them from running down her face. She took a deep breath before continuing.

"One of Cooper's older brothers, I think it was Garrett, was one of the paramedics at the scene. He told me that Gavin may have saved EJ's life. That, by the way they were positioned in the vehicle when they arrived, if Gavin's body had not been on top of EJ, the frame most likely would have hit her in the face."

Becca felt as though she'd just been karate kicked in the stomach. She once again felt as though she might throw up. She didn't know if that feeling came from Ms. Elisabeth's description of the accident, how close her friend may have been to dying or hearing Cooper's name. Maybe it was a combination of the three. Not that the reason seemed to matter; she needed to sit down. Scrambling over to the chair next to Xan, she plopped down and put her head between her legs. Becca had no idea if that action would prevent the contents of her stomach from coming up, but she hoped it would make her feel better. And soon. She could hear her mom and Ms. Elisabeth continuing their conversation but it was the underwater thing all over again. There was no clarity in what they were saying. And then, as quickly as the sick feeling came, it went away. She was able to pick up her head without losing her supper. Her mom and Ms. Elisabeth seemed to have huddled closer to the entrance, their backs both slightly turned toward Becca and Xan. The underwater sensation had ceased but she still could not make out what they were saying. Becca leaned back slightly in her chair and then realized she felt better leaning in the opposite direction. She snuck a look at Xan, who appeared to be unaware of anything other than his game, and propped her elbows on her knees, resting her chin on her hands.

Becca pondered what would make EJ so angry that she would take Gavin's jeep. She hoped it wasn't her. Their one-sided phone call had been hours ago, although to Becca it felt like days ago, but could that have been the reason that EJ was so angry? Given how much she yelled on the phone, it was possible. Becca dropped her face into her hands and tried not to let the guilt she felt overwhelm her. She felt a squeeze on her shoulder and looked up to see Ms. Elisabeth smiling down at her.

"Thank you for being here, Becca," she said softly. "I know the last few months have been difficult for the both of you, but I also know your friendship is immensely important to EJ. Even if she has a hard time showing it right now. Everything will work itself out."

Becca could feel her eyes welling up with tears and struggled to maintain eye contact. Her voice caught in her throat as she started to speak.

"-elcome."

It was all she could bring herself to say. The tears started to run down her face. Ms. Elisabeth seemed to understand her plight and leaned down to give Becca a hug. She then took her place on the other side on Xan, and they settled in for what Becca prayed would be a short wait.

CHAPTER 49

Becca was getting restless. It had only been about forty-five minutes since she and her mom had arrived at the hospital but sitting and waiting was never something that she'd done well. Apparently, neither did her mom. While Ms. Elisabeth had sat back down after her talk with Becca, Becca's mom had disappeared. She returned a little while later, sat down for about five minutes, and then left again. Maybe she was out making calls to other parents and people at church. Or checking in on the boys at home. Whatever it was, it certainly didn't help Becca's impatience.

She must have dozed off for a minute or two because she jumped when she heard someone call out, "Mrs. Jones?"

Ms. Elisabeth stood and answered what looked to be a very tired doctor.

"Your daughter is out of surgery. She had a significant break in her left femur which required the insertion of a rod. There was a laceration to the left side of her abdomen, but it missed all of her organs. She will be sore. Otherwise, there doesn't seem to be any other damage. A neurologist will be by to assess her brain function when she wakes from anesthesia, but we saw no evidence of trauma on the scans. She was very lucky."

Ms. Elisabeth let out a breath of relief and a, "Thank you Jesus."

"And the boy?"

Becca was so focused on the doctor and his words that she didn't notice that her mother had reentered the room. She watched her walk over and put her arm around EJ's mom, who now seemed torn between relief and concern.

"Still in surgery. It will be a while. He sustained considerably more damage than she did." The doctor paused as he thought about his next words. Whatever he wanted to say, he seemed to decide against it, because his head gave a quick shake and then he said,

"Your daughter is being moved to a room in ICU. Give the nurses about ten to fifteen minutes and then you can go see her."

"Thank you, Doctor," Ms. Elisabeth said.

Becca's mom gave Ms. Elisabeth a hug and then followed the doctor out of the waiting room, mumbling something about 'information' and then immediately walked back in. She walked directly to Becca, pulled her out of her seat and wrapped her in the biggest hug that Becca could ever remember getting.

"She's ok. I'll be right back, and we can go see EJ together."

Becca nodded and wiped her very wet eyes on her mom's shoulder.

"I love you, Bec." She kissed the side of Becca's head, released the hug and walked back out of the waiting room.

Becca stood there, tears streaming down her face, unsure of why, with good news about EJ, she was crying. Ms. Elisabeth took the place of her mom and wrapped her in a hug of her own. Becca felt another arm wrap around her and looked down to see Xan joining in. He said what Becca was sure they all were thinking.

"Gavin's going to be ok, right?"

"Gavin is strong. He's a fighter. We will keep praying, but I already believe that he will make it through," Ms. Elisabeth answered.

Just then, Becca's dad walked into the waiting room with both Bryson and Brendan. Xan turned, trying to hide his tears from his buddy, but Bry, in a rare display of concern and sympathy, put his arm around Xan and told him that he was happy that EJ was ok.

"She's been filling me in," Becca's dad said with a head nod toward the hallway. Becca took that to mean her mother. *She must be busy making phone calls.* Her dad gave Ms. Elisabeth a quick hug and said, "I'm here to collect Xan. He can stay with us for as long as needed. Hang with the boys, get his mind off things."

"Thank you, Ben. He will be eager to go, I'm sure. I'm a bit restless in this place myself so I can only imagine what he is feeling right now."

"No problem. Anything else you need right now? Food? Coffee?" her dad asked.

He walked over to Becca, put his arm around her shoulder and pulled her close to him. Becca allowed herself to be swallowed by his embrace. Her dad was a rock, physically but also emotionally. But a soft, lovable, compassionate rock. No matter the situation, be it teenage mood swings or nearly losing a best friend, Becca's father kept her anchored. Maybe it was the military in him. Or maybe it was just him; strong, steady, anchored in his faith. His strength renewed hers.

"Coffee's taken care of."

Becca's mom reentered the waiting room holding a cup of coffee and a bottle of soda. She handed the coffee cup to EJ's mom and gave her husband a kiss. He leaned over and whispered something in her ear, to which she made a face and gave a bit of a shrug. Becca watched this encounter from her nook against her father's side. Under normal circumstances, Becca didn't think she would notice that parental interaction, let alone care. But nothing about tonight could be considered normal circumstances. She wondered if this had anything to do with the way her mom had been acting since she heard about the accident.

Accident. That word triggered something in Becca's subconscious and her mind exploded with activity, trying to piece together all these fragments of information. She barely noticed her father squeezing her tightly and kissing the top of her head before heading out with the boys. Or the nurse who popped in to tell Ms. Elisabeth that she could go back to see EJ. At some point, Becca must have sat down because she found herself leaning back in a chair and watching her mom slowly pace around the waiting area. Becca noticed that she strategically avoided the left side of the room, even though it was now unoccupied. She paced along the right side of the room, past the old television and weird fish pictures, along the back wall and back, never even looking toward the other walkway. Every so often, her mom would stop at a particular picture along the back wall that looked like an old treasure map. *So strange*, Becca thought to herself. *What is she looking at?* Her thought process was interrupted by her name being called.

"Becca!" Lindy came barreling into the waiting room and nearly knocked Becca to the floor with a hug, chair and all. "How's EJ? We heard about the accident. Is she ok? Is her brother? How are you?"

"Whoa, slow down there, kiddo." A tall woman with her dark brown hair tied up into a bun walked in behind Lindy. They were not twins, but the resemblance was strong enough to know that this was Lindy's mom. Becca remembered seeing her once but for the most part, Lindy and Will's dad was the primary presence at their activities. Becca's mom had turned at all the commotion and was staring at them with a funny expression.

"Becca, this is my mom. Mom, this is Becca and that's her mom, Mrs. Scott."

"Hey Sadie," Lindy's mom said, as if she already knew Becca's mom. Becca watched as her mom's face scrunched in confusion and then her eyes bolted wide open. Her soda bottle slipped from her hand and dumped its contents all over the tile floor.

CHAPTER 50

SADIE

She was lost in thought, staring at the old map. It had been a mentally grueling night. She hadn't been to this part of the hospital in nineteen years. In fact, she had always gone out of her way to avoid it. And now, on an eerily similar night, she was back here, awaiting news about another car accident. It was only by the grace of God that she hadn't fallen apart when she got the news about Gavin and EJ. Walking into this room took a strength she knew that she didn't possess on her own, especially because she was there for the only part of her childhood best friend that she had left. For what it was worth, and until recently, JJ had done well for himself and for Gavin. If she herself could have handpicked a mother for Gavin, she still wouldn't have found one as wonderful as Elisabeth. She loved him and treated him as if he was her own. And as far as everyone knew, she was his mother. But he was Kat's. And Sadie couldn't fathom God taking away the only thing she'd left. The commotion behind her registered in her subconscious but on a nearly imperceivable level. She was somewhat surprised that she caught the next sentence.

"Whoa, slow down there, kiddo."

She started at the words. Aside from herself, she knew no one who still used the term kiddo. Turning toward the noise behind her, she saw Becca and Lindy, along with whom she assumed to be Lindy's mom. She'd always thought there was something familiar about Lindy, in her look, her bubbly personality and even in the way she moved. It was purely coincidental. But then she saw Lindy's mother. That familiarity came flooding back like a tsunami. Her ears heard Lindy introducing her mother, but her focus was on Lindy's mom's face. The nose was thinner, and the cheek bones a little higher. There was a faint but visible scar that ran from her left eye down to the left side of her chin and one above her right eyebrow. But the eyes were the same ocean blue. The hair was now a dark chestnut color, much like her own, but the bun was exactly. . .there's absolutely no way.

"Hey Sadie."

The voice: the way she said her name. It couldn't be. But as she looked into Lindy's mom's eyes, she knew. The bottle fell from her hand and spilled dark soda all over the old tile floor. Sadie felt her knees go weak, exactly as they did nineteen years ago. She reached out to steady herself and grabbed the same magazine rack that had bruised her knee all those years ago. If she'd been in her right state of mind, she would have made some sarcastic quip about that but all she could think about was not faceplanting into the spreading puddle of brown liquid.

"Kat? It can't. . .you're de. . .," Sadie stammered as she awkwardly made her way into a chair, face full of confusion and bewilderment. She felt as though there was an elephant sitting on her chest, whose sole purpose was to keep her from breathing. The ghost that was Kat O'Malley was walking toward her. Sadie felt her head shaking but wasn't sure if she was controlling it or if it was performing the same unintentional spasm as the rest of her body. *This must be some sort of a bad dream. That's the only explanation; a bad dream set about by Gavin and EJ's accident. Like a PTSD event.* Sadie experienced plenty of them after Kat's death. She recovered enough control of her body to punch herself in the leg. Hard. *Crap, that hurt. This isn't a dream.* She saw a small chuckle escape from Kat, probably in response to Sadie's self-inflicted injury. As she got closer, Kat's pace slowed. At least Sadie thought that it slowed. Everything was moving in slow motion, so it was hard to tell. Everything except Sadie's brain. That was moving at light speed with so many half thoughts and questions. Kat, or at least the figment that was Kat, sat in a chair across from Sadie. All of sudden, her motherly instincts kicked in and her head popped up to see both Becca and Lindy staring at them, fear and confusion written all over their faces. Kat noticed Sadie's reaction and turned back to the girls as well.

"It's ok. I promise," Kat said.

Sadie watched Lindy's features settle, making her look more like Kat than Sadie had ever noticed before. Becca still looked terrified and ready to run. Sadie tried to speak to calm her daughter, but nothing came out. She merely nodded in agreement and held up a hand to keep Becca where she was. She saw Becca sit down but Becca still looked completely perplexed. *Me too, kid.*

"I'm not sure where to start," the Kat imposter began, "so I'll start with this; no this is not a bad dream."

If Sadie hadn't been so terrified, she might have laughed at the fact that Kat still knew exactly what she was thinking.

"Yeah, I can still read you like a children's book." Kat said, once again reading Sadie's thoughts. She sighed and continued, "I know that I have a lot to explain."

"Yeah, you do," Sadie interrupted. "Who are you? Why are you doing this to me?"

The woman across from her took a deep breath and looked at the ceiling, as if willing God to intervene. Sadie was hoping He would as well. There was no physical way for Kat to be sitting in the seat across from her. She died nineteen years ago in a car crash. Sadie had gone to her funeral. Dumped her ashes. She'd been living for the past two decades without her best friend. The evidence was clear that this could not be Kat O'Malley. Yet, something in Sadie's soul told her that it was. She needed divine intervention to help her understand what was happening.

"My name is Anne Walker Stevens." Sadie noticed that she put an extra emphasis on the middle, or maiden, name. "But I was born Katherine Anne O'Malley on June 17. You're Sadie Leigh Thompson, now Scott, born May 4, daughter of Henry and Tess Thompson, granddaughter of Jack and Marnie Walker." Emphasis on the 'Walker' again.

"That's not exactly privileged information," Sadie whispered. "Everyone knows that. Even Google."

The woman across from her sighed. She moved forward in her seat and looked directly into Sadie's eyes. "Just accept it. I speak truth and there's nothing you can do about it," she said, matter-of-factly.

Instantly, Sadie was transported to her grandfather's dock and to conversations that were nearly twenty-five years old. There was no way anyone other than the real Kat would know that statement. And then something clicked.

"You took my grandfather's name?" Sadie shouted, although she still had yet to find her voice, so it was more of a whispered shout. But she was suddenly angry that Kat would steal something as precious as her grandfather's name to aid her nearly twenty years of deception. And in a move that proved that this could be no one other than Kat herself, the woman across from Sadie replied calmly, with the same certain smirk that was so prevalent throughout their formative years,

"At least now you believe that I really am Kat."

Sadie crumbled against the back of the chair. The dam that had been holding back her tears for the duration of this horrible night broke and the tears flowed like the river that she thought had taken so much from her.

CHAPTER 51

Becca watched with near horror at the scene unfolding in front of her. Her mom looked as if she had seen a ghost. Her face had turned pale, and she seemed to be shaking uncontrollably as she grappled for a chair. Lindy's mom started walking toward her and Becca's mom appeared both scared and confused. Part of Becca wanted to jump up and save her mom but a bigger part of her wanted to watch what was about to unfold. She was nearly one hundred percent certain that this played a part in why her mom was acting so strange tonight. She heard her mom say the name 'Kat' and it vaguely registered in her memory. But she also was pretty sure that Lindy had told her that her mom's name was Anne. Becca wondered if at any point anything about tonight was going to make sense. She heard Lindy's mom say that it was ok, but she was still very unsure. She felt kind of funny. It wasn't until her mom nodded and held up a hand that Becca realized she'd been holding her breath. She inhaled deeply and tried to sit down but she was still feeling very unsettled about everything. She turned her head toward Lindy, keeping her eyes on the moms, and whispered,

"Do you have any idea what is going on?"

"No," Lindy whispered in return. "But it seems like my mom already knows your mom somehow. Which is strange because she rarely goes out. She's so busy with Jackson."

"Yeah," Becca replied, still focused on the conversation in front of her. "Wait, who's Jackson?" she asked, leaning forward as she strained to hear what was being said.

"Um, my little brother," Lindy said, slightly annoyed. "You know that."

"Shh." Becca interrupted.

"You asked." Lindy retorted but she, too, was preoccupied with the incident at the other end of the waiting room.

They sat silently for a few moments, although neither could hear anything that was taking place. Even though the women couldn't have been more than thirty feet from them, their voices were so quiet that they might as well have been three hundred feet away. Becca could only speculate on the situation based on her mother's facial features. The color in her face slowly started to return and the fear in her eyes seemed to have turned to skepticism and then back to confusion. And then, suddenly, her mom looked angry. She seemed to try to yell something, but all Becca could make out was the word 'grandfather,' which certainly didn't aid in figuring out the puzzle.

"What was that?" Lindy asked.

"I think she said something about a grandfather, but I don't have a clue what that means."

And then her mother did something that Becca had never seen in her fourteen years on this earth. She broke down into a mess of tears. Sure, she had seen her mother shed a tear or two a couple of times, but Becca had never experienced this. Her mom was nearly convulsing, she was crying so hard. Becca was suddenly concerned that Lindy's mom had some news about Gavin and that it wasn't good. Becca hopped out of her seat and bolted to her mother.

"Mom, Mom, are you ok? Is it Gavin? Did something happen to him?" She ran and buried her face into her mom's shoulder as she hugged her. "Is he ok?"

*****

Becca's voice echoed in Sadie's ears as she felt her daughter's body meld into her own. She had to pull herself together. There was so much to process and figure out but in front of Becca and Lindy, in the middle of a waiting room, especially this one, was not the place to do so. Sadie desperately tried to compose herself but when she looked across the aisle and saw the tears in Kat's eyes, she nearly lost it again. Gavin. The boy who had already survived a car accident in the Broken River. The car accident that supposedly took his mother. The lightbulb finally went off. That's why Kat's here right now. Because it was her son that was once again fighting for his life. Sadie wrapped one arm around her daughter and extended the other out toward Kat. Despite the anger and confusion and the multitude of questions that Sadie had, compassion for her former friend won out. Kat moved to the seat next to Sadie and leaned hard into the embrace.

CHAPTER 52

SADIE

"**I**'m not sure that I'm ever going to understand but start from the beginning. And please, go slow," Sadie said.

Sadie and Kat were back on her grandfather's dock, just like old times. Except that it wasn't anything at all like old times. It had been over a month since Kat reappeared as Anne, however, this was their first opportunity to air out the details of that reemergence. Gavin had once again survived the clutches of the Broken River, but his injuries were extensive, and he required significant help. He had been their primary focus for the past few weeks. Elisabeth, still regarded by almost everyone as his mother, had taken the reigns but Kat and Sadie had also been assisting in various ways and at various times. Kat had, for the most part, slipped back into the shadows, Sadie never seeing her outside of Elisabeth's house or her own. They did tell the kids that 'Anne' was Gavin's biological mother, but not about anything else. That had gone just about how everyone expected it to: chaotically. The kids were asked to keep that information quiet for the time being, but kids are kids, and no one expected them to stay quiet for long. But no one in Edgewater outside of Sadie and Ben, Kat/Anne and her husband, Jake, and Elisabeth, knew the truth about Kat. How Elisabeth found out and why she never told Sadie was an issue for another time. Right now, Sadie only needed answers from the source herself.

Kat took a deep breath and slowly let the air escape from her lips, her eyes searching the river below as if it possessed the words she was trying to say. She lifted her head toward the sky and then righted it, keeping her eyes straight ahead on the opposing bank.

"OK," she started. "I don't remember a whole lot about the accident and the immediate aftermath, and that's not just because of the amount of time that has passed. I never remembered much of it. JJ, or James as I guess he is called now, had called the day before asking me to meet him in Edgewater. He was getting ready to leave for Europe and had something to give me. I remember being a little skeptical because I hadn't spoken to him in a while, and I was still a little concerned about the threats. But I hadn't received any in a couple of months, so I figured that I was safe in that department. And, if you remember, I never thought that JJ was a part of that."

Sadie rolled her eyes. And even though Kat was still looking across the water, she seemed to see.

"Yes, I know that you were solidly on the JJ threat train, but you also hated him. So, you were not exactly an unbiased source of opinions."

Sadie's disagreement with that statement was written all over her face but Kat chose to ignore it and continued.

"Anyway, he sounded excited. He said that he had set up a bank account that would help take care of the baby for a long time, so long as I held to my promise not to disclose his identity as the father. Yes, it was annoying, but it was really the first time that he had offered to help at all. And I needed the money."

"That's what he told me at the hospital that morning," Sadie said. "Right after I decked him in the jaw and accused him of killing you. He even showed me the bank book with the account information."

"You hit him?" Kat turned towards Sadie and laughed. "Of course you hit him. You'd been wanting to do that for years. Glad you finally got your chance."

Sadie was not the least bit amused. Kat sensed her irritation and continued with her story.

"Getting back to it, I called you to tell you that I was going to meet with him, which you warned me, again, to be careful. It's amazing how much I can remember before the accident. It's almost as if it's a video reel that my mind can retrieve whenever I want. And then suddenly, it's all blank. Like the tape was erased. But I digress. I knew that JJ was going to be at a party at the yacht club that night, so I didn't drive into town until nearly nine thirty. I got a text message from his phone number to meet him at the old fishing shack opposite the Banks. It sat almost exactly where his house is today, actually. I found that kind of odd. Anyway, that's where I was going. And then, bam, the car flipped off the road and apparently, I went flying out of it. At least that's what Grandpa Jack told me."

Sadie tensed at hearing her grandfather's name. Over the past few weeks, she was able to put two and two together and figure out that her grandfather had been complicit in the lying and scheming. There was no other way for Kat to have disappeared off the operating table and out of the state. The realization had caused a fit of rage that resulted in a hole in her garage wall courtesy of Becca's lacrosse ball and hours upon hours of crying in the solitude of her bathroom. The only silver lining was that her throwing arm hadn't lost too much zip over the past eighteen years.

"But there is one detail that I remember more clearly than I remember anything else. Right as I was coming around the curve towards the old bridge, I saw JJ's truck."

Sadie's head swung around in shock. "It was him, after all? I'm swear I'm going to. . ."

"No, no," Kat interrupted, trying to quell the rage that was coming from Sadie. "JJ wasn't driving. It was Rosemary. It was his mother."

"What?" Sadie nearly screamed. "Rosemary? Come on, Kat. First of all, it was dark, how could you even tell who was driving? And second, yeah, she was kind of a witch, but there's no way."

"I promise you Sadie, it was her. Remember the light pole that was there by the road that leads to the Banks? The one that never worked? Well, it was working that night. And I remember her face in his truck. That is the very last thing that

I remember clearly. Grandpa Jack told me that I woke up on the way to the operating room and said her name. He said that was all he needed to know to make his decision. And that decision was to fake my death and get me the heck out of dodge."

"Well, that was the last time that light pole worked because your car knocked it completely out of commission," Sadie said quietly, her mind trying to comprehend the information that she had just been given. It seemed too ridiculous to be real, yet so ridiculous that it had to be the truth.

"I didn't know that," Kat said.

"How would you? You were dead. Only you weren't."

"Sadie," Kat said painfully.

"If he was going to fake a death, why not fake both your death and Gavin's and then send you both away? Why just you? Why take you away from your son? It doesn't make any sense."

"I was in no shape to take care of a newborn. Your grandfather moved me to another hospital, under an alias, Anne Walker, where I remained in a coma for two weeks. After that, I spent four weeks learning to walk again at a rehab facility in Sheffield. I had a broken jaw, broken orbital bone, broken arm, broken pelvis, and had to have my spleen removed. The new face was done a few months later."

Sadie put her head in her hands, in a vain attempt to stave off the immense headache that was brewing.

"I don't know how he knew what he knew, but he told me afterwards that if he didn't fake my death and get me out of town, Rosemary would never stop hunting me down. He told me that Rosemary's hatred of me spawned from a sordid affair between JJ's dad and my mother."

"What?" Sadie mumbled incredulously as she gently shook her head, still cradled in her hands, from side to side. Given Kat's mom's propensity for wealthy men, maybe it shouldn't have been so surprising, but Sadie's brain was having difficulty processing the most basic of information right now.

"He told me that I was not the product of said affair, but that it went on for some time. And since my mom was rarely around, Rosemary took out her ire on me. And she would have taken it out on the baby, on Gavin, too, if I was still in the picture. So, he removed me from it, to save both my life and Gavin's. It worked. Once I had recovered from my injuries, he put me on a plane to Colorado, with a new face and a new name. Why Colorado, I never found out, but he knew people everywhere and I'm sure had them looking out for me."

Sadie shook her head in disbelief. Her earlier statement was proving correct; she didn't think she would ever understand. Especially because Grandpa Jack wasn't around to answer any questions regarding his part in this life-altering lie. It all seemed so unlike him. At times, he could be quite enigmatic, but Sadie never thought that 'deceitful' would be a term she would use to describe him. Ever.

"He looked me in the eyes and told me you were gone. That the damage was so bad that I couldn't even go in and see you. Now I know why. I'd kill him right now if he wasn't already dead."

Sadie burned with anger, but it was only the manifestation of deep seeded pain. The two people who were the closest to her during that period of her life had deceived her in the cruelest manner that she could think of. She wasn't sure she had ever felt so hurt.

"Cut him some slack," Kat said. "Lying to you hurt him more than anything else in the world. Even more than losing his wife."

"Then why'd he do it?" Sadie yelled.

"You know why."

"He could have filled me in. I mean, you were my best friend for years. Did you guys think I wasn't trustworthy or something? Or did you just want to destroy me?"

Kat dropped her head in sorrow as Sadie looked away. It had taken years to repair the brokenness that Sadie had felt from Kat's death. After Kat's funeral, Sadie returned to school, her broken right hand encased in plaster, and finished her senior year of college. She had thrown her whole self into softball; it felt like the only thing she had left, until that, too, ended prematurely and completely outside of her control. The grief that she was so desperately trying to stave off with that softball field then swallowed her whole. She fell hard and broke into thousands of pieces. She did the only thing she could even think of doing: she ran away from everything and everyone. Sadie left the state for graduate school, with no intention of ever returning, especially not to Edgewater. And no hope of ever being put back together.

"None of it was easy, Sadie," Kat said, breaking the deafening silence between them. "None of it. We both knew how much you were hurting. But you had to believe that I was dead almost as much as JJ's parents did. Grandpa Jack couldn't risk you looking for me and Rosemary somehow finding out. And you were the only one left to ensure that Gavin was taken care of, to make sure that no one hurt him. You did, and you are still doing that. You and I both know that you would have never come back here if it weren't for him."

Kat paused and when she continued, her voice cracked and quivered. Sadie turned her head slightly and, out of her peripheral vision, could see tears running down the side of Kat's face.

"I mourned too. A lot. I mourned for my baby and for the loss of my old life. I mourned for the loss of my new life as a mother. I mourned you and for the lost future of raising kids together. I was broken too, Sadie, and not just physically. But knowing that you were going to be Gavin's biggest ally and advocate for the rest of his life was one of the only things that got me through. He was your only connection to the past. But it's more than that. You love him, and you swore that you would always protect him. And that gave me hope that he would be ok. And he is."

Sadie felt her heart strings start to tug. She thought about how difficult it would be if she had to walk away from her children. And she felt a twinge of sympathy for Kat's pain. But neither that nor the return of her best friend was going to undo the pain and guilt and crushing hurt she'd experienced on that dreaded night, and in the years that followed. Sadie's heart had completely shattered, and it had taken far too long to put it back together. She didn't think it could ever handle that type of agony again. And now, just like her, her heart was sitting on the banks of the broken once again.

CHAPTER 53

BECCA

*N*ear death experiences tend to separate the important things in life from all the others. When EJ saw Becca enter her hospital room, she broke down in tears. Through those tears, EJ managed to ask Becca why she was here, especially after the way that EJ had treated her over the past school year. Becca, through tears of her own, told the truth; EJ was her best friend, no matter what, and she didn't want to lose her. That answer caused EJ to cry harder, but she somehow managed to get out an apology. For everything. It's what Becca had been waiting months to hear. And when she heard them, she realized it was not the apology that she needed; it was her friend. Becca had sat down gingerly on the edge of EJ's hospital bed and started talking as if the past year hadn't happened. They laughed and cried and gossiped as teenagers often do, and there seemed to be no strain whatsoever. It was the most liberating day of Becca's young life.

Once EJ returned home, Becca returned to spending nearly every day at EJ's house, helping her with once easy tasks such as climbing the stairs and putting on her shoes. But mostly working on their emotional and mental restoration, with lots of laughter and silliness. Lindy was also a consistent presence during this time, as her mother was helping both Ms. Elisabeth and Becca's mom with Gavin's care. It was odd to see Lindy's mom around, seeing as she'd been pretty much missing in action throughout the entire school year. But given the bizarre circumstances, it made sense. The girls found comfort in each other's presence as they had all been profoundly changed by the events of the previous few weeks. One physically. All mentally and emotionally. The transition from middle to high school that seemed so tumultuous to most, passed by unnoticed to them. There were bigger issues to attend to.

They'd all been floored by the revelation that Ms. Elisabeth was not Gavin's biological mom, and even more so by the fact that Lindy and Will's mom was. EJ seemed to handle this material with ease as compared to how she reacted upon hearing about her parents' divorce. She said she had always felt like there was something different in the way that both her mom and her dad interacted with Gavin that seemed to make this information fit. It was nothing EJ could find the words to explain, just a feeling. It also gave her a solid explanation for the change in Gavin's behavior and lifestyle over the past few years. His major pendulum swing from normal teenage boy to alcohol abuser to overprotective big brother over the course of two plus years made little sense outside of the context of finding out your birth mother wasn't the mother you'd known for sixteen years. And given EJ's reaction to finding out about her dad's behavior that led to the divorce of her parents, she understood Gavin's plight better than ever.

Speaking of the divorce, EJ finally allowed Becca and Lindy into the hurting spaces of her heart by revealing the details, as well as her feelings, regarding the dissolution of her parents' marriage. Her father had been unfaithful to her mother, more than once, so the hurt went much deeper than just a parental split. EJ's relationship with her dad was one in which she thought her father walked on water, and to have this awful revelation thrown into her face had wrecked her world. At first, she blamed everyone except him, lashing out at her mom in ways that she deeply regretted. And then, when he never came back home, she started to lose hope in him and in everything that she believed. So, she did the only thing she could think of doing; she tried to forget the life she knew. She ran away from the people who truly loved her, and never even attempted to deal with the reality of the situation or lean into the truths that she knew. EJ now knew what a monumental mistake that had been.

EJ also revealed the specifics about the night of the accident. Shortly before EJ had called Becca and blamed her for ruining her life, Weston had broken up with her. Via text. EJ was so distraught by someone else leaving her that she had blamed all her problems on Becca. Later that night, EJ heard Gavin's jeep coming down the driveway and decided that he was just as responsible for her problems as Becca was. She had sprinted down the stairs and out the front door, then committed to standing in front of his Jeep in the driveway until he got out to yell at her. Amid their argument, EJ noticed that his Jeep was still running so she made the ridiculous decision to drive away in it. She ran and jumped into the open driver's side door. By the time he realized what was happening, all Gavin could do was jump into the passenger's seat as EJ spun the car through the grass and drove away. They continued to argue until EJ told Gavin she didn't want to live anymore and didn't care if they both died. EJ said that she then let go of the steering wheel completely. Gavin had reached over and tried to grab the wheel but as he did, he pulled too hard, and the Jeep clipped a tree and flipped. The next thing EJ remembered was lying in a hospital room with her mom sitting next to her. Gavin had taken the brunt of the accident, suffering multiple internal injuries, a significant head injury and a broken back.

Becca cried when EJ retold the story. She was crushed by EJ's admission that she had lost her desire to live, even if it was only for a moment. EJ had cried too, wishing that she had handled everything differently and allowed Becca and Cooper, and even Lindy, to help her. It would have prevented so much pain. But they all knew that they couldn't go back, only forward. And that's what they were trying to do. Together.

Fridays were for the Grove, again. EJ's leg was improving, although she was still very weak and seemed to have difficulty maintaining her balance on uneven surfaces so navigating the mangroves proved a bit tricky. Lindy and Becca helped her onto the piece of seawall that Cooper typically occupied, as there was no way she was climbing into her normal resting place. Becca grabbed a stone that was resting on the sandy bank and flipped it over in her hands. Her mind transported her back to the last time she was here, and she struggled to believe that a full year had passed since then. So much had transpired in that year; things that she would have never imagined if she had tried. Her knee was as good as new and both she and Lindy were starting on the varsity volleyball team as freshmen. She and Lindy. Becca had also come so far in her mindset toward Lindy since being here last. It was hard to believe that she ever held any animosity toward this person who was fast becoming one of her closest friends. Becca kissed the stone and sent it skipping across the river.

"Five, not bad for your first try," EJ said, mimicking both Cooper's voice and his words from the last time they were here. It made Becca smile in remembrance. Cooper. That had been another web to untangle and wound to repair. Becca had finally apologized for the month of ignoring him. Thankfully, he simply acted like the same old kind, crazy Cooper. The relief was enormous but something inside of her told her that there would always be a hint of awkwardness between them from now on. But that was for another season. The rest of the group would be rejoining them soon enough, but right now it was just Becca, Lindy and EJ. They needed this time to sort stuff out.

"I've missed this," Becca said.

"Me too," EJ admitted. "I am really sorry for how everything went down. I guess I just needed someone else to feel the hurt that I was feeling. And it happened to fall on you. I'm sorry."

Lindy piped up from the mangrove hammock in which EJ normally sat. Her long legs were bent nearly up to her face as she tried to fold all five foot eleven of her into the space that seemed perfectly suited for EJ's five-foot four body.

"My mom says that it's the people that you feel most comfortable with that you will end up hurting the most. And that will hurt you the most. Because you've allowed them to see inside of you, to be inside those walls that we put up."

Becca shot EJ a look and they both started laughing. Lindy stared at them wide-eyed.

"See what I mean," she said. "I try to say something profound, and you both laugh like it's a comedy show."

They both started laughing even harder. This time Lindy joined in, unaware as to why she was laughing, but unable to withstand their infectious amusement. Becca inhaled a mouth full of air as she tried to gather herself to tell Lindy why they were in such hysterics. "You comfortable over there?" she asked, her laughter increasing once again.

"You look like you're eating your knees," EJ said. "How do they taste?" EJ was laughing so much that she nearly fell off the seawall and into the water. And this only served to make them laugh even harder.

After a few minutes, and without anyone taking a dip in the river, the three caught their breath and quieted down. They could hear the cicadas picking up their harmony as the sun began to dip to the west. Songbirds chirped along melodically. It created an arena of peace that seemed to have been missing over the past month. Or maybe even the past year. EJ was the first to interrupt the symphony.

"I needed that. Like, really needed that. Thanks, you guys."

"I think we all did. It's been a heck of a year," Becca replied.

"You can say that again," said Lindy.

"It's been a heck of a year," Becca replied with a smirk.

Both EJ and Lindy simultaneously rolled their eyes at her. Becca glanced back and forth between the two and the gears in her mind started to turn.

"So, how are we feeling about the whole 'sisters' thing?" Becca asked, because she was genuinely curious. The whole Gavin-is-the-older-brother-of-both-EJ-and-Lindy revelation was so mind blowing. She wasn't sure how she felt about it so she could only imagine how Lindy and EJ felt. Her question was met with silence. Lindy looked at EJ and EJ looked at Lindy, still folded up in the mangrove tree.

"I mean, we're not really sisters, we just have the same brother but still, I guess it's kind of cool. Strange, but cool," Lindy said.

"Yeah, agreed," EJ said. "It's definitely a little sus, but like I said, there was always some tension there so it sort of fits. Plus, I always wanted a sister."

"It is weird that my mom would keep something like that from us," Lindy admitted. "Even weirder that she'd leave him. That's not the mom I know. I think she might still be keeping something from us."

"Speaking of keeping something from someone. Bec, I think I remember the last time we were here you were in the middle of a secret feud with Lindy," EJ announced, her change of direction so swift it caught everyone off guard.

"What?" asked Lindy, sitting up so quickly that she nearly hit her head on the mangrove branch above her.

"Here we go," Becca said sarcastically, her face reddening with embarrassment. "You had to bring that up, didn't you?"

"Yep."

"You had a feud with me?" Lindy asked.

Becca sighed, wishing that tidbit of old news would have remained undiscovered, but also not necessarily afraid to talk about it.

"Yeah, I was jealous. I thought you were going to come in and dethrone me as the best volleyball player. And you did. But that's ok. Getting hurt and watching you and the team succeed without me helped me to realize that I am not defined by volleyball. Or lacrosse. Or my grades. Those are merely things that I do; gifts God has given me and ones that He can also take away. He says who I am, and I'm His child. Loved, cherished, redeemed. My job is just to glorify Him in all that I do. So, I'm not jealous of you anymore. In fact, I'm super glad we are as close as we are. All of us."

EJ nodded in agreement. She swung her bad leg off the seawall and planted both feet firmly on the sandy surface below. She looked as though she finally had her glow back. Maybe it was the sunlight reflecting off her face, but Becca didn't think so.

"Do we get to laugh at you for saying something profound?" Lindy asked as she struggled out of the hammock. They all started laughing again.

"I guess so," Becca replied as she grabbed another stone and sent it skipping across the water. Seven skips, the number of perfection. That's what this afternoon felt like. She wondered if there would be more days like this. Or more struggles. She figured it would probably be a mixture of both. But with God, her family, and with friends like this, she would make it through them all. She heard EJ's voice call out.

"Get over here, sisses. Group hug!"

Becca and Lindy followed EJ's instructions, the perfect ending to the perfect afternoon.

CHAPTER 54

SADIE

"**I** asked JJ to move back here," Kat announced, as their dockside conversation continued.

Sadie could have sworn that she heard wrong. Because if she heard what she thought she heard, it meant that Kat had revealed herself to someone and that someone wasn't Sadie. It also meant that James freaking Jones had known that Kat was alive for at least thirteen years and hadn't said a word of it to her. Or to Elisabeth. Or had Elisabeth known the entire time and joined in on the deception? Sadie wasn't sure that she wanted to hear anymore. Each new piece of information caused her heart to teeter closer to the edge. But her desire for truth won out. However, instead of simply asking a question to get to said truth, she stupidly spoke out of her pain.

"I'm glad you felt comfortable telling *him* you were still alive. I see you're still choosing JJ."

"Sadie," Kat huffed.

"Yeah, yeah, go ahead and break me some more and tell me how that happened."

Kat lowered her head and wiped her eyes. A part of Sadie wished that she would keep her mouth shut and make this easier on both of them, but that part was being smothered by hurt, pain and bitterness. She knew that the only way forward was to hear Kat out, and to do a heck of a lot of praying for help in forgiving her, but she didn't realize it would be this difficult. That was a lie; she knew. It's why she'd been dreading this day instead of rejoicing that Kat was alive. The pain was too much the first time, and it was only by the grace of God that she made it through. She didn't know if she'd be strong enough for a second time. Or maybe she didn't trust that God would rescue her once again. She was starting to wonder if she'd truly learned all the lessons He'd been teaching her, or if her advice to Becca was merely words coming out of her mouth.

"I didn't search him out to tell him," Kat said adamantly. "Jake and I had only been married a short time when he received orders to go to England. I freaked out because I knew that JJ was still in London, and I was hormonal because I was pregnant with the twins. I'd also never been out of Colorado since Jack had sent me there. There's another story in that but that's not important right now. Anyway, we get over there and Jake decides to spend a few days in London before reporting to the base. I told myself that London was huge and that there was no way that I'd ever run into JJ. And for three days, I didn't. And then I decided to go out on my own to shop for the babies. I literally ran into him on the street. I don't know if he would have recognized me if I had just said 'excuse me' and kept walking but I was so stunned and freaked out that I just stood there and stared at him. It took a second, but when he realized that I was alive, he freaked out."

"I can relate," Sadie murmured.

"I explained everything as best I could," Kat said.

"I'm sure he loved you accusing his mother of trying to kill you and the baby."

"Shockingly, he believed me. His mother was apparently still pretty hostile toward Gavin."

"So, he just up and left London because you were alive and were there and you told him to go home because his mother tried to kill you?" Sadie believed none of this.

"Not exactly. I had other motives. You being one of them."

Sadie was beyond perplexed. She'd been listening to Kat but had kept her gaze fixed toward the setting sun. At this, she turned to face her, eager to learn how she had now become a 'motive' in all this scheming.

"I can't wait to hear this," Sadie said, sarcastically, rolling her eyes in the process before allowing her gaze to settle on Kat's face.

Kat took a deep breath before continuing. Whether it was because she needed a moment to gather her thoughts or to gather her breath, Sadie did not know. But a good five minutes passed before Kat stopped to breathe again. And when she did, Sadie noticed that she needed help catching hers. Kat's life as Anne was great, and she was about to have twins with her husband who was nothing short of amazing. After she saw JJ, she feared that it may all come crashing down. Again. She barely made it through losing one life; she couldn't bear the thought of losing another. Even if it wasn't completely true. She'd come clean and told Jake everything. He had a ton of questions, of course, mainly regarding Kat's feelings toward JJ but also with Gavin. Together they decided that the best way forward for their own family, and for the safety of both them and Gavin, was to maintain the façade and stay away. Together, they met with JJ and told him their plans. Kat asked if, since she couldn't leave England right now, JJ would move back home. His father was sick, and JJ had already been contemplating the move, so it hadn't taken much persuading. The other part of that push was Grandpa Jack. Their communication was extremely rare and always one way, him sending her letters postmarked in random cities with tidbits of information about Gavin and occasionally about Sadie, whom he hadn't seen in almost five years. In his last message, he revealed his sickness to Kat and intimated that what he wanted more than anything was for Sadie to come home. But he knew, as did Kat, that the only way that was going to happen was for JJ to bring Gavin back. So, when fate, or circumstance, or maybe God, brought about that run in in front of a clothing store in London, Kat knew she had an opportunity to help everyone that she'd hurt by faking her death. Gavin would get to experience life surrounded by family, both blood and not, that loved him, Grandpa Jack and Sadie's parents would get

Sadie back, and Sadie could be close to the son that Kat left behind.

"That's as far as I thought it would go. It was not much, and it still hurt to be away, but it was something positive. I knew Gavin would be protected even more with you around, especially if Rosemary was still holding a grudge against him. And I hoped that with JJ getting married and having another child, she'd be more excited about him being home than concerned with the illegitimate son he was bringing with him."

Sadie's head felt like it had just stumbled off the teacups at Disney. The information and subsequent thoughts and feelings were spinning with such force, she felt like she was going to be sick. She pressed her hands hard against her eyes, willing her brain to slow down. She didn't have the slightest clue how to process all of this, let alone what to say, yet her mouth opened, and words came out.

"That still doesn't explain why you are here now, after nineteen years. Why come back at all?" Sadie stunned herself with her own words. It was definitely the most pressing question, and one that she'd been wanting to ask this entire time, but she was still surprised that she managed to ask it. And at a time when there were a million different questions that she could have asked. She may have been most surprised by the tone in which she asked the question. There were no accusatory undertones or pointed sarcasm, just pure exhaustion. And maybe a hint of concern under the surface that she herself didn't recognize.

"Right," Kat said, with resignation in her voice. "That answer will probably take a long time to answer properly, but the short of it is that Gavin found out that Elisabeth was not his biological mom. His method of coping was, to say the least, not healthy. As you well know. About two years ago, I received a phone call from JJ asking me to meet him in Frankfurt to talk about Gavin. He said it was important. I don't know how he found me but at that point it wasn't as concerning because both his parents had passed. Anyway, we were living outside Ramstein Air Base, so I made the drive over. And there was my nearly seventeen-year-old son, whom I had never ever seen. I've never cried that hard in my entire life. I don't know the entire story surrounding his finding out or what led to JJ asking me to meet him, but I was told that it was Gavin's idea. When I returned home, I told Jake about the meeting and suggested moving here. We were getting ready to return stateside anyway, and he would only have a year or two before retirement, so we were already looking for a place in which we could settle for good. I knew there was a base close enough for him to commute to and his rank was such that he could almost choose his assignment. He agreed. We spent the next six months arranging the moving parts and then six months in Colorado awaiting the official orders. We moved here one month shy of Gavin's eighteenth birthday. My kids didn't know anything about him, or my past, and despite Gavin and Elisabeth's acceptance of me and my past, I was incredibly nervous to be found out by anyone else. Especially you. I didn't know how to tell you. And Jackson was the perfect excuse to keep my distance. But then Lindy and Becca became such good friends – I can see so much of us in them, and I wanted to tell you. I wanted to tell my kids and your kids, and live the life that we should have had, but I was so scared. Mainly of this moment right here. God gave me the opportunity to meet my son and to build a relationship with him, and to ask his forgiveness for my mistakes. But he only had to deal with the knowledge of me and my absence for about six months, not nineteen years of me being 'dead.' I was far more afraid of this than of reconciling with him. But then the accident happened, and I realized I couldn't be scared any more. My son that I had just gotten back, that I had just gotten to know, was once again fighting for his life. I needed him. And I needed you."

Sadie felt herself starting to crumble. All these sentiments that Kat was expressing brought her solidly back to that hot August night nineteen years ago, when she was pleading with God for the very same things. It was the night that she started to lose her faith in the God she thought she knew. Her college boyfriend had then broken up with her just before Christmas break, telling her that her singular focus on sports and lack of socialization was the cause. What he really meant was that he was tired of getting pushed away, and she couldn't blame him for his decision because she was pushing. Hard. So hard that she felt more indifference than pain at the breakup. But it was one more person God was taking away from her, and it made her run farther away from Him. Then came the broken ankle in early April, effectively ending both her softball career and her faith. Senior day was the last time she ever stepped, or hobbled, onto a softball field. Consequently, it was also the last time she went to church for about half a decade. She never lost her morality, or her sense of right and wrong, but began to question everything regarding her faith and belief in a good God. The whys became more abundant, or maybe they were just louder than normal, and Kat was no longer there to pull her out of her own way. No one was. Sunday mornings became days for sleeping in, or for long runs in the Virginia hills. Her Bible collected dust on a shelf that was overrun by medical journals, classic novels and the occasional self-help book, that she found were anything but helpful. Family and friends stopped calling to check on her, probably because she stopped answering. There were only so many ways she could lie about being fine. She found solace on the lake, not fishing but in rowing, pushing her body to its limits in yet another way to escape the mental darkness that enveloped her when she stopped the doing.

The days had floated by in a cloud of apathy. She would paint on a smile when going to class and in her required interactions with the rest of the human race, but her lonely nights were spent in tears, curled in the fetal position, trying to manage her anguish. She spent years running, from God, from close personal relationships, from her family, from really any meaningful thing in this life, all in effort to prevent the one small, functioning piece of her heart from breaking too.

Sadie inhaled deeply, allowing the smell of seawater to invade her senses. Kat knew none of this, nor anything about God rescuing Sadie from herself, and Sadie wasn't sure how much she wanted to reveal. She'd worked too hard to put those days behind her and she wasn't sure that reliving them now would be good for anyone. How she wished that Kat would have been around to do life with, to plan weddings with and raise kids with! But would she be in the same place spiritually if Kat had never died, or if she hadn't had to endure the subsequent pain and suffering of God reestablishing His rightful place in her life? Only Kat hadn't died and to make matters worse, both she and Sadie's grandfather had lied about it and then had apparently been pulling some strings from afar to manipulate Sadie's life. Was it all for naught? Was any of it necessary? Or was she caught in the fallout of someone else's bad decisions? Sadie's brain was starting to spin again so she found the horizon and fixed her gaze there.

The sun was slowly succumbing to pull of the skyline, and the cicadas were serenading its descent with dramatic tones. Sadie watched a family of ducks float along with the current and wished for the ease with which they appeared to coast. But she knew that under the surface, their little webbed feet were moving at a furious pace. The overall setting seemed to parallel her current situation, calm on the surface and a mess of desperate paddling within to avoid the coming tumble into agony. She needed to talk this through but had no idea what to say. Grabbing the wooden dock tightly with both hands, she took a deep breath and simply allowed her mouth to start moving.

"This is the first time that I've been on the dock since your funeral," Sadie confessed.

"Seriously? This was your favorite pla. . .," Kat's words drifted as realization struck.

Sadie nodded slowly, keeping her sunglass covered eyes looking toward the horizon.

"I dumped your ashes here. Well, I guess they weren't your ashes after all. But I dumped what I thought were your ashes here, jumped in my car and went back to school. Didn't come home at all, which you apparently know, for nearly five years. Not for holidays, not for birthdays, nothing. I couldn't handle it." She turned slightly away from Kat, discreetly wiping away the tear that was forming in her eye.

"Sade, I'm so sor. . ." Kat stopped again, probably realizing that no words were going to lessen the pain or take back nearly two decades of blatant dishonesty.

"Grandpa Jack left me the house and the surrounding land in his will. I was never really sure why, since he knew that I avoided this place like the plague. Even when I moved back, I would only enter his house through the back door. Never even wanted to look this way." Sadie paused and turned her head back towards Kat but kept her eyes firmly on the river below.

"We had to tear the house down a few years back when a hurricane came through and did more damage than the house was worth. I was going to sell the land – too many painful memories. But for some reason, I couldn't bring myself to come over and stick a sign in the yard."

Sadie took another deep breath. She reached into her pocket and pulled out a worn piece of paper. She flipped it over in her hands a few times and then handed it to Kat.

"He also gave me this." Sadie didn't watch as Kat unfolded it. She knew very well what was written on the yellowing piece of stationary. In typical Jack Walker fashion, it was a quote from a book followed by a Bible verse. It read:

"The world breaks everyone, and afterward, many are strong at the broken places." From Hemingway's *A Farewell To Arms*. And underneath was Psalm 34:18, *"The Lord is near to the brokenhearted and saves the crushed in spirit."*

A tiny gasp escaped Kat's lips as she saw Grandpa Jack's handwriting. "My heart broke when he passed. And I couldn't come say goodbye."

"Should we celebrate your entry into the broken heart club?" Sadie asked pointedly. Her sympathy toward Kat and her grandfather was negligible at this moment. Sadie inhaled deeply, trying to calm her soul and regain her composure. It took a minute, but then she, through gritted teeth, continued.

"He gave that to me shortly after your funeral," she continued. "I wanted so badly to tear it up or throw it away but, just like the land, I couldn't bring myself to do it for some reason. Knowing what I know now, we probably wouldn't be sitting here looking at that."

All this talk of the past and of her grandfather was not as cathartic as she'd hoped, and she could feel the anger and pain of betrayal bubble up inside of her. She couldn't yell at him, but she could at Kat and right now Sadie needed Kat to know exactly what they did to her. She needed someone to feel the pain that she felt and to understand the damage that they had inflicted. And she needed to know why. Sadie clenched her jaw, turned her head toward Kat and allowed the fountain of hurt to explode.

"How could you do this? Any of this? How could you willingly walk away from your child? How could you lie to everyone for nineteen years and then reappear like you've just been on vacation? How is Gavin ok with this? How am I supposed to be ok with this? You and my grandfather lied to me and deceived me and then watched me flounder in a sea of despair. For years! And now I'm just supposed to pretend like nothing happened?" Sadie watched as Kat dropped her head, casting her eyes down toward the water. She could read the regret in Kat's body language.

"It's taken a lot of time for him. But we've also had almost two years to get to this point. Not that this point is great, but it's better than it was before. He still asks questions," Kat replied. "I know it's going to take more time.

With you too. And I don't expect you to forget anything. I was just hoping you could find it in your heart to forgive me."

Sadie huffed and turned her head away again. Everything in her wanted to yell and scream and somehow make Kat truly understand the hurt that she had endured. But seeing Kat, hearing the regret in her voice, physically sitting next to this person who was, for a good portion of her life, closer to her than a sister, caused a piece of her heart to move toward forgiveness and reconciliation. This is what she had always wanted; to live life with her very best friend. And despite all the odds, seemingly despite reality, she was getting that chance. But her heart had been ripped out once before and she knew she couldn't handle that again. This internal turmoil was most likely going to break her as it was. She could only hope that God would put her back together again this time. She shook her head as she felt another tear run down the side of her face like a fugitive from the cops. Sadie's mind wasn't running though, it was waging war against itself. *Just be honest. You've always been able to be honest with her. But you don't know this 'her'. How can you trust her, especially after what she did? But she's here, she's alive, you get a second chance. Is it worth it?*

"Kat," Sadie started and then paused, trying to collect her thoughts and emotions. Another tear escaped. She closed her eyes and silently prayed for wisdom and guidance. This was not something that she could handle on her own. Sadie opened her eyes and looked down at the river just below her feet. She could almost see the swirl beneath the surface. A stream of thought quietly entered her conscious mind.

Not everything is as it seems. On your surface, you look calm and steady, but underneath you're a swirling mess of confusion and pain. You've taken so much from me, but you've also given me so much peace. You're broken, but you're resilient. Your banks are muddy and trampled and worn out from centuries of gentle reshaping and refining, but

they allow you to flow along to the places that God has
intended for you to occupy.

She inhaled deeply once again as realization set in.

We are each our own river. We are here because this is
where God intended for us to be. She inhaled the briny air
once more and then let the words cascade like a waterfall.

"Kat, your death broke me. I mean, absolutely shattered
me. Years went by, years of sleepless nights because I'd
close my eyes and be in that waiting room again, hearing
those words. Years of mental breakdowns, some of which
were only mended by the grace of God. Years of wondering if
life was worth it, of keeping everyone at arm's length because
I was absolutely petrified of losing anyone else. The pain, and
the prospect of dealing with that pain again, outweighed the
loneliness. I spent so much time questioning everything I
knew and believed. I even went to therapy once and I know
you remember how difficult talking about stuff is for me."

Sadie turned to look at her former best friend to find that
Kat was staring back at her with tears streaming down her
face. A piece of her wanted to reach out and give Kat a hug
but she refused her sense of empathy any more than just that
piece. Sadie looked away again.

"I'm finally put back together. Or at least I thought I was
until all of this. Right now, I feel like I'm tiptoeing the edge of a
cliff and one stiff breeze will push me over, causing me to
shatter once again. I don't really know how to do this. To do
us. I don't know how to undo two decades of you being
dead."

Sadie removed her sunglasses with one hand and wiped
the wetness from her face with the other. She had tried to
keep her emotions in check, but the tears came anyway. She
kept her eyes averted because she knew that if she looked at
Kat again, the tears would never stop. But even without
looking, she knew Kat was sobbing. Sadie could sense Kat's
body shaking beside her. After a while, the movement
stopped and for a long while they both sat in silence. For how
long, Sadie was unsure, and she contemplated leaving Kat

here alone. But as the sun kissed the edge of the horizon, Sadie noticed what looked like golden flecked minnows popping around her feet. She allowed her eyes just a glance, and she saw Kat's toes lightly kicking the top of the water, creating tiny splashes that looked golden in the setting sun. Sadie looked toward the disappearing yellow balloon, hiding not tears this time, but the very hints of a smile. She felt a tap on her shoulder and when she turned, she was greeted by big, ocean blue eyes and a smile. And the words,

"My name is Anne Stevens, but you can call me Kat."

ACKNOWLEDGEMENTS

All glory and honor to Jesus Christ, the Lord and Savior of my life. He has reconciled my brokenness to Himself through His blood and death on the cross, and defeated death forever with His resurrection. And He wants you to know His love and mercy and inexhaustible grace as well. He's waiting patiently to put all your broken pieces back together. Seek Him, trust Him. I'm so grateful for the opportunity to share His love and graciousness with you through these characters.

To my amazing husband, thank you for your unwavering support, your unconditional love, and your godly leadership. Thank you for providing so well for our family and allowing me the opportunity to try something new. You make me a better person every day. I love you with all that I am!

To my children, you are the best and I could not imagine life without you. I'm so grateful that God has revealed Himself to you both at so young an age and I pray that you will continue to follow Him all of your days. And I hope one day you enjoy reading, even if it's not anything that I've written! I love you "one less than Jesus!"

Nicole G, thank you for twenty plus years of friendship, for constantly pushing me out of my comfort zone and for believing in me even when I didn't believe in myself. I know for a fact that this would have remained a story in my head if it weren't for you. LYLAS, A&F.

Layne, thanks for the assist, kiddo. You'll always be my favorite! And Lynne, thank you for your editing skills and your willingness to be the self-proclaimed 'hype woman'. Because you know I won't do that myself. You guys are the best!

To the readers, THANK YOU for spending your time with Sadie and Becca. They are near and dear to my heart, and I hope that their relationship with each other, as well as with their closest friends, stirred something in your heart. God desires that relationship with you. Actually, He desires a more intimate relationship than anything humanly possible. I pray that each of you will know Him in that manner. Thank you again for choosing this book.